LAST FLIGHT OUT OF KHAM DUC

"The evac was complete—except for the three members of the combat control team. They'd been going from one bunker to another to find survivors. They didn't find any.

"So now they're stuck on an airfield that's completely overrun with North Vietnamese. The enemy has complete possession of the airfield. They have gun positions set up alongside the runway. They've taken over the camp completely. I could see the automatic weapons and antiaircraft fire coming out of the jungle on the southwest end of the airfield.

"The runway was full of shell holes and mortar rounds. There's an enemy gun position directly across the runway. You could see the tracers right in front of the airplane . . ."

Berkley Books by Timothy S. Lowry

AND BRAVE MEN, TOO
VALOR

Valor

TIMOTHY S. LOWRY

BERKLEY BOOKS, NEW YORK

VALOR

A Berkley Book / published by arrangement with
the author

PRINTING HISTORY
Berkley edition / December 1989

ISBN: 0-425-11916-5

A BERKLEY BOOK® TM 757,375
Berkley Books are published by The Berkley Publishing Group,
200 Madison Avenue, New York, New York 10016.
The name "BERKLEY" and the "B" logo
are trademarks belonging to Berkley Publishing Corporation.

PRINTED IN THE UNITED STATES OF AMERICA

10 9 8 7 6 5 4 3 2 1

Contents

v

Valor

Introduction

VIETNAM was America's longest and most controversial war. It had its roots in the Forties, escalated in the Fifties, peaked in the Sixties, and began to fade in the Seventies. While each of these decades contributed to the puzzle of Vietnam, it was the frantic nature of the Sixties that had the most profound impact on the war.

This decade was unconventional in almost every aspect and left its mark on everything it touched. Music went from Lawrence Welk and Dinah Shore to the Beatles and Janis Joplin; for boys, hair went from crew cuts to ponytails and for girls the styles went from ponytails to crew cuts; headlines in college newspapers switched from fraternities and sororities to Students for a Democratic Society (SDS) and the National Organization for Women (NOW); racially the country saw Rap Brown and Stokeley Carmichael replace *Amos and Andy*; and the political selection process changed from politicians plotting in smoke-filled back rooms to young people rioting on tear gas–clouded streets.

Another change in our culture was the relationship between the military and society. Politicians under the scrutiny of unrestricted and uncensored media coverage had redefined the rules for waging war. No longer did we seek an "unconditional surrender" as in World War II; in Vietnam, it became "Peace with Honor." As a result, political considerations took precedence over military objectives.

The American experience in Vietnam consisted of two wars, and what separated these two wars was the Tet Offensive of 1968. America was dying to get into Vietnam before Tet, and then we were dying to get out. This nationwide offensive is considered today by many to have been the turning point in the war.

By military standards, the Tet Offensive had been a major victory for the Allies. "This is the Vietcong's Bay of Pigs," a Washington official noted. "The Vietnamese people did not arise and overthrow the government as Hanoi predicted."

Not only did the Communist insurrection fail to materialize, but because of the numerous executions and atrocities committed by the North Vietnamese soldiers and the Vietcong against civilians, many previously nonaligned South Vietnamese came out and openly opposed the Communists. However, this went unreported because Tet had caused many news reporters to question America's involvement in the war.

Objectivity and balanced reporting had become casualties of the war.

In battles subsequent to Tet, photographers clicked off rolls and rolls of film—pictures of downed aircraft, devastated villages, rows of body bags: Sometimes televised pictures, sometimes still photographs, but always emotional images of the painful aspects of war.

Cameramen bombarded the nation with on-the-scene coverage: An enemy soldier was shown being executed by a Vietnamese policeman; a twelve-year-old girl was pictured screaming as napalm cooked her alive; civilian bodies littered a country road. Several Pulitzer Prizes were won for showing the horrible aspects of war.

Our soldiers' bravery and pride, though, went mostly unnoticed. Sure, there was a My Lai, and it was trumpeted across the land. But there was also Dai Do, and few at home heard much about that.

Courage had taken a backseat to cruelty.

Some Americans began to equate opposition to the war with honor and participation with shame. One result of this fragmentation was that many Americans, once the war was over, wanted to put Vietnam behind us quickly. "Forgive and forget," they said, but it soon became fashionable to forgive the protester and forget the vet.

The Vietnam veteran wasn't totally forgotten. There were movies such as *Apocalypse Now, The Deer Hunter,* and *Platoon.* Many people came away from these films saying, "That's what Vietnam was really like." It didn't matter that they had never been to Vietnam, never smelled it. They had seen the make-believe version on the screen, and they believed it.

Conversely, when heroics and Vietnam came up in conversations, some people opined, "No, there weren't any heroes in Vietnam; not like in World War II." More than one barroom discussion exploded into a brawl over that one.

There were American heroes in Vietnam, brave men who put it all on the line, but because of a difficult time in American history they went unregarded and unremembered. Recent parades like those in New York, Chicago, and Los Angeles honoring the Vietnam veterans indicate that America is beginning to recognize this.

It just took a little while.

1

Point

RONALD L. COKER

Rank: Private First Class   **Date:** March 24, 1969
Unit: Company M, 3rd Battalion, 3rd Marines   **Place:** Northwest Section Quang Tri Province
Born: Alliance, Nebraska, August 9, 1947

HE was walking point.

In another time and another place, the twenty-one-year-old Nebraska native might have been racing across a college campus for class; or he might have been strolling down a shady lane hand in hand with a pretty girl; or he might have been dashing over to a neighborhood tavern for a beer and a burger with his pals.

But the time was now—March 24, 1969—and the place was there—Quang Tri Province, South Vietnam—and Private First Class Ron Coker was walking point.

The rifleman of the 2nd Platoon of Company M, 3rd Battalion, 3rd Marine Regiment (Three-Three in Marine slang), 3rd Marine Division, were returning from a routine Search-and-Destroy patrol in the heavily wooded, moun-

4

tainous region near the DMZ. The weather was clear that morning as PFC Coker lead his platoon down a narrow jungle trail hunting the soldiers from North Vietnam.

From the television broadcasts and newspaper reports about Vietnam, many Americans believed that the United States was only fighting an elusive guerrilla force of pajama-clad farmers. However, as often as not, Americans faced well-equipped and well-trained regular army units from North Vietnam.

Consequently, walking point was an extremely dangerous job in Vietnam. You never knew whom you were going to confront on a trail. Anyone who has ever walked point knows the danger, the apprehension, the tension, the fear.

Ron Coker had walked point before and he knew all about it.

In addition to looking for enemy soldiers, the point man had to be ever vigilant for trip wires that could be strung anywhere from a few inches off the deck to chest-high. The trip wires could be attached to explosive devices ranging from hand grenades to 155-mm refitted artillery rounds that had not exploded during an American artillery barrage.

If the point man tripped a hand grenade, it could shatter his legs and cripple him for life; or if it was an artillery round, he probably would be dead before he heard the bang.

Or worse, it might be a decoy attached to nothing but jungle brush. More than one point man had been scanning the jungle trail when he came upon a thigh-high wire strung across his path. His adrenaline would surge; Death was lurking nearby.

"I've got one!" he might yell, instantly stopping the patrol behind him.

Carefully, oh, so carefully, he would pinch the wire, delicately testing its tautness. If he was in a hurry, careless or uneducated, he might maintain his delicate hold and step over the wire. When his foot touched down, it might settle on the real danger, a trip wire attached to a Bouncing Betsy: a booby trap that exploded groin-high.

The men who followed depended on the point man for their lives too.

Once, in the early days of the war, a squad was patrolling outside of Da Nang. There was an opening in a hedgerow that the Americans had used before. The point man went through, and the squad bunched up as it hurried to follow him through. From somewhere a hidden Vietcong detonated the booby trap, wounding half the squad and killing the rest.

The only clue: det cord leading to a hidden position.

There were also punji pits of up to six feet deep that were lined on the bottom with sharp, barbed metal or bamboo spears that a hapless American might fall into. The enemy covered the punji sticks with excrement so that, if the sticks didn't kill you, the infection might; gangrene might set in, requiring amputation of one or both legs.

There were Malaya whips, too: head- and chest-high branches that were bent back and, when tripped, snapped forward, sending barbed darts whistling through the air at the patrolling Americans.

Or there could be snakes.

The enemy would capture the lethal reptiles, drive bamboo slivers through their tails, and attach them to the dangling vines that hung from overhead. An unsuspecting point man could be bitten on the neck by a deadly krait. His buddies could only call in a medevac chopper and watch him die.

And, of course, the enemy was there, waiting. If the point man concentrated entirely on the trip wires, det cords, punji pits and suspicious vines, he might look up and see the last thing he'd ever see: the flash from the wrong end of an AK-47.

Yeah, walking point was hazardous duty.

As he continued down the well-traveled trail that March morning, PFC Coker was scanning the area looking for any trace of the enemy. Suddenly he came upon five NVA soldiers. He shouted a warning back to the rest of the platoon, dove for cover, and opened fire with his M16, wounding one of the enemy soldiers.

The enemy withdrew from the area, and the lead squad of the 2nd Platoon aggressively pursued the fleeing NVA soldiers as they ran down the trail. The Marines had traveled the trail often and knew that just up ahead it bent sharply to the left. Immediately after the initial contact, the second squad charged off the trail to the left, flanking the NVA soldiers and effectively cutting off their avenue of escape.

With the trail blocked ahead, the enemy soldiers vanished into the thick underbrush off the trail. The Marines continued to the cutoff point, and when they found no trace of the enemy, they backtracked along the path until they found their trail. Carefully, they followed it along a small stream.

The NVA had taken refuge in a cave down a small ravine that was protected on all sides. An overhang provided protection from above. As the Marines approached, the enemy opened fire, seriously wounding a Marine named Playford in the stomach, groin and legs.

The rest of the squad dove for cover and took up positions, leaving the wounded Marine exposed in the killing zone. PFC Tim Barrett, PFC Jimmy Murphy, and Lance Corporal Warren Vanaman took up positions on the right while Staff Sergeant Clifford Goodau, Corporal Gifford Foley, and Lance Corporal Willie Terrell were on the left side of the cave.

PFC Coker, also on the left flank, realizing the imminent danger to his buddy, jumped up and ran forward to get Playford out of there. The AK-47s immediately began clattering away as he dashed forward.

When he entered the fire zone, PFC Coker was hit in the neck and chest by enemy small-arms fire, and he went down. Despite his own serious wounds, the young Marine continued on his mission.

With the AK-47s blasting and the Marines returning the fire, Coker threw a hand grenade at the enemy. Although the resulting explosion did not eliminate the enemy position, the NVA fire abated sufficiently to allow him to reach his destination—his wounded comrade.

Ignoring his own pain, PFC Coker began dragging the wounded American back to his squad. Once again, the sound of battle roared to a crescendo; AK-47s clamored away and M16s answered in return as both friendly and enemy hand grenades exploded.

The fierce battle continued all around while PFC Coker continued pulling his wounded buddy back. The enemy threw a Chi-Com (Chinese Communist) grenade, which landed on Playford's back and rolled to his side. The time bomb was ticking and could explode at any second, causing death or serious injury to Playford.

Without hesitation, PFC Coker snatched it up with both hands and turned away from his wounded buddy. However, before he could dispose of the grenade, the clock ran out and it detonated.

"The grenade blew up in Coker's hands," Jimmy Murphy recalled later, "and completely blew his hands off at the wrists."

Despite the fact that his hands were gone, PFC Ron Coker still couldn't be stopped.

As the firefight raged on, Ron rammed the stumps of his arms into his comrade's cartridge belt and continued to drag him back to the Marine lines and cover.

The enemy threw another grenade and another, and they landed next to Coker. He had no hands to attempt to throw them away, and they both exploded. The explosions blew away half his jaw and severely wounded the struggling point man in the legs and head, according to a later statement by Captain M. B. Riley, commanding officer for Company M, Three-Three.

Still, the valiant Marine refused to yield. He crawled back, dragging, pulling, muscling the wounded man with him.

Finally, one of the American fire teams was able to gain

fire superiority and suppress the NVA fire sufficiently for one of the Marines to dash forward and bring in both mortally wounded Americans.

Hospital Corpsman Roberto Valencia worked feverishly over Ron Coker, but the wounds were too savage, too numerous. "I worked on him," Valencia stated later, "but he died a short time later from loss of blood due to his many shrapnel wounds."

It was 1969 and the media had much to report:

In sports, the Jets upset the Colts in the Super Bowl, the Amazing Mets beat the Orioles in the Series and Muhammad Ali said, "I don't have to prove I'm better than Joe Frazier or anyone else. You're the champion until somebody beats you, and nobody has beaten me."

Students were rebelling at Harvard and black militants carried guns onto the Cornell campus.

In Washington, Richard Nixon became the thirty-seventh President of the United States, Vice President Spiro Agnew lashed out at the news media, and Attorney General John Mitchell was labeled Mr. Law and Order.

In a stream near Chappaquiddick, a girl named Mary Jo Kopeckne drowned and a U.S. Senator named Teddy Kennedy swam to safety.

In the obituaries were John Steinbeck, Norman Thomas, Allen Dulles, Boris Karloff, Gabby Hayes, Dwight D. Eisenhower, Judy Garland, John L. Lewis, Tate and LaBianca (victims of cult killer Charley Manson), Everett Dirksen and Ho Chi Minh.

In Beirut, the Israelis launched a reprisal against the Palestinians.

In Northern Ireland, the Catholics and the Protestants began an undeclared war.

In Libya, a twenty-eight-year-old military officer named Muammar Khadaffy overthrew King Idris I and raised the price of crude oil 20 cents to $2 a barrel.

In Paris, American and North Vietnamese officials bickered over the shape of the peace conference table.

In the Sea of Tranquillity, Neil Armstrong became the first man to walk on the moon.

And in Quang Tri Province, Ron Coker walked point.

2

The Unconquerable Soul

IT was cloudy and cool—typical weather for northern California in the fall—as the middle-aged educator and his guest strolled across the Stanford University campus. They had just eaten lunch at the faculty lounge where they had discussed history, humanities, philosophy, and yes, the war.

Both had served in Vietnam, but the older man had been there from beginning to end. He flew to the aid of the U.S.S. *Maddox* after it was attacked by North Vietnamese PT boats. Two days later, when she and the U.S.S. *Turner Joy* were "attacked" by sonar echoes, this aviator again flew to the rescue. These two incidents in the Gulf of Tonkin in August 1964 led to passage of the Gulf of Tonkin Resolution that bestowed unprecedented war powers upon President Lyndon Johnson.

A little over a year later this former Navy pilot was shot down over North Vietnam.

The visitor had many questions to ask this educator, but the approach of a student interrupted the discussion.

"Hi, Jim," the young man said to the teacher. "How's it going?"

"Fine, just fine," replied the retired Navy vice admiral. "Busy as usual. How are you doing?"

The young man rolled his eyes and said, "Midterms coming up, and you know how that is."

The teacher knew well the strain of college from his undergraduate days at Annapolis after World War II and his graduate studies at Stanford. "If you have the time and ever need someone to listen," he said, "you know where my office is." The student nodded and rushed off.

"I knew his dad in the Navy," the professor said to the visitor. About the departing student he added, "A real nice young man."

The visitor thought to himself, "Does the student know how you got that limp or how your arm was mangled? Does he know about the torture or the years of solitary confinement? Does he know about the sacrifice you offered for your prison mates?"

Possibly not; college students today—as always—have so many other things on their minds.

"I thank God for the other Americans I was imprisoned with," the former pilot said as they continued across campus. "The respect one develops for others in a POW situation is really indescribable.

"I think it might be best illustrated with a story of something that happened once when I was in solitary and under extremely close surveillance. I was in dire need of a morale boost when two other POWs, Dave Hatcher and Jerry Coffee, sent me a note at great risk to themselves.

"I opened it and found written the complete poem 'Invictus'.

> 'Out of the night that covers me,
> Black as the pit from pole to pole,
> I thank whatever gods may be,
> For my unconquerable soul."

JAMES BOND STOCKDALE

Rank: Vice Admiral (Ret.),   **Date:** September 4, 1969
(then Captain)   **Place:** Hoa Lo Prison,
Unit: U.S. Navy   North Vietnam
    Born: Abingdon, Illinois, December 23, 1923

The war—the air war over North Vietnam, anyway—
began August 2, 1964 when American and North Vietnamese naval vessels clashed in the Gulf of Tonkin.

The U.S.S. *Maddox*, according to an intelligence briefing for pilots aboard the aircraft carrier *Ticonderoga* that
morning, was moving up the coast of North Vietnam to
affirm its right to passage in international waters. As it
steamed about thirty miles off the coast, three North
Vietnamese PT boats closed on the American destroyer and
fired a couple of torpedoes at the *Maddox*, as well as a
couple of bursts of machine gun fire.

When the *Maddox* notified the *Ticonderoga* that she was
being shadowed by torpedo boats, four Crusaders, led by
then-Commander James Bond Stockdale converged on the
destroyer about three hundred miles away.

By the time the Crusaders soared over the *Maddox*, the
North Vietnamese had broken off the attack and were sailing
away. The jets attacked the fleeing PT boats and the North
Vietnamese returned fire. After several strafing runs, Commander Stockdale radioed the *Maddox*. "All boats hit, two
still underway to the coast, one dead in the water and
burning."

After the attack, the U.S.S. *Turner Joy* joined the
Maddox, and they patrolled together. Sometime after nine
P.M., Tuesday, August 4th, the two ships reported radar
contact five miles away.

For the next couple of hours there were confusing radio reports and the destroyers conducted evasive maneuvers. However, the *Turner Joy* was firing on "targets" the *Maddox* could not track on radar, and the *Maddox* was dodging "torpedoes" the *Turner Joy* could not hear on sonar. Neither ship was able to detect any enemy radio or radar emissions in the area.

Jim Stockdale had been flying support, diving on the patches of water immediately after they had come under fire by the destroyers, following up by spraying the area with his 20-mm cannon while trying to *find* enemy boats. For an hour and a half he tried in vain to pick up any sign of a PT boat, or even the wake of one in the highly luminescent water that made the destroyers' wakes glow persistently. Finally, desperately low on fuel, he headed back to his aircraft carrier, convinced that whatever enemy somebody thought was heading out toward the destroyers never showed up.

"When I went to bed about one o'clock on the *Ticonderoga*," Stockdale recalled in his office at the Hoover Institution, "everybody in the pilots' ready room was in a giddy, silly mood, laughing. At eight-thirty we had been getting messages from the destroyers saying they were expecting to be attacked any minute, and we were rushing to our planes like World War III was beginning. But by midnight even the destroyers were saying that there hadn't been any boats out there after all. We had gone through the complete fire drill, changing emotions like a roller-coaster ride, and fell drained, in total relief into our bunks.

"Over on the destroyer *Maddox*, the same thing. After the captain had announced to the crew that they had not been hearing echoes from torpedo boats or their torpedoes but aberrations caused by aiming the sonar aft while running at thirty knots with the rudder full over, a kind of crazy hilarity had set in, and those not on duty also turned into their bunks, totally relieved that it was all over. This was in a book I read by the medical officer on the destroyer.

"In the nineteenth century, before instant worldwide radio communications, that would have been the end of the whole matter. After such an exercise in false signals, seamen would have calmed themselves down with about three swigs of a bottle of booze and hit the sack, writing off that chapter as one big screwup. But in the twentieth century, those who command at sea have lost the authority to write off screwups.

"The messages of what was initially thought to be happening in the midst of earlier excitement continue to pour into busy headquarters at distant locations. And the eager beavers who make a profession of drawing word pictures for the commander in chief as messages spill in off the wire eventually have trouble finding words to explain that what they had been screaming at him for hours now turns out to be all bunk, and pretty soon the headquarters machine is running away with itself.

"In this case, we now know that the headquarters machine started running away with itself very early that evening, even before my planes took off from the carrier. When the messages that set the wheels moving—the ones that resulted in our launching—were read to the President, the House Majority Leader, Carl Albert was with him in the Oval Office.

"Albert remembered the President's reply and later quoted him as follows: 'I not only want retaliation, I want to go all the way into the shore establishments that support these PT boats and bomb them out of existence.' When you take into account the fact that he gave that order even before the destroyers issued their first alert messages, well over an hour before the first American gun fired a 'shot in the dark' up in the gulf, you can see what I mean.

"I think as the day wore on and the further we got into it, messages about what really happened that morning (Washington time) began coming in, and people were reluctant to go down into the lion's den (LBJ's office) and say, 'Hey, boss, you know what we've been saying for the last five hours? Well, that's all been bullshit.'

"Now who would want to do that? The President probably would have strangled the guy."

A tinderbox situation prevailed in Southeast Asia and there would be war in due course, but for the long pull it seemed important for Jim Stockdale that the entry of the United States be on more solid footing.

"When you go to war, you have got to do it in a way that will wash, because there will be many times when people will try to discredit your entry into the war. If there is any scandal and it is found out, then it is really inhibiting."

Three days later the Gulf of Tonkin Resolution was passed, and American's slippery slide into Vietnam began in earnest.

"The Tonkin Resolution was the engine of the war. It certainly started the air war in the north and is the closest thing we have to a watershed event in that war. I am somewhat impressed by Barbara Tuchman's statement in *March of Folly* when she said that it was no less significant than Fort Sumter or Pearl Harbor."

Thirteen months later, Jim Stockdale was in the midst of his second combat cruise in Vietnam as air group commander of the aircraft carrier *Oriskany*, flying sorties against North Vietnamese installations. Early on he discovered that enemy targets were being selected in Washington based on the belief that by not targeting key military installations peacemaking signals would be conveyed to the North Vietnamese leadership.

Political restraints employed by the United States government in the Vietnam War were one reason it became so frustrating, painful, and tragic for the men and women who fought under the new rules.

This frustration was apparent in September 1965, when a young Crusader photo pilot was killed. A week before he was shot down, the pilot had photographed a Russian cargo vessel unloading guns, ammunition, and Soviet surface-

to-air missiles at Haiphong. These munitions could not be
bombed because of the stipulations imposed by Washington.

"What a way to fight a war!" Stockdale reported later.
"Give Communist merchantmen free access to Haiphong
docks and watch them peaceably wave to you as they pass
your flight deck returning south while you hold a memorial
service for a pilot killed by the missiles they delivered."

American lives were being lost attacking worthless targets while U.S. warplanes overflew prohibited targets that
were crucial to the North Vietnamese war machine.

The day after the photo pilot was killed, possibly by one
of the missiles he had photographed, Jim Stockdale was
downed by antiaircraft fire while on a "milk run" against
low-risk targets between Vinh and Thanh Hoa.

The original target was the Thanh Hoa bridge, but
because of zero-zero visibility in the bridge area, he ordered
the thirty-five airplanes in his formation to split up and
proceed in pairs to the secondary targets specified in the
contingency briefing aboard the *Oriskany*.

He broke off and proceeded to his secondary target—the
boxcars on the siding between Vinh and Thanh Hoa. He
passed down the middle of the boxcars and dropped his
bombs in a neat pattern. As he was pulling up he heard the
distinctive *boom-boom-boom* of a 57-mm antiaircraft gun.

As the rounds impacted his Skyhawk, all of his red
warning lights went on. The forty-one-year-old commander
radioed "Mayday" as he pulled the ejection lever between
his legs. His parachute deployed, and as he descended, he
heard rifle fire from below. That's when he noticed the
bullets cutting into his parachute.

When he landed, Stockdale was set upon by North
Vietnamese villagers who pummeled and kicked him until
local authorities separated the American from the crowd. It
was then that he noticed his left leg had been shattered at the
knee. He couldn't lift his left arm, indicating either a broken
shoulder or back or both.

Jim Stockdale was crippled and escape for him would be impossible. He would be a POW for the duration. "I thought five years." He chuckled, "That wasn't the only thing I was naive about going in.

"The North Vietnamese prison where we American pilots were locked up was not a POW camp in the usual sense. It was a political prison.

"The conditions under which the American POWs existed [in Vietnam] had changed radically from those in Germany in World War II. It was no longer simply a matter of being shot down, descending in your parachute, going to a reasonably pleasant *Hogan's Heroes* prison camp, and sweating out the end of the war.

"At least, it was not that way in Vietnam.

"In Vietnam the American POW did not suddenly find himself on the war's sidelines. Rather, he found himself on one of the major battlefronts—the propaganda battlefront.

"Our enemy in Vietnam hoped to win his war with propaganda. It was his main weapon. Our captors told us they never expected to defeat us on the battlefield, but did believe they could defeat us on the propaganda front.

"Unlike the World War II POW, who was considered a liability, a drain on the enemy's resources and manpower, the American POW in Vietnam was considered a prime political asset. The enemy believed that sooner or later every one of us could be broken and used as ammunition on the propaganda front. Some of us might take more breaking than others, but all of us could be broken.

"Thus, for Americans who became POWs in Vietnam, capture meant not that we had been neutralized, but that a different kind of war had begun—a war of extortion."

This new type of war began for Stockdale when his North Vietnamese captors took him to a hospital in Hanoi to operate on his injuries, so he could get into some sort of prison routine.

After three operations they tried to get military informa-

tion from him to test his gratitude. He was given an Air
Force map and told to draw in-flight refueling areas.

The Navy didn't have specific in-flight fueling areas, and
he told this to the interrogator, named Eagle by the POWs.
That was logical and Stockdale believed that Eagle knew it.
Nevertheless, Eagle told Stockdale he had to make a mark
on the map to show his good attitude. Eagle had to have
something to show his superiors.

Stockdale realized that if he drew even fake marks on the
map, his captors would try to blackmail him with it later.
They were experts on blackmail and shame. He knew he
had to fight back. "It took me a while to get a handle on
how the game had to be played. At the time, I felt like a bug
on the floor, I felt like a beetle upside down being eaten by
ants. At that point it came to me.

"I said, 'I've got to get up on my feet and fight. I can't
just lie around and be a comatose turtle and not say
anything, be an oafish grouch. I've got to get up on my feet
and fight! I've got to have at that son of a bitch!'

"This was a great boon to my morale. I was crippled and
I had to have some outlet."

Stockdale refused the North Vietnamese attempt to elicit
information, and the enemy responded with torture. It was
simple but effective.

First, they knocked the injured American to a sitting
position on the ground and spread-eagled his legs. Then a
guard called Little Scruffy held his arms back as another
guard, Pigeye, began wrapping rope around his upper arms
while they screamed at him for his insolence and ingrati-
tude.

As they shouted, Pigeye put his foot in Stockdale's back
as he yanked on the rope, pulling his arms and shoulders
together, bending him forward at the waist.

He cried out in pain, and they stuffed a gag in his mouth.
Then Pigeye put his foot on the back of his neck and
pressed him forward as he continued yanking on the rope
until, finally, his head was touching the ground between his

legs. This stopped the circulation to his arms and they began to throb.

His guard removed the gag and told him to keep quiet, but in that position he was having trouble breathing. The pain in his shoulders and arms was incredible, and everything was beginning to close in.

As he thought about the possibility of suffocating, he began to get claustrophobic. He thought he was going to die.

"Do you submit, do you submit!" his tormentors shrieked.

Finally, he gasped, "Okay! My God! Yeah, I submit, I submit."

After a couple of minutes more, so that Stockdale wouldn't forget, Pigeye got off his back and began loosening the ropes. "What kind of airplane were you flying?"

So he told his guards which plane he had been flying.

"It doesn't sound like much, but they never got anything out of me that they didn't already know, and I don't think I am unusual.

"They know you know what type of airplane you are flying, what the target was, what unit you were in. If they want it, they are going to get it.

"They don't do it by boxing your ears or hitting you in the jaw, because those kinds of blows do not lend themselves to giving up information. They do it by putting you in the ropes and shutting off your blood circulation, by giving you claustrophobia, and so forth.

"If you can come out of one of those torture sessions and make the son of a bitch really give it to you, you go back to your cell feeling exuberant, because it didn't hurt anything.

"Sure, you had given the enemy information, but it had taken its toll on him, too, and all for something he already knew.

"But if you get yourself into such a state as to believe there is something sacred in revealing only the big four—a total misunderstanding of what the writers of our Code of Conduct had in mind—you might get a guilty conscience and that might start to destroy you from within. And guilt is what kills you.

"I can't imagine what would have happened to me if I had only tried to stay with just name, rank, serial number and date of birth over a four-year period and four hundred interrogations.

"We had a rule over there that it was best to give ground grudgingly before you lost your mental skills. The last thing you want to do is react to every little challenge as though it were your ultimate test of manhood and goad them into forcing you to spill your guts. You have to retain a credibility of defiance and save something to fight with the next day. This is a very hard thing to coach. Everybody is different.

"This is the same problem you have with a green football team. You tell them on the one hand to go out there and die for Dear Old Siwash, yet not lose control of their own destiny. The great majority of them will get the picture. But out of a squad of a hundred, there will be a small percentage that will cave in at the smallest twinge of pain; at the other extreme end of the spectrum, a couple of others will probably make it that test of their manhood and wind up choking on their own vomit. You have to allow for that.

"You have to get the feel of the ring, to get bloodied and disarrayed but still have your marbles and hopefully still have the finesse and the cunning to appear to have lost your marbles.

"This [being a successful prisoner] is hard to learn, and it takes getting the 'feel' of the thing. You will know when you are getting the hang of it when you begin feeling competitive and are able to manipulate *them* for a change, to plant misleading seeds in their minds.

"I was told in survival school that if you tough it out for a couple of weeks, they will leave you alone. That may work in a German prison camp, but Communist jailers are never going to leave you alone. You never want to say, 'That is my last torture.' Figure there is always going to be another one. Get it through your head that it's never too late to become a hero in a prison camp.

"In a prison camp, you've got to maintain your ego, you've got to have a belly for a fight.

"People ask, 'What do you hang on to? Is it God, is it country?'

"It's both, but more than that, it's to have a fixation on personal honor, that 'enigmatic mixture of conscience and egoism.'

"There are those who say, 'Well, if you love America and you love God, that's all you need.' There are a lot of people who love America and who love God who are pretty poor prisoners.

"In our situation in Hanoi, closeted in tiny cells, alone, or maybe with one other prisoner, the 'thing to hang on to' was the guy next door—to communicate with him, to tap through the wall to him, to level with him, to encourage him. By sowing the seeds of comradeship you become enveloped in a feeling of unified strength and selflessness. Our motto in prison was 'Unity over self.'

"When people ask, 'What is it that is going to keep you going in a prisoner-of-war environment? Is it a concept of this or a concept of that? How do you do it?'

"I'll tell you how you do it.

"You have to feel good about yourself and for that you've got to make them hurt you. It sounds dumb, but when you're in there, you've got to do a lot of things that sound dumb. There is a limit to what they can do in torture. They can't get anything out of you they don't know you have.

"When you are out there in combat on the floor—in the torture room with the interrogator, with the torture guard—you have to be a helluva lot more than a stoic Indian, or they will eat you alive.

"You have got to be able to know how you can make them stop their torture short of losing your rational skills and not give them the idea you are playing games with them.

"You can scare yourself to death if you think about it abstractly and rationally. Abstractions don't pass the test of combat. Once you've been in the torture room, been cinched up a few times, made them take you down to where you are pulp, you see that there is a limit and you can get used to that.

"You can't beat them but you can play games with them.

"You also learn when to submit. When they are getting into dangerous territory, you can submit early enough so as not to let them carry it on to where you go over the edge, to the point where you spill the family secrets."

The "family secrets" for Jim Stockdale was his participation in the Gulf of Tonkin Incident, particularly the August 4 aspect where there were apparently no attacking enemy PT boats.

When he was first captured, the North Vietnamese commander showed Stockdale a story in the *Pacific Stars & Stripes* concerning an air raid launched off the *Oriskany* a couple of weeks earlier. Since the North Vietnamese were reading the *Stars & Stripes*, then surely they knew of his involvement in the Tonkin Gulf incident. Stockdale's involvement was noted in the August 12, 1964 European edition which a friend in Germany had sent him.

If the North Vietnamese government were aware of this, it could create headlines around the world. Stockdale must not yield that information; he had to learn how not to give it up.

"I'm telling you how it is. If they know you know something, they are probably going to get you to say it. That's the nature of the torture system. They might not have gotten it at first, but they would have gotten it.

"I was worried sick.

"If they could get me to say that it didn't happen and President Johnson's justification for expenditures for the Vietnam War was based on fabrication, it would have caused a lot of trouble.

"I just didn't know what to do. I would have done

anything, including probably kill myself, to avoid being made a stooge of the enemies of America."

The fear that the North Vietnamese would pounce on him with the Gulf of Tonkin article was always lurking. Surely they had a copy and were just waiting. That in itself was torture: not knowing when the interrogators would spring the trap and ask him about Tonkin. Luck was on Stockdale's side, because they never read the article.

The paragraph about Stockdale had appeared in the European edition of *Stars & Stripes*, but somehow that paragraph—and only that paragraph—had been deleted in the Asian edition. Stockdale didn't discover this until after his release, so every time he faced his interrogators, he waited for the shoe to drop.

While he was never confronted with this shoe, there were others.

There was an interrogator, named Rabbit by the prisoners, who was one-on-one with Stockdale for about three years.

"He was an officer and his job was to get my number. Well, after a fashion, he got mine, and I got his. It's impossible to spend an hour a day with a guy for years and not get to know what makes him tick. Now don't get the idea we ever met on even terms. I was always seated in the inferior position, on a stool if he was on a chair, on the floor if he indicated that was where he wanted me; he steered the conversation and I volunteered nothing. There was no familiarity. But flashes of anger erupted, particularly when he was trying to put the make on me for some kind of propaganda stunt, and we would both lose our cool and start calling each other sonsofbitches.

"We didn't come to the point of personal expressions of vindictiveness overnight. It came about over months of contact. It was when we both had a measure of each other's strengths. My strength was that I knew that he had deadlines to meet. He had a boss, a commissar, and bureaucratic pressures to produce a stream of intimidated prisoners to meet the commissar's propaganda requirements laid down by *his* boss.

"Rabbit's strength was the ropes, but ordinarily he didn't have the authority to have them applied unless he had some sort of 'moral' justification, like my breaking a prison rule. So our battleground was framed with these limitations, and over time our tempers tended ever more frequently to explode into shouting matches.

"It was for these shouting matches that I saved up disquieting seeds that I wanted to plant in his mind. Once the barriers are dropped and shouting starts, a man acquires a license to say things that he could not get away with in measured conversation. A smart prisoner learns to feign spontaneity.

"Sure, he had the ropes and I was going in them again, but it wasn't a stoic Indian versus an oriental ogre. It was two pretty smart guys. Each had assets and each was going after the other.

"I always lost, but when we started shouting, I knew I could feign a response. It was like a cheap act, but every so often I would come to the end of my string and would start shouting things at him that I had no business shouting.

"In a sense, after prolonged association with extortionists with total power on their side, one learns that his best defense often lies in the field of drama.

"My mother was a drama coach and I learned to act from her, and this was very helpful in prison. When I talk about drama, I mean over a period of months to find ways to express sullenness and contempt short of a point that will get you slapped silly every day. You want to avoid that because it will cause you to lose energy. This—theatrics—would come in handy when Rabbit was being pressured to get me to make a public statement or an appearance before a visiting delegation.

"He came in one time after I had submitted and said that there was a visiting delegation and I had to talk to it. The questions were prearranged, as were my 'answers.'

"I had to do something that he thought was spontaneous, a product of my total loss of control. I had to give him the signal that I was a high risk of embarrassment to him, and to his boss, and his boss' boss, in public.

"So, I came to my feet without being given permission— violating all rules of prisoner conduct—upset the table, and shouted with conviction and a wild expression on my face, 'No, goddamnit! I won't do it!'

"This caught him completely off guard and he said, 'Now, calm down, Stockdale, calm down.' He had a deadline to meet and this was throwing a monkey wrench in it because he would be held responsible if I acted up before a delegation.

"However, this was a dangerous tactic, because if Rabbit thought for one minute that I had only been acting, he would have put me in the ropes and had me crying like a baby. I had to make him believe I was beyond my limit."

Another tool in Stockdale's arsenal was disfigurement. Once he was given a razor and told to shave, but he had already learned that there was no such thing as a free shave. A public display was imminent, and he had to sabotage the enemy's plan.

When the guard left, the cagey American lathered his hair and began shaving a swath down the middle of his head, sort of a reverse Mohawk. His hair was dry and matted. In his hurry to get it cut before the guard returned, he dug into his scalp with the razor. When the guard returned, he screamed and took the insolent American to Rabbit. As blood ran down his shoulders, Stockdale quietly assumed a sitting position on the floor and waited for the inevitable.

But Rabbit yelled, "No! You don't deserve the ropes."

The North Vietnamese had planned to use him in a propaganda film before his "haircut". Rabbit was pretty cagey, too; he said that the movie would be filmed anyway. Stockdale would wear a hat.

He was locked up again, and he thought about countering their hat move. Time had also become his enemy. He had to do something immediately. The only thing in the room was a small stool. Not much, but it was all he needed.

He took the stool and began hitting himself in the face. Before they were able to stop him, Stockdale bashed, hammered and pummeled himself until he was not presentable for public display.

Blood flowed down his face when the stool was taken from him. Rabbit looked at him and went to report Stockdale's belligerence to the camp authority. Left alone again, Stockdale went over to a wall and banged his face against it a couple of times for good measure.

Planned irrationality and disfigurement were only two weapons in Stockdale's arsenal that helped keep his enemy off-balance. There was a third; one that frightened his foe and helped end the terror in the POW camps.

The POWs in North Vietnam were forbidden to communicate with one another. If caught talking without permission or transmitting notes, the likely result would be a session in the ropes. The North Vietnamese understood Morse code, so the Americans developed a specialized tap code.

This, too, was banned, and the punishment when caught was just as severe. More than one American POW had been killed in the torture room, but basic communication with other Americans was needed to avoid the desperate feeling of being alone.

In September 1969, Jim Stockdale was caught writing to a fellow prisoner. In the note was information that with help of the ropes would reveal the names of other POWs who were also guilty of transmitting communications. Those with whom he had been in direct contact would be uncovered and, in turn, they would be tortured and name others.

Initially, Stockdale was worked over all day, including being slapped with a fan belt to the face, but he held out. At the end, though, his tormentor warned that the following day Stockdale would yield the details his interrogator was seeking.

Stockdale thought about what would happen if he gave up the names the North Vietnamese sought: For his comrades there would be more beatings, more ropes, more deaths.

The imminent interrogation had to be avoided, but how? The year before he had successfully fought off the hat move, but this was different, more extreme. Extreme problems sometimes require extreme solutions.

Again he went on the offensive.

After a roving guard had checked his cell, Jim Stockdale popped out a windowpane and went to work on his wrists with the shattered glass. He slashed, stabbed, punctured the artery. His blood gushed from the self-inflicted wounds, and he waited alone for Death and one final victory.

As he drifted into semiconsciousness, the guards discovered his plot and rushed into his cell. They had arrived in time, and the unconquerable American was saved.

The next day a guard offered Stockdale a cup of tea and asked why he did such a terrible thing.

"I'm tired of being treated like an animal, being followed, questioned, hounded," Stockdale answered. "I'm a prisoner of war and I'm tired of being nagged to death."

He was told that he would be moved, but nothing was said about him being a communicator or about continuing the interrogation. After his wounds had healed, Stockdale was told that the North Vietnamese were investigating the possibility of improving living conditions for the Americans.

The brutality of the previous four years was behind him and he had won.

"Sometimes I could get Rabbit so mad at me, he would start telling me things I knew he wasn't supposed to tell me. I had to do the same thing—make him believe that I was so angry, that I had lost control and was telling him something I shouldn't. I had to know when he thought I was at that point, so I could say things I wanted to get across.

"I remember one time when I had been photographed after I had come out of the ropes. When I was talking to

Rabbit a couple of years later, I said, 'Do you remember that time about two years ago after you had me in the ropes and you said I pleased you because I gave you all of that propaganda? Well, you get that film out and look at it! See what my right hand is doing? It looked like this!

" 'Do you know what that means to a Western audience? That means bullshit! Everything I said was bullshit! And that has been spread all over the world! Now, goddamn you, you go back and look at that photograph and think it over!'

"Normally, that is not a smart thing to say, and if I had said it as a matter of rationality, he would have thought that something was funny. Therefore it had to appear spontaneous.

"When that picture was being taken, I knew then that there would come a time it could be seeded back and perhaps give my captors second thoughts about releasing other photographs of other prisoners of war.

"One time Rabbit went off his rocker.

"They were not to tell us anything about their personal lives; they were not to tell us their names, whether they were married or anything about themselves.

"But Rabbit was a braggart, and during one of these sessions, he started talking about how I thought I was a scholar, yet didn't know anything about Marxism. I had taken a course here at Stanford—Comparative Marxist Thought—and I did know more about it than he did. I know what Lenin said; I read his books.

"Sometimes I would tell Rabbit, 'That's bullshit; Lenin didn't say that and you don't understand the dialectic.'

"Well, he would get mad at this, and one time he blurted out, 'I am a party member.'

"He wasn't supposed to tell me that, but that was his trump card in this particular argument. I replied—not too cleverly—'Okay, what are the criteria to get in that party?'

"He said, 'There are only four: one, you've got to be seventeen years of age; two, you have to be smart enough to understand the theories; three, you have to be selfless, you have to give with no compensation; and four,—this is the most important—you have to have the *innate* ability to influence others.

"He spelled this out, and that told me something. It told me that party members, to pick other members, probably had practiced eyes that could detect this innate leadership ability. I had come to realize that those prisoners I valued as the best leaders were seen by the Vietnamese as their worst trouble-makers. What are troublemakers to one side in such a standoff as this are leaders to the other.

"This explained why we all had so many seemingly pointless hours of interrogation by the political officers. They were trying to separate us out in terms of innate leadership/troublemaking qualities. They had to keep our natural leaders in solitary if they wanted to control the population.

"I had been interrogated by Rabbit at least two hundred times, thirty to forty minutes at a stretch. That doesn't mean he put the ropes on me that many times; he didn't. I think he put me in the ropes fifteen times. I had a good idea not only of Rabbit's personality, but also of what sort of acts he was capable and not capable. And, of course, that was the same data he was gathering on me. 'What sort of threat to our regime is this guy?' That is *the* question Communists concentrate on.

"They study nature. And they are good at it. To minimize damage to their prison regime, they put the right people in solitary. This became my best American performance indicator: 'Show me a prisoner with over two years in solitary, and I'll show you an American leader.'

"I remember what Rabbit said to me as he walked out of what became his last-ever interrogation of me. 'You know,' he said, 'I am sick of you. I am going to get off of this detail. I can't stand you. You are a very clever actor. For four years, all I've done is provide you a stage on which to perform.' That was a great shot in the arm for me, a high compliment.

"I did see him the last day, the day I got out of prison. He was standing at the gate with a clipboard, and he read each guy's name as we were individually marched through the tent. I thought I recognized his voice as I approached the tent—you couldn't see into the tent until you were first in line.

"When I marched in he said, 'James Bond Stockdale,' with a half glower, a half sneer as I walked out. And as I walked right past him into freedom, I could sense his eyes scanning my face.

"What would I do if I ran into him in a bar in Paris? Probably buy him a beer. There wasn't much room in a prison underground leader's life for hatred. Hatred tends to take command of you just when you have to keep so many other things in mind."

3

Grenade

HE was a quiet man, and he and his visitor sat unnoticed by a swimming pool in Arlington, Virginia, sipped beer and talked about events that had happened ten thousand miles away, fifteen years and fifty-eight thousand lifetimes ago—from Tonkin to Tet and beyond. The man had been seriously wounded, yet he hadn't lost his youthful appearance.

While he was recovering from his injuries at the Balboa Naval Hospital in San Diego, cities were exploding in racial violence, universities were being forced to shut down, and soldiers were being cursed.

The man shook his head, and then told a story of courage and compassion that only combat soldiers know. It began with a conscious act of kindness and ended with the President of the United States awarding John Baca the Medal of Honor as his proud mother looked on.

But there is more to his story—yes, much more.

JOHN P. BACA

Rank: Specialist Fourth   **Date:** February 10, 1970
Class
Unit: Company D, 12th   **Place:** Phuoc Long Prov-
Cavalry, 1st Cavalry Division   ience, Vietnam
  Born: Providence, Rhode Island, January 10, 1949

"I got to Vietnam July 20, 1969; funny how a date like that will stick in your mind.

"I was in-country about four months, and some enemy soldiers walked along the trail where we were setting up an ambush. I had seen them coming and was ready—I had my 90 [millimeter recoilless rifle] set up—but our OPs [outposts] weren't set up yet. I had a beehive in the 90, and had I fired, I would have blow away the OPs, so I didn't fire.

"However, my company CO got ticked off because we hadn't done anything to keep the NVA from going back where they had come from. So he radioed the colonel and they made us start walking point. I didn't mind.

"There I was, out on point.

"I think I was the only point man in the company who, up to that time, hadn't been hit. Every other point man in the company had been either wounded or had gotten killed.

"It must have been late December. We had just moved from the Long Binh area up to the Quang Loi Song Bay area; that was where our company was set up, where we operated out of. I guess I called home Christmas.

"They flew us into this one area and we were marching along this mountainside; a path had been carved into the mountain. On the other side was a big river, I don't remember the name.

"We had come into an abandoned bunker complex to set up for anybody coming up the trail. We searched it out for a couple of days, looking for any trace of the enemy, and to see if they had left anything behind.

"I was looking around and I found what appeared to be a barbershop, where they had set up a barber chair out there in the jungle to cut hair. I was kind of curious and I was looking around.

"I came up on a hill and heard some voices down below. The voices carried and it sounded like a few people—NVA, gooks, the enemy, whatever—together.

"They had been sniping at us for a couple of days, and we were looking for somebody to blow away. We had been carrying some of our own bodies with us for a while, looking for a clear place to bring in a chopper and evac them out.

"I got a little ahead of the backup men, and I kept hearing the voices. They kept getting louder and louder, and I got close enough to throw a grenade to where the voices were coming from.

"There was a little valley, a ravine, and I threw a grenade, but it went a little too far and exploded up on the hillside. But then it seemed like just one voice. He must have been with this other fellow who split. Maybe they were setting up an ambush.

"Anyway, he was looking down the trail expecting help, and I just kind of maneuvered in and saw this guy down there; I guess he was Vietcong. I don't know—it's hard to say—but I do know he had a lot of information on him.

"I had come up and exposed myself, looking right at him. I had a clear view. He was looking at me, talking to me in his language, and I was waiting for the guys to hurry up and get behind me.

"They were either coming up or setting up, because there was movement around me.

"He had his weapon along side him—a 47. I knew what to say to him to ask him to surrender. I guess that was what he was waiting to hear. When I said, 'Chu Hoi?' he said, 'Yeah.'

"I was waiting for that.

"He had been wounded in the leg, I think from artillery fire—my grenade had gone by him—and had been left behind by his squad because he might have slowed them up.

"My friend Art James was with me. We have always kept in contact; we were wounded together and I guess our friendship will last forever.

"You depend on the man next to you. I guess if anybody had any love, it was when they were overseas with their buddies. Maybe they didn't know how to verbalize it, yet it was experienced every day. You knew you could count on the guy next to you. He was with me when I got the prisoner.

"Anyway, I got the enemy soldier to move over a little, and Art came over and helped me pick him up and carry him back up the hill. We brought him back and patched him up. We were talking to him. He was scared. He had a couple of hundred dollars in their money and gold chains on him. He also had a lot of documents.

"He was talking his head off, and we fed him some lousy C rations. We patched him up and he kept saying to me, 'You Number One GI, you Number One GI.'

"I was really happy to take that guy alive.

"When we were back in the rear, the lieutenant and some of the guys wanted to talk to me. They wanted to commend me for what I did.

"They hadn't seen a prisoner till then; it was the first time we had taken anyone alive. They were coming around just to see the guy close up. I could have killed him; anybody could have killed him.

"They were saying, 'Thanks for taking him alive. It helped me and my attitude.' Seeing them alive made you wonder. Shooting guys who were two, three, four years younger than we were—taking their lives. It also made you anxious to come home.

"He had pictures of his family. He started talking to us

with the interpreter, a Kit Carson scout. It made you want to cry.

"If it's him or you, you are going to blow him away; that's the way it is in combat. I don't know why I didn't kill him. I went over as a Christian person, and I wanted to remain a Christian. If anybody else would have come across him before I did, I know they would have killed him. That is what they were telling me.

"Taking that prisoner alive, that was nice, real nice. He heard us coming, a hundred people walking through the jungle make a lot of noise. He must have had some people with him setting up an ambush, waiting for us to get exposed and then blow us away. I knew I could shoot him, kill him, and that would have been okay, but I didn't.

"He had documents and he talked to the interrogators, because the colonel gave us an R & R, our squad. Apparently, that fellow revealed a lot about the enemy movements in that area. Our squad got an in-country R & R for three days for that, just the one guy.

"It was December 1969, I think, when I captured him. I'm sure of it, because I had called my mom for Christmas. This would have been about two months before I got wounded.

"At that same time a lieutenant got shot in the neck and died. He had been following a trail of blood when he was hit. That's what was scary, following blood trails. Sometimes the other platoons would wound somebody and run up and wouldn't find them.

"There were no dead, just wounded and they'd have the 4th Platoon—the heavy-weapons platoon—follow the blood trails. That was frightening, seeing the blood traces.

"I don't know if I killed anybody over there. We always had mad minutes where you waste your ammo and you might hear, 'Oh, yeah, we got some wounded or killed,' and never find any traces of them.

"The night I got wounded, we had been selected to go on

patrol and set up an ambush. I had a feeling something was going to happen; call it intuition, a feeling, a premonition.

"Just prior to that, our machine gunner had blown away two guys walking down the trail. We knew there were people all around us. We had moved into the area maybe a week prior to that, and there were flashlights and all of this noise and commotion.

"We landed at nighttime and scared the hell out of them. We had just come in from a fire base in the field after thirty days for a couple of days of rest.

"My friend Art, another fellow, and I went out with another platoon. A helicopter dropped us off and we set up a couple of automatic-weapons ambush positions; we set up trip wires and all that kind of stuff. That was to let us know when there was somebody else in the area.

"I don't think we dug any foxholes.

"There was movement out front and then several explosions. I guess the NVA walked into one of our ambushes. I don't know how many were involved, but a few of our guys went to check it out and they got fired at.

"The rest of us in the squad went out and we had a couple of people wounded. The machine gunner got shot, a sniper got wounded, and another guy got hit.

"It was really confusing; I was trying to set up the 90-mm and was about to fire a round when a grenade came in. I guess one of them had gotten close enough to throw one in.

"I saw it and was trying to get the other people's attention. I don't know how many people were around, but I think there were eight.

"I was aware of what I did when I put my helmet on it. Most people don't believe you are conscious of what you are doing in a situation like that, but I was fully aware of what I was doing, and I was scared.

"I alerted them, put my helmet on it and covered over it. I don't know why I did it. It was there and I don't think anybody else saw it. I noticed it and, well, somebody had to do something.

"I thought I was going to get killed, but I thought it better one person than a bunch of people. I knew when I put my helmet on it that it was all over; anyway, I was pretty sure.

"I yelled, got their attention. I'm not sure what I yelled. 'Grenade!' or 'Grenade in our midst!' [He chuckles.] Right, John, yeah, sure. 'It's right here!'

"When I realized it was going to go off, I guess I screamed. It would have been embarrassing if it had been a dud, but, oh boy, would I have liked it to have been a dud!

"As soon as I screamed, it went off, *BOOOOOM-MMMM,* and blew me up and backward. It blew up inside the helmet and I screamed. It blew out some of my stomach and ripped parts of my legs away.

"I remained conscious all of the time.

"I didn't feel anything.

"I was numb.

"It was peaceful, really peaceful. I was lying on my back and there was confusion all around. It was kind of frightening, but I was more or less just numb and I didn't feel the pain. I wasn't sure if my legs were still on.

"I was thirsty, all of the liquids drained right out of me. I was calling for Art, and he was yelling to see if I was all right. I could hear him yelling, and I think he tried to get up and run over to me.

"I was afraid the enemy was going to overrun us. Everyone was running around, and I didn't know exactly what was going on. I wanted to warn people to watch over me, because, well . . . that's what scared me then, that one of the enemy soldiers just might walk up and shoot me.

"But then I was almost absent from it all, detached. I don't mean to say that there was any out-of-body movement. It wasn't like I was above looking down on my body. But I wasn't really there, either; I was out of it. That's what was peaceful about it.

"I didn't feel the pain for a while. I sensed that there was a presence there, a kind of peace. It was like it was over behind me and I looked. It was comforting me.

"It was a very peaceful moment, and I was ready to die at that point. I mean, I was ready, it was such a peaceful moment.

"I was thinking, 'Oh, this is not so bad.' I realized that my stomach was hanging out—that's why they didn't give me any morphine, or any liquids to drink—and I still wasn't sure about my legs.

"I looked up and could see my stomach coming out, one leg was sticking out and I could see rips in it. I started crying because I realized what had happened, and I was hoping that I wouldn't die.

"But then I realized that I wasn't going to die, and I began waiting for the helicopters to come in and medevac us out. I didn't know if they were going to be able to get in, because we were still in a firefight.

"Bullets were flying around and I knew the choppers weren't going to come in if there was still action.

"There was a new medic who had just broken in, and he didn't know what to do. My guts were all blown away and he just panicked. He put a dressing over it. He had never seen a wound like that before—nobody had.

"I was thinking, 'Boy! Is Mom going to be pissed at me when she sees this! She's really going to bawl me out when I get home.'

"I think they all thought I was dead, or dying right there.

"I was in shock, but I was conscious all of the time. Art James was with me; he had had his legs messed up. When the grenade blew up in the helmet, it blew out the side and got Art in the ankles; it messed up his legs.

"They eventually medevaced us out together. When we came back to the States, our company was in contact almost every day. I was in the Balboa Naval Hospital in San Diego, and his dad found out where I was at. He said to me, 'You brought my boy back.'

"I later saw Art James at Friendship Field in Baltimore— what an appropriate name—and we both had our casts on, had our khaki uniforms on, canes; we looked like bookends.

"It was frightening, coming back to the World, though, and adjusting with all of the riots and stuff. War and rebellion here in our own country.

"If I knew then what I know now, I probably would have been a protester against the war. Having government officials back here deciding how the war should be fought without having been there or [having] any idea what it was like over there, that bothered me. That bothered all of us.

"But I trusted in the Lord. 'If He wants me to go, I'll go.' I didn't have anything against it—against the war, I mean. A lot of people were demonstrating against it then, but I felt I had to go; it was my duty.

"But I'm glad I was there. I'm glad I did what I did. I would have stayed in the Army had they not medically discharged me. Looking back, I still feel I did the right thing. Sure, it was where I seemed to be at the time.

"When I came home I was a little different and adjusted better than most veterans, because of the time I spent in the hospital. I had a lot of attention. Everyone there had heard what had happened to me, and they wanted to help.

"There were a couple of nurses who I cared about, and who really cared about me. A couple of the guys I hung around with came to see me; one guy had been wounded in the head and the other lost his leg. All of the people I knew prior to the service, though, never came around.

"If someone came around when they were changing my dressing, they never came back again. I guess they didn't want to see it. They cared, but you just get wore out.

"I spent a year in the hospital and then I went to a liberal arts college and took some Bible classes as well as some general education classes.

"The president of the college knew what happened; he got the phone call that I was going to see President Nixon at the White House and receive the Medal of Honor. But most people were unaware.

"It was funny. I was in school all that semester and nobody even said hi, and all of a sudden they wanted to hear about what went on overseas. I went through a semester of school and they finally talked to me the last day of school. They were curious and wanted to know what happened.

" 'What was it like to kill somebody? What was it like to have your guts blown up?' They just want to hear the gory stories.

"I just kind of closed myself off. I hung out with a few veterans. I spent a lot of time in prayer and meditation.

"But I like to tell kids today, 'Hey, I didn't kill anyone.'

"If somebody just comes up and asks point-blank, I don't say anything. It's too personal.

"I've had a few interviews with newspapers and television stations and I've seen what they do, what they cut out. When you are talking to them, you can see the emotion in them and they sometimes say, 'John, what you have said really touches the heart.'

"But the news, well, they don't seem to pick that up. It's all cut out and edited. I think that last time I talked to a Channel 9 newsman for fifteen or twenty minutes, and all that got on was twenty seconds.

"They flew my mom to Japan when I got wounded, because I was on the border; the border of whether I would live or die. But I knew I was going to make it. I figured that if I didn't die when I was wounded, I would make it through whatever operations and stay alive in the hospital.

"The guy in the bed next to me lost both arms and a leg. Just a young kid. Another guy next to me lost most of his back. My mom watched them change the dressings. Those guys had to have morphine to change their dressings.

"A couple of guys had their eyes blown out from [mine explosions]. You could smell their burned flesh. They had third-degree burns, and when there was no one around, they'd freak out. I would go and hold their hands.

"A general came in and gave the guys a Purple Heart.

"It was a sad time in the hospital.

"They didn't show that back here. The news never picked up on that."

4

Harvest Moon

IT was Military Day at Cheshire High School, Cheshire, Connecticut, and the military service representatives were attempting to recruit students into their respective branches. The junior and senior boys were assembled in the school auditorium, with faculty members observing from the rear of the room as each recruiter got up to give his pitch.

The Air Force recruiter got up to explain the advantages of joining the United States Air Force. He was greeted with catcalls and whistles from the young high-schoolers.

The Army recruiter received the same treatment, as did the Navy recruiter.

Then the Marine recruiter, a seasoned gunnery sergeant, rose and glared.

"There is no one here worthy of being a United States Marine," he growled. "I'm deplored that the faculty in the back of the room would let the students carry on like this. There isn't anybody here I want in my Marine Corps."

When he sat back down, several eager students swarmed around his table.

One of those hovering around the gunny's table was Cheshire High School Senior Class President Harvey Barnum, Jr. He did the paperwork to enlist as a senior in high school and joined the Platoon Leadership Class when he got to St. Anselm College in Manchester, New Hampshire.

He joined the Marine Corps—raised his hand—November 12, 1958.

HARVEY C. "BARNEY" BARNUM, JR.

Rank: Colonel (then Lieutenant) **Date:** December 18, 1965
Unit: H Company, 2nd Battalion, 9th Marines **Place:** Ky Phu, Quang Tin Province
Born: Cheshire, Connecticut, July 21, 1940

"Let's go back a few years before my initial assignment to Vietnam.

"I was stationed in Okinawa with the 3rd Marine Division in '63 as the fire-support coordinator for the 9th Marine Infantry Regiment. As you recall, we mounted out on three or four different occasions that year to go to Vietnam to secure the hills around the Da Nang air base.

"We never got there.

"On one occasion I was in the Philippines, firing naval gunfire, and was called back in from the naval gunfire range to Subic. The ships were going to pick up my forward observers and naval gunfire spotters on the way to Vietnam. That never materialized.

"I was aware of what was going on, because I was in on the preparation. On two other occasions, we boarded aircraft, took off, and returned to secure Kadena Air Base on Okinawa. The missions changed from contingency movements to exercises when entry into Vietnam was called off.

"That was twenty-one years ago.

"I was stationed at Marine Barracks, Pearl Harbor, when one of the officers at Marine Barracks, Barber's Point, a

Captain Gardner said, 'You know, it's kind of tough, having these young troops here in the Pacific guarding doors, classified information and buildings while there is a war going on.'

"After commenting about this situation to his fellow officers, Captain Gardner drafted a proposal, suggesting an alternative. He proposed sending company-grade officers and staff NCOs to combat in Vietnam for a two-month period, serve in their individual MOS [military specialty], and come back to the barracks in the Pacific to tell the troops what was going on over there. He felt that this would help motivate the troops by showing them that what they were doing in Hawaii was very important even though there was a conflict going on at the time in Southeast Asia.

"The program was approved by General Victor Krulak, Commanding General Fleet Marine Force (Pacific), and Marine Barracks, Pearl Harbor, was assigned the first quota—an officer and a staff NCO. At that time there were, I believe, twenty-four officers in the barracks, and I was the only bachelor.

"I had already augmented, indicating that I was planning to stick around the Marine Corps for a while. Consequently, I volunteered to go do what I had come into the Marine Corps to do.

"'If this is going to be my chosen way of life,' I reasoned, 'then I'd better find out what it's all about.' Of course, in addition to career considerations, there was a great deal of adventure, excitement, anticipation—launching off into the unknown.

"I went to my commanding officer and said, 'You know, it's going to be over the holiday season, Christmas and New Year's, so I feel that I should be the one to volunteer. Why send a married man? He'll get his opportunity in the months to come.' Boy, was that a ploy to get that assignment, but it worked.

"My CO approved my request, and myself and First Sergeant [John] Matson—a big man from security company—were the first to go to Vietnam on the program. I was assigned to Echo Battery, 2nd Battalion, 12th Marines, the same battery that I commanded later during my '68–'69 tour.

"The purpose of the program, in my particular instance, was to allow me the opportunity to serve as a forward observer, fire-direction officer and XO, and then come back and relate my experiences to the troops.

"But it was more than that—Vietnam, I mean. There was another side that people back home didn't hear about.

"We were involved in the military side of the war, of course, but we also participated in the people-to-people aspect of the war. We did a lot of work with the people and the local orphanages, and we worked hard. These activities didn't receive much press, but it was still something we all were proud of.

"After my [Medal of Honor] action, I also served with Lima Battery, Four-Twelve, for a couple of weeks to get a feel for the '55s. There were major differences between the '05s and the '55s and it was vital to understand them with regard to the security aspects for movements, employment and deployment of the towed, self-propelled guns.

"When I got in-country, the first thing I noticed about Vietnam was the smell—latrines burning at Da Nang; it was really something. We used fifty-five gallon drums cut in half and they were burned off every day—a smell no Vietnam vet will ever forget.

"Another thing was that when I got there in December 1965, there had been a lot of rain and the red mud was knee-deep. This was before there were many roads in Da Nang, before the buildup.

"When I arrived, I joined my unit south of Da Nang. We were located near the CP of 2nd Battalion, 9th Marines in a stationary position firing in support of Two-Nine when they went out on their daily patrols.

"I was assigned as the forward observer for Hotel Company and I joined them in their position on the battalion perimeter. We were on patrol on the Anderson Trail, where one of the first big ambushes took place—VC ambushed Marines—and we were recalled. If I remember, this happened on my second patrol with the unit.

"We immediately terminated the patrol and were airlifted out to replace Fox Company from Two-Seven. They had been in a firefight and had several battlefield casualties, as well as a great number of immersion foot casualties. They had been participating in Operation Harvest Moon for several days. Hotel Company joined Two-Seven for the remainder of the operation."

"It was around noon on the 18th of December. The lead elements of the battalion march column had entered into Ky Phu and had proceeded through. H & S Company was just entering the village and we heard firing.

"Hotel Company was the rear element, tail security. I was thirty or thirty-five yards behind Hotel Company commander Captain Paul Gormley. His radioman was right behind him. We were coming around this little hill with rice paddies to the right and about two or three hundred meters between our lead element and the village of Ky Phu.

"I still say the initial round that triggered the ambush on the rear element hit the company commander. I'm pretty sure it was a rocket, probably a B-40 rocket, and then all hell broke loose.

"It happened that quick.

"It was a matter of minutes. I had heard firing in the distance, up toward Ky Phu, and all of a sudden we were right in the middle of it. The commander was walking along with the radio antenna sticking up and they picked it out. And, boy, they did it right; they took out the commander.

"Of course, we all took cover and started returning fire. I remember the corpsman running by me—Wesley 'Doc Wes' Berrard, a black corpsman from the Chicago area if I recall.

"He called back and said, 'The company commander is seriously wounded.' Then Doc Wes was shot. My scout sergeant ran forward to help the Doc and cover him with return fire. Then he was shot.

"At that point I ran forward to the company commander and his radio operator. The young radio operator had been killed outright, and Captain Gormley was mortally wounded. I picked him up, carried him back to safety, and he died in my arms.

"I went back out and carried Doc Wes back.

"I returned to where Captain Gormley and the radio operator had been hit and took the radio off the dead operator, a PRC-25, and strapped it to myself. I called in artillery, but we were at max range. Jerry Black was battery commander, and boy, he was giving it all he had. We also had Huey gunfire support.

"It wasn't a VC ambush; it was NVA, tenacious little bastards.

"I got close to some of the NVA and fired my .45 a couple times. I also had an M14 rifle and went through my ammunition rather rapidly, because you could see where the enemy fire was coming from across the rice paddy less than fifty meters away.

"As I used up my ammunition, I went from the firing mode into the listening, analyzing, and giving direction mode.

"I got on the radio and told our battalion commander, Lieutenant Colonel Leon Utter, what had happened, the condition we were in and that I had assumed command of the company. I don't think there was an XO, I don't remember, it's been so long, but I was not the senior guy. One of the platoon commanders had seniority and could have assumed command of the company, but I was there and I had things in motion.

"I told Colonel Utter, 'The platoon commanders have their hands full. I am aware of what is going on and I have assumed command.'

"He told me, 'Continue to march and make sure everyone knows you are the boss.'

"I did.

"I think one of the things that was phenomenal about the battle is for the next three or four hours all company commanders, the battalion commander, and the helicopters were on the same radio frequency. By listening, you could tell what was going on.

"When you figured that you were in a worse situation than the other guy, then you would butt in on the frequency.

"I led a couple of counter-attacks against the enemy positions to our right flank and rear.

"There was incoming fire off to our right flank, and I went up on this little hill to get a better view. I could see where the fire was coming from and I pointed out targets for our Huey gunships to take under fire.

"I knew that I would have better luck with the gunships than the artillery, because the enemy was entrenched at the edge of the artillery's maximum range. In order for the artillery to bring fire to bear on them to get to the targets, the artillery would have had to fire directly over our heads; we were right on the gun-target line. At that range the chance of error was significantly greater than closer in. The Hueys were there, so I used them.

"I pointed out targets for the choppers and I remember firing a 3.5 Willy Peter rocket as a marking round once. Hell, those Hueys were coming in right over our heads and I was standing up pointing at the damn targets and talking to the pilots.

"I would give them a target heading, and when they could pick me out visually, pointing with my arm to the target, they would come in. By that time, though, they were getting shot at, too, so they could see where the fire was coming from. At the same time I was directing one of my platoons in a successful counterattack against the NVA positions on our right flank.

"We were getting pretty low on ammunition and we suffered a number of casualties. It was starting to get dark—it was also an overcast day, if I recall—so we cleared an area of some trees to bring in the H-34 choppers to take out the wounded and dead.

"The battalion commander said, 'You've got to come out and join up with the remainder of the battalion, and you've got to come out by yourself.' The rest of the battalion was having a hell of a battle in the village and could not come to our aid.

"So I told everyone to lighten their load, to drop their packs in a pile, and any equipment that was not working, including radios and machine guns, and I had the engineers blow it up.

"The Marines in the village set down a base of fire and we commenced squad rushes across three hundred yards of open fire-swept ground. If someone fell, someone else picked him up, and we brought everybody out. It was really something to see. Teamwork at its best.

"That was about four and a half hours of battle.

"I did what I had been trained to do. I made decisions and people carried them out. That was the most amazing thing. Here I was company commander, and most people didn't know who I was.

"I was the officer who stepped forward and took command. Despite being relatively unknown, people did what I told them to do, when I told them, and in the manner I told them to do it. Some of them got hurt, some of them got killed, but they still carried out their orders. The result was success.

"When we rejoined the battalion, I met with the battalion commander and he assigned Hotel Company a sector of the perimeter to defend. I set my people out on the perimeter and sat down with the gunny to account for the dead and wounded and make arrangements for resupply.

"They mortared us that night, pretty much throughout the night. The next morning I remember crawling on my belly with General Jonas Platt, the task-force commander, and surveying the battlefield. Of course, they had removed most of the bodies by that time.

"The rest of that day we maneuvered to Route 1. Two-Seven mounted up and went south to Chu Lai and we got on trucks and went north to Da Nang to rejoin Two-Nine.

"When we started loading the trucks, we took small-arms fire from a nearby village. We had just come through one hell of a battle and these Marines were some pretty seasoned guys. After you come through what we had come through, you don't know what incoming rounds might turn into. We were grouped up to load the trucks and it was a dangerous time to get bunched up.

"An Ontos [a small, tracked vehicle armed with six 106-mm recoilless rifles] had come down the road to meet us for road security, and I told the Ontos crew to turn around and fire on the hut from where we had received that incoming fire.

"The Ontos fired, leveled the hut, and the fire ceased. Someone later criticized me for this, saying that I had over-reacted. Well, I had seen that one round could signal the start of a hell of a fight. Therefore I made the decision to eliminate that hut as a threat. It was eliminated, and I stand by my decision.

"Anyway, the Battle of Ky Phu and Harvest Moon was over, and they figured we overcame twelve-to-one odds.

"We got on the trucks and went north and stayed the night a FSLG [Force Service Logistics Group] between Da Nang and Chu Lai.

"I was awakened by a colonel from Division HQ around midnight who took me to a tent and started asking questions about the battle. He said, 'You're probably going to get a Sunday School Award out of this.'

"The next morning a new company commander came in and I turned Hotel Company over to him.

"When I got back [to Da Nang] my feet were in pretty bad shape from immersion foot. I was taken over to the hospital and had the water blisters drained. Then I went over and got cleaned up—we hadn't showered or shaved for five or six days—and I went to bed.

"I wasn't sent out on any more patrols and stayed in the battery area until I went over to Lima, Four-Twelve, to work with that battery.

"One night the battery commander woke me up and said, 'Boy, you've got to get up. General Walt [Commanding General, 3rd Marine Amphibious Force] wants to see you.' That's when he told me that General Walt had recommended me for the Medal of Honor.

"I can remember waiting to see him and being scared. I thought, 'I'm going to meet a three-star general.'

"I don't think I had ever met a three-star general, much less the MAF commander.

"He talked to me like a son, though. I realized very quickly that there was a lot of compassion, a lot of concern in the general. But I remember how those blue eyes of his penetrated right through me.

"Later, when he came in to speak to the 9th Marines, I remember he jumped up on the hood of a jeep and commented on my action. I guess I was his teaching point. People treated me with a great deal of respect, because they knew that I'd been recommended for the Medal of Honor. I recall [that] on Christmas I was able to attend Cardinal Spellman's Mass.

"I wanted to stay in Vietnam for a full tour but left in February at the termination of my temporary duty. When I returned to Marine barracks in Hawaii, two more officers and two more NCOs from Security Forces [Pacific] went on this program."

"I was at Fort Sill in the summer of '67, and went to the Marine Corps League Convention in St. Louis. General Walt was there and one of his aides told me the general was looking for another aide and asked if I was interested.

"I said, 'Well, I've got orders for the 2nd Division.'

"From St. Louis I flew to New Orleans, where I got the Military Man of the Year Award and General Walt presented it. After he hung it around my neck he said, 'I want to see you afterwards.'

"I went to see him and he said, 'Do you want to be my aide?'

"I said, 'I'd be honored, but I've got orders for the 2nd Marine Division.'

"He said, 'Go home and you'll receive orders when you get there to report to Headquarters Marine Corps.'

"When I got home, I had orders assigning me as his administrative assistant. I was his aide for a year. At the time General Walt had said he didn't think an aide should be an aide for more than a year.

"When you complete an aide assignment and have done a good job, it's pretty much understood that you will get the next assignment you want. So, after I completed my assignment as his aide I said, 'I want to go back to Vietnam.'

"There was a little pressure at the time about me not going back into combat. He felt the way I did; that Vietnam was the place to be—where Marines should be. Here I am wearing the Medal of Honor, and I hadn't even served a full tour of duty in Vietnam. I still had fire in my eyes, and that's where I wanted to be.

"After I served as his aide for a year, I got my orders back to Vietnam. He was a man of his word.

"Going back, there's a week refresher course at Camp Pendleton and, unbeknownst to me, General Walt had contacted General Ray Davis—Medal of Honor Korea—who had the division, and they had a battery all set for me when I got there.

"I got to Camp Pendleton and checked in at four o'clock one morning, and a young lance corporal said, 'Sir, the next company grade officer coming in is supposed to take C Company through staging battalion.'

"I said, 'If these are your orders, I am ready to carry them out.'

"I stayed at staging battalion for a month and got to Vietnam six weeks later. All this time that battery assignment awaited me. When I finally showed up, General Davis said, 'Where have you been?'

"I'm glad I took that company through staging, though. Not only did I help prepare the young Marines for combat in Vietnam, but it also got me prepared physically and mentally. I took over Echo Two-Twelve, my old unit.

"We were fire basing all the time; we built or reoccupied over twenty fire bases. I've got a diary at home with all the details. We saw a good deal of action. Went through the A Shau Valley with the Ninth Marines—Operation Dewey Canyon. We were firing in support of Wes Fox's Alpha One-Nine during his Medal of Honor action [See Chapter 15, p. 153].

"That's pretty much what happened."

5

The Refitted Gliders

DURING World War II, gliders were used by the Allies as an assault vehicle to ferry men and supplies across the English Channel following the invasion of Europe on June 6, 1944. After defeating the Axis Powers in 1945, several thousand surplus glider airframes were stockpiled as the Pentagon tried to find a place for them in America's arsenal.

The "hot" war was over, but a new, undeclared Cold War had begun as an Iron Curtain descended, dividing Europe between East and West. When the Russians blockaded Berlin in 1948, the American Air Force scrambled to resupply the isolated Free World bastion.

As the Russian siege continued, several attempts to fit the gliders with engines were unsuccessful, and the idea was temporarily scrapped. Conventional American aircraft such as the DC-3 were used to break the stranglehold.

After several years of research, the perfect match was made—an R-2800 engine was put on each wing of the glider, and the C-123 was born. For years they were used as mission support and light transport airplanes, but the C-123s still had the tow hook in the nose of the aircraft, reminiscent of World War II days.

That seemed appropriate, because Joe Jackson—Vietnam's 115th Medal of Honor recipient—was a flyer in World War II and before.

In March 1941, just after his eighteenth birthday, Joe enlisted in the Army Air Corps and was stationed at Orlando, Florida, with the 13th Bomber Group. He went through cadet training, graduated in April 1943 and then went on to gunnery school, where he towed targets and helped train gunners for B-17s and B-24s.

He also served in the Korean War.

In December 1950 after the Chinese entered the war on the side of the North Koreans, Joe's group was transferred overseas. He left the States on November 17, and off-loaded in Japan on December 2, just outside Tokyo at Yokohama. Sixteen years later he was called to combat duty again.

JOE M. JACKSON

Rank: Lieutenant Colonel   **Date:** May 12, 1968
Unit: 311th Air Commando   **Place:** Kham Duc, South
Squadron, U.S. Air Force   Vietnam
          Born: Heard County, Georgia, March 14, 1923

"I went to Vietnam as well," Joe, who retired from the U.S. Air Force after thirty-three years, said from his home in Kent, Washington, one rainy afternoon in 1986. "I flew C-123s."

"When Vietnam started up, they sent the 123s in because they had the ability to land and take off using rather short airfields. They got good use out of it, and later on they discovered that if they lost an engine—if it was shot out or failed—the airplane had rather marginal performance. As a matter of fact, it was rotten with only one engine.

"As a result, they added two small jet engines—one on each wing—and that made a tremendous difference. They saved a lot of lives in Vietnam. In normal operations, we would start up the jet engines and leave them idling for takeoff and shut them off once airborne.

"We would then start them up and have them on idle during landings for a safety backup. However, if operating with a short field or heavy load, the jets were used for take-off.

"I had a friend who was flying in supplies during the Battle of Khe Sanh. The VC and the North Vietnamese controlled the eastern end of the Khe Sanh runway; they had slit trenches right alongside the runway. As he was taking off, his right engine was shot out. Had it not been for the jet engine installed on his aircraft, he would never have gotten out of there.

"Another pilot was flying out of Chu Lai, and both recips [engines] failed as he passed the end of the runway. Fortunately, he had both jet engines running. He just ran them up, flew around the pattern and landed.

"The day before, a C-123 without the jet engines had both engines fail right after takeoff. He crashed and everybody on board was killed. When they investigated the crash, they found that the fuel tanks had been serviced with JP-4 instead of aviation gasoline. If he had the jets, he would have made it.

"My squadron didn't have a detachment at Khe Sanh, but we flew in and out, taking supplies in and casualties out. We were stationed at Phan Rang, which was down in the south, and I was detachment commander at Da Nang with eight airplanes. We primarily worked in I Corps.

"My tour began in August 1967 and ended in August 1968. It was a twelve-month tour. Fighter pilots who were going up north over the DMZ had their tours based on the number of missions they flew.

"It was the twelfth of May; everything was normal, routine. I was due to get a check flight that day. We had to do that every six months to ensure that we had maintained our proficiency. I had gotten up early—as I usually did—

and went down for an intelligence briefing and a weather briefing.

"I came back and briefed my pilots. It was mentioned that there had been some trouble over at Kham Duc, but no significance was placed on it. My job that day was to haul supplies and people up along the coast from Chu Lai to Hue-Phu Bai and to a little dirt strip between Hue and Dong Ha.

"I had a load and went into Dong Ha and flew out to Da Nang. Somewhere around noon I landed at Chu Lai and the airlift control element gave me a change in my itinerary.

"He said, 'Go back to Da Nang immediately.' So we took off for Da Nang.

"When we landed we were told that we had been diverted for an operational emergency mission. We then began getting an intelligence briefing and we knew we were getting into something pretty hot.

"They issued us additional ammunition for the pilot and the copilot; we got extra .38-caliber ammunition. The loadmaster and the flight engineer drew M16s and extra ammo. We all got flak vests, and we were told to fly to Kham Duc and report in.

"We refueled and left Da Nang about two-thirty and got to Kham Duc around three o'clock. It's not too far.

"We checked in with the airborne command post, which was an orbiting C-130 high above everything; it was the main control for all of the aircraft in there. It seemed like there were thousands of airplanes in the Kham Duc area—there weren't that many but because it was such a small, restricted area, it just seemed like that.

"We were in a holding pattern to the southwest of the field at nine thousand feet. As we circled, we listened to the action until about four o'clock in the afternoon.

"The Special Forces camp at Kham Duc was there to observe enemy movement on Route 14 just across the border in Laos. Movement could be seen, but not very well.

"There was a smaller outpost south of Kham Duc called

Ngoc Tavak, and from there Route 14 could be observed directly. They could see it much better from Ngoc Tavak than from Kham Duc.

"Somewhere around the ninth of May there had been a lot of probing attacks in the area. One of them was at Kham Duc, and a North Vietnamese soldier was captured.

"He told interrogators that Kham Duc was on the North Vietnamese hit list, and they were going to take it. On the tenth of May, both the main camp and the outpost came under increased enemy attack. This was down in a valley almost completely surrounded by mountains.

"The North Vietnamese regulars held all of the high ground around the camp, so they were really looking down the throats of the guys down on the ground. It is estimated that there were between three and six thousand North Vietnamese regulars attacking Kham Duc.

"Initially, there were approximately seven hundred people at Kham Duc, including the Army, the CIDG (Civilian Irregular Defense Group), and their families.

"Someone at headquarters in Saigon realized that it was going to be a pretty tough fight, so the camp was augmented and replacements were sent in. The augmentation force was commanded by a Lieutenant Colonel Nelson, and it consisted of a battalion of about one thousand troops.

"At that time, Ngoc Tavak came under very heavy attack. At the insistence of some of the CIDG leaders, a retreat back to the main camp at Kham Duc was initiated. However, while they were en route back to the main camp, they were ambushed.

"All of the Americans except two—there were forty-four—were either killed or wounded, so they returned to Ngoc Tavak. It was then decided that instead of going directly to Kham Duc, the Ngoc Tavak force would proceed south instead of north. They circled around and got on a hill where they were picked up by helicopters and dropped into the main camp at Kham Duc.

"Because a lot of the people had been wounded by M16s,

they figured that some of the CIDG troops were Charlie.
Anyway, they got everything consolidated back at the main
camp at Kham Duc on the night of the tenth.

"When Colonel Nelson got to Kham Duc, he established
seven outposts around the camp. During the night of the
tenth right after he had gotten there and set up these outposts, they started falling one by one.

"They would be overrun, sometimes there would be survivors and sometimes there weren't. By the next morning,
the eleventh, every one of the outposts had fallen.

"That's when the attack started hot and heavy. Kham Duc
was completely surrounded, and it really was brought under
heavy fire. All sorts of [Allied] air power were called
in—helicopter gunships and everything you can imagine—
to try to ward off the attack.

"On the night of the eleventh, the decision was made in
Saigon to evacuate the camp the next morning. Despite the
fact that the orders were to evacuate the camp, the first
plane in to Kham Duc—a C-130—was bringing in cargo for
resupply instead of evacuation. As it was on its final
approach to land, it had one of its main gear tires shot out.

"A flat tire creates all sorts of drag when you land. When
the crippled 130 pulled into the parking ramp and stopped,
the airplane filled up with the dependents of the CIDG, and
they couldn't get them off. And since they couldn't get them
off, they couldn't unload the cargo. They also had the flat,
and the civilians wouldn't move. Something had to be done.

"The pilot decided that the only thing he could do was
attempt to take off, which he did. But he didn't make it. He
pulled back into the parking ramp. When the civilians saw
that they couldn't get off the ground, they left the airplane.
Then the cargo was unloaded.

"After the cargo was unloaded, they began cutting off the
flat tire with bayonets and a fire ax to help cut down on the
drag.

"There was an O2 observation plane that had been
directing fighter strikes around the airfield and it went

down. It had the aileron controls shot out and the elevator was jammed. The only control the pilot had was with power and rudder. He was able to maneuver around and get it on the ground, but he ran off the runway, too.

"It was fortunate that it was able to get on the ground as safely as it did. Since there were no hydraulics for the brakes, it ran off the runway and ran into a ditch, wrinkled the fuselage, and collapsed the nose gear. The crew was able to get out.

"A C-123 from my outfit was able to land, pick up a load of passengers and bring them out.

"Anyway, we had the O2 pilot, Captain Smotherman, and a combat control team on the airfield. The combat control team was a crew that was sent in to control the air traffic that was coming in to land, and to line up cargo and people who were to go out.

"That group of people got on the airplane that had had the tire shot out with a few civilians and got off the ground and headed back to Saigon.

"One of the reasons they called off the evacuation was that two helicopters had been shot down on the airfield and one of them had crashed on the runway, blocking it.

"At this time, one of the engineers got in a front-end loader and was scraping the wreckage off the runway to open it up again after they had stopped the evacuation. He got most of it off the runway when he was killed by a sniper.

"The front-end loader went on running cross-country, hit a ditch, and turned over. However, because the engineer had been able to get most of the wreckage off the runway before he was killed, the evacuation would be able to continue if necessary.

"Sometime later in the day, it was decided that they were going to call the evacuation back on again, because there was no way those troops could survive with the pressure the North Vietnamese were putting on the airfield. So they started up the evacuation again. There is some confusion as to what happened next, but as I understand it, it was at that time that they decided to call off the evacuation. The first aircraft in after the evacuation was resumed had all four engines shot out, as well as the hydraulic system. So it was a glider and not under control.

"Almost every airplane that went in there—mostly C-130s—got some kind of battle damage, one way or another. One airplane that had an estimated one hundred fifty people on board was shot down on takeoff and everyone on board was lost. That happened just off the northeast end of the runway.

"When the airplane with the tire shot out got down to Saigon, it had the combat control team on board. They were told, 'We have started evacuation again. You stay on board that C-130, return to Kham Duc and control those airplanes.'

"They headed back to Kham Duc and arrived somewhere around four o'clock in the afternoon. I'm not quite sure about the time because nobody was keeping track of the time.

"They landed and the combat control team jumped off and headed for the bunker where their jeep and radio stuff had been stored. They got there and their jeep was riddled, their radio gear was useless and their emergency radios didn't even work.

"In the meantime the C-130 took off. Since their radio didn't work and they didn't see anybody, the three members of the combat control team began going from one bunker to another, trying to find survivors. They went to all they could get to, and didn't find anyone.

"But now they are stuck on the airfield that had been completely overrun with North Vietnamese; the enemy has complete possession of the airfield. They have gun positions set up alongside the runways, and they have taken over the camp completely.

"They were the only three Americans there, and they were in the bunker by their radios.

"The next to the last aircraft took off and said that he had picked up the last of the survivors.

"At that time the airborne command post gave the order for the fighter commanders to go down and destroy the camp.

"The last airplane that had just let off the command control team said, 'Negative, negative! I just let the combat control team off.'

"Up to that time you could hardly get a word in edgewise on the radio. Then suddenly it was absolute silence; nobody said anything. Absolute quiet for what seemed like ten minutes, probably not that long, but it seemed like it.

"The airborne command post took charge and directed some observation planes to go down and look at the camp to see if they could find the three guys. They flew around over the camp and drew very heavy automatic-weapons fire, so they got the hell out of the way.

"They sent some fighters in and they couldn't see anything, either. The command post had been trying to locate the combat control team for about fifty minutes. Then they asked another guy who was flying a C-123 just ahead of me to land on the airfield and see if he could bring them out.

"In the meantime while all of this was going on, my circles kept going farther and farther north, and when they asked this guy—his name was Al Jeanotte—to go down, I was right over the airfield at nine thousand feet. I watched him.

"As he was coming in on final approach, I could see the automatic-weapons and antiaircraft fire coming out of the jungle on the southwest end of the airfield.

"He went in and made a touch-and-go landing, which he had been instructed to do. As he was rolling down the runway, the combat control team saw him make his final approach. As soon he touched down, the team left the bunker and headed for the runway. Before he saw them, he applied the power for takeoff.

"Just as he rotated and lifted off, he saw them running for the airfield.

"He had been in there quite a while and he said that he didn't have enough fuel to make another pass at the field. When he reported seeing the control team, the airborne command post asked, 'Is there anybody in the vicinity who can go in and get the guys?'

"I was there; I had seen what was going on and I figured that I was the most logical person to do it. I nodded to the copilot and he called in and said that we were going in.

"I did my entire landing checklist, my assault checklist and everything at nine thousand feet. Since I had seen the heavy fire Jeanotte was drawing during his approach, I decided I wanted no part of that.

"So I made an extremely steep approach, one that is not acceptable for the standards of safety. I figured that it was the safest way to go.

"In the C-123, if you exceed a certain speed, the flaps will begin to come up, because the pressure on the flaps will exceed the pressure in the hydraulic system. That is 135 knots; that is pretty fast because that is faster than the airplane actually cruises.

"I had the propellers in full low pitch, which was creating maximum drag; I had the flaps fully extended to the assault position and I was going down just like I was diving into the ground.

"At any rate, I rolled out and leveled the wings about a quarter of a mile from the end of the runway out of a really steep approach. I had just enough time for the speed to drop off to the landing speed and I touched down right on the end of the runway. There was a lot of luck involved in that.

"I couldn't put the prop engines in reverse to stop the airplane, because if we put them in reverse, it would automatically shut the jets down and close the flapper doors on the front of the jet engines.

"This was a safety precaution to keep the props from

throwing stones up into the jets, because if these were ingested by the jets, it would destroy them.

"I got right down to the end of the runway and stood on the brakes as much as I could. The runway was full of shell holes and mortar rounds, and stuff like that. Anyway, we were able to get stopped exactly opposite those three guys. When we stopped, they jumped out of a ditch.

"As soon as we came to a stop, I was going to turn the airplane around so the guys could enter through the back door. But they jumped out of the ditch and ran directly toward the airplane. I had to stop my turn, because I didn't know exactly what they were going to do, and I didn't want them to run through the props.

"At any rate, the back door was open and they ran around the airplane.

"At that point Major Campbell, who originally was my flight instructor for my flight test—it ended as soon as we had gotten the call—was now my copilot. I said to him, 'I wish they had stayed still. I can turn this airplane around faster than they can run.' They were fully exposed and weren't about to stand still, though. There was so much fire directed at us.

"There had been an enemy gun position directly across the runway which had been involved in a firefight with those three guys. The three guys had killed everyone in the gun position.

"They belly-flopped on board and I was looking back through the airplane to see when they were on board, and about that time Major Campbell yelled out, 'Oh, my God! Would you look at that!'

"The NVA had fired a 122-mm rocket directly at the airplane, and it was scooting down the runway toward us. It was really coming in, but it stopped, oh, from here to the other side of this room, in front of the airplane. It broke in half, and somehow it failed to explode.

"We could also see tracers going under the airplane and ricocheting.

"When the loadmaster called and said that they were all on board, I immediately applied power and we took off. They kept firing at us during takeoff. You could see the tracers right in front of the airplane. We lifted off, and the tracers kept coming out of the jungle and they began to taper off at about fifteen hundred feet. They quit altogether at about thirty-five hundred feet.

"We figured we were pretty safe about then, and we headed on back to Da Nang. We got in there about five-thirty or a quarter to six. We no sooner got on the ground than the base came under moderately heavy rocket attack, so we were in the bunker about thirty minutes or so.

"We went through debriefing and then headed for the chow hall. It was getting kind of late—about nine o'clock—and we had another rocket attack. We dove out of our van and into a ditch.

"I think we had four more rocket attacks after that. It was enough to curl your hair.

"Every airplane that went in there that day, except for two 130s, had heavy battle damage. We had no battle damage, no rounds went into our airplane, none. That was one of the amazing things about it. I know that thousands—and maybe tens of thousands—of rounds were fired at the airplane and we didn't get a single hit. I can't explain it; I figure I was riding copilot for Somebody Else.

"I don't give myself a heck of a lot of credit for that. I was doing just exactly what I had been trained to do and what I was expected to do.

"Six months later I came home.

"For the most part, I enjoyed my tour in Vietnam, because I liked to fly, and flying was good there. I was in transport and not in a shoot-'em-up and bombing group. So to me, the flying part was really fun.

"There was an awful lot of work too. You'd get up at four-thirty or five o'clock in the morning and still be working at ten o'clock at night. Then you'd get in bed and there would be a rocket attack and you couldn't get back to sleep for a couple of hours.

"But that made the time go fast. We were busy and we thought we were doing a good job.

"We went into a lot of rinky-dink airports and places that weren't even airports. We'd land on roads, cow pastures. A lot of times they'd scrape off the brush with a bulldozer and that was an airport as far as we were concerned.

"I remember seeing a guy after the war, and he said, 'Yeah, I remember you. You brought in turkey for us on Thanksgiving.' We liked doing things like that.

"There might have been only ten guys way out in the boonies. They were out there for God only knows how long and hadn't seen another American in six or eight months.

"Well, we would go to the PX and buy up a case of beer or a case of Coke and take it to them. It wasn't a lot, but I'm telling you, they were the happiest guys in the world to see us coming.

"I remember one day—on, somewhere along the spring of '68—there was an Army colonel who came into our shack and asked me, 'Are you going up north tomorrow?'

"I said, 'Yeah, as a matter of fact, I am going up to Dong Ha and back to different airfields.'

"'Could you take in a few cases of beer for my men?'

"I checked my load—two pallets of milk—and asked the airlift people if there was going to be any more cargo to go on board.

"They said no.

"I went back to the colonel and said, 'If you buy it, get it down here and guard it overnight, I'll haul a pallet of beer for you.' His face lit up like a Christmas tree. I don't know how many cases it was, but it was a big stack of beer.

"He had an enlisted guy with him, and I think he detailed that enlisted guy to stand guard on that beer all night long.

"We took off and were headed north the next morning, and he came up to the cockpit and handed me a slip of paper with a frequency, a call sign, and a sergeant's name on it.

He said, 'Would you radio this call sign and tell this sergeant to meet the airplane with a truck?'

"I said sure, and when we landed, they met us with the truck. They loaded the beer on the truck, and the last I saw of them, they were going down this dirt road with a pallet of beer on the truck.

"You know how dirty you would get in Vietnam with all of that red clay dirt and how when you'd sweat, the dust would stick all over you. Well, two weeks later, this grungy ol' GI came into our shack, covered all over with the stuff.

"He had a dirty old barracks bag slung over his shoulder. He asked for me and they called me out of my office. He threw this grungy barracks bag on the counter and said, 'These are compliments of the colonel'—the guy I had hauled the beer for—and it was a case of steaks.

"I told him, 'I really don't want anything in return for that.'

"The guy said, 'It's too late now. I'm on my way home, and I'm sure as hell not going to take them back up there.'

"We didn't get steaks down there at Da Nang. We'd get bully beef and dehydrated potatoes most of the time.

"At any rate, I had an old oil drum that had been made into a barbecue pit. I called over all of the guys in the squadron and said, 'Now, don't eat supper, because we are going to barbecue some steaks tonight.'

"So we had a little squadron barbecue and everyone got a steak. I don't know where the colonel got them, but they were the best darn steaks."

6

Khe Sanh

THE Khe Sanh Combat Base (KSCB) was located on a plateau overlooking the village of Khe Sanh on Highway 9. Although sparsely populated, the seizure of this region would have cleared the way for the North Vietnamese to advance into Quang Tri and the heavily populated coastal regions.

"Had we withdrawn to fight the enemy's force of over two divisions in the heavily populated coastal region," General William Westmoreland reported later, "the use of our firepower would have been severely restricted because of our precautionary measures to avoid civilian casualties and minimize damage to civilian property."

This was a touchy subject for the Allies and so General William Westmoreland, commander of the United States Military Assistance Command—Vietnam (MACV) decided to hold the plateau and thereby deny the enemy access to the coastal region.

Due to the massive numbers of NVA and VC troops that were committed to the nationwide Tet Offensive, it was not possible for the Allies to reinforce the plateau. Consequently, the Marines at the KSCB were outnumbered but not outfought.

The Battle for the Khe Sanh Combat Base lasted seventy-seven days and pitted the 26th Marine Regiment against two crack NVA Divisions, the 325-C and the 304th—a force of six infantry regiments, two artillery regiments, and an unknown number of tanks and other supporting units.

Numerous press reports about the Battle for Khe Sanh were centered primarily on the enemy artillery and mortar barrages and their effect. An ammunition depot took a direct hit in one attack, a C-130 cargo plane was destroyed during another, a C-123 in still another.

During one twenty-four-hour period, the KSCB received 1,307 incoming rounds and, consequently, many people believed that the Battle for the Khe Sanh was a shooting gallery where the Americans and their South Vietnamese allies were just targets for North Vietnamese gunners and mortarmen.

However, in addition to the daily barrages, there were several fights that were often brief, bloody, and hand-to-hand.

They were on a pockmarked plateau in northwestern South Vietnam and were waiting for Captain Bill Dabney to give the order. A few—those old enough—had scraggly beards; most wore salty jungle utilities; and all of them knew what was going to happen when the captain gave the order.

They had gone through it daily.

The captain knew it too, but it was a matter of pride, a matter of honor. "Attention to colors," he shouted across the hilltop, and he and the other Marines in I Company, 3rd Battalion, 26th Marines scrambled from their bunkers and trenches, snapped to attention, saluted the RC-292 radio antenna, and waited.

Second Lieutenant Owen S. Matthews blew into a battered bugle and what emerged was a choppy version of "To the Colors." Two enlisted men quickly raced to the antenna that served temporarily as a flagpole and attached the Stars and Stripes.

As the battered banner was raised, the Marines heard the *thunk-thunk-thunk* of the enemy's 120-mm mortars leaving their tubes. It would take twenty-one seconds for the mortar rounds to land on the hilltop, but the Marines remained standing until the flag had been raised and the lieutenant had finished his tune.

There may have been a few prayers for a double-time version, yet no one budged until the last note floated over the hilltop. Then Company I disappeared into trenches, bunkers, and foxholes just as the mortars exploded, sending shrapnel and shell fragments whistling over the makeshift parade field.

The attack ended quickly as smoke and dust blanketed the compound. As usual, there were no casualties, the Marines waved a pair of red, silk panties—Maggie's Drawers—at the errant NVA mortarmen signifying that they had missed again.

Some of the Marines added a few choice phrases while others defiantly flipped the enemy the appropriate single-digit salute.

The day on Hill 881 South, which towered over the garrison at the Khe Sanh Combat Base, had begun.

Although encircled, the defenders of the KSCB were able to make excursions outside the wire defenses for security and reconnaissance purposes. Because they wanted to avoid getting into a slugging match with the numerically superior NVA, the Marines broke contact when the enemy was encountered and withdrew while supporting arms were employed.

However, in the early-morning hours of February 5, a battalion from the 325-C NVA Division launched a major attack against Hill 861, a hilltop owned by Company E, Two-Twenty-Six. The attack for Hill 861 began with a two-hundred-round artillery barrage from the NVA gunners followed by a heavy volley of RPG rounds.

E Company's 1st Platoon, under the command of Second Lieutenant Donald Shanley, was pushed back to supplementary positions by the enemy who, it was thought, was under the influence of narcotics.

After taking the 1st Platoon's trenches, there was a lull in the fighting, and the North Vietnamese soldiers paused and went souvenir hunting through the Marine gear. Magazines and paperbacks were the most popular.

The NVA apparently believed that the struggle was over; but it had hardly even begun.

Lieutenant Shanley reorganized his men, and after showering the enemy with grenades, the enraged Marines charged back to their original positions. Because of the darkness and the low-hanging fog, the counterattack was hand-to-hand. The melee quickly developed into a bloody brawl as the men of the 1st Platoon swarmed on the NVA using knives, bayonets, rifle butts and fists.

Captain Earle G. Breeding, E Company CO, saw one of his men come up against an NVA soldier in the darkness. The Marine delivered a crushing roundhouse right to the jaw, leveling his opponent. The Marine jumped on the fallen soldier and finished the job with his knife.

Nearby, an NVA jumped one of Breeding's men and was preparing to slit his throat. However, one of the Marine's buddies rushed to his aid. He put the muzzle of his M16 between the two combatants and opened fire on full automatic with a full clip. Chunks of the Marine's flak jacket were blown away, but so was the NVA's chest.

Another advantage of the flak jacket in this close-in fighting was apparent when both sides began throwing hand grenades. The Marines would throw grenades, turn, and absorb the fragments with the flak jackets and the backs of their legs. Captain Breeding saw several enemy soldiers "blown away" at less than ten yards.

During the fighting, four-man fire teams from the 2nd

and 3rd Platoons attacked the NVA penetration point from both flanks. The "new Marines" ripped into the NVA as if they were making up for lost time.

"It was like watching a World War II movie," Captain Breeding recalled later. "Charlie didn't know how to cope with it . . . we walked all over them."

The NVA retreated down the hill and ran into recoilless rifle fire from Marines on Hill 558, to the east.

The North Vietnamese withdrew and at 6:10 A.M. they re-formed what was left of their battalion and attacked again. This attack was thwarted by heavy artillery fire and radar-controlled bombing missions. The enemy's reserves were shredded as they attacked.

After the second attack fizzled, the North Vietnamese withdrew, and at 2:30 P.M., replacements for E Company were heli-lifted to Hill 861. The fight—this one anyway—was over.

Seven Marines were killed and thirty-five were Medevaced. Most of the KIAs came during the initial NVA barrage and, to Captain Breeding's knowledge, none died in the hand-to-hand fighting.

The NVA suffered 109 known dead, of which many had been shot, slashed or beaten to death.

In April, the weather cleared and the NVA began to withdraw from the battlefield. A combined force of U.S. Marine and South Vietnamese units, coordinated by the U.S. Army 1st Cavalry Division (Airmobile), linked up with the Marines at Khe Sanh and routed the remaining enemy elements.

7

Dai Do—Vargas

THE first half of 1968 was one of the most disruptive periods in American history. It began with the seizure of the U.S.S. *Pueblo* by the North Koreans, and almost simultaneously the North Vietnamese launched the nationwide Tet Offensive against several major South Vietnamese cities and provincial capitals.

This offensive by the NVA and VC was labeled a success because, according to newspaper, magazine, and television reports, it had caught the Allies off guard. However, two months earlier, several magazines reported that, according to Defense Department analysts, a New Year offensive was being planned by Hanoi.

General Westmoreland ended his four-year tour as the Allied military commander in Vietnam and was to be named Army Chief of Staff.

President Johnson was being criticized on all sides. Despite the 32,000 enemy troops reportedly killed during Tet according to Pentagon figures, many critics labeled it a defeat for U.S. forces. The Marines were still being attacked at Khe Sanh by ground assaults, as well as by daily artillery barrages that sometimes exceeded a thousand rounds of incoming.

When the battle was ended by advancing American and South Vietnamese units in April, the President told the nation that he would not seek renomination. This opened the field as Democrats scrambled for position.

A week after President Johnson made the announcement that he wouldn't run again, Martin Luther King, Jr., was assassinated in Memphis. Dozens of cities around the country erupted in racial violence. This seemed to indicate that America was in for another long, hot summer of rioting.

The frustration of the nation was exemplified when a black man shot his neighbor for no apparent reason. After the shooting, the man sobbed, "They've killed my King, they've killed my King."

Two months later, after winning the California primary, Bobby Kennedy grinned, raised his hand in victory and was murdered.

America was being deprived of some of its finest leaders, and this led some to violence, e.g., the summer racial riots and the disruptions surrounding the Democratic National Convention in Chicago.

Against this backdrop of violence and disruption at home, a Marine battalion landing team battled elements of a North Vietnamese Army division near Dai Do in Quang Tri Province. Like the Battle of Khe Sanh to the west, it was a multiservice and multinational operation, but unlike Khe Sanh, except for those directly involved in the battle, few remember.

Brigadier General William Weise, USMC (Ret.) was the battalion commander; he remembers. In an article for the Marine Corps *Gazette*, General Weise wrote, "The Battle of Dai Do was a fierce and bloody struggle between an under-strength Marine battalion landing team (BLT Two-Four) and major elements of the 320th (NVA) Division during three hot days in 1968.

"I was privileged to command those magnificent Marines

and Sailors who stopped the well-equipped 320th in its tracks."[1]

One of those Marines was Golf Company Commander Jay Vargas, who today is the Force Marine Officer/Amphibious Plans Officer for Vice Admiral Kehune, COMNAVSURPAC, at Coronado, California.

"I look back at what happened at Dai Do and think, 'Holy Jesus! Why am I here?'" Jay's eyes glisten like the eagles on his collar as he remembers an all but forgotten struggle.

The Battle of Dai Do was fought several months after the 1968 Tet Offensive. The war for Jay Vargas, though, began four years earlier when Navy Commander James Bond Stockdale was leading air strikes against North Vietnamese naval vessels during the Gulf of Tonkin incident.

JAY R. VARGAS

Rank: Colonel (then Captain)   **Date:** April 30 to May 2, 1968

Unit: G Company, 2nd Battalion 4th Marines   **Place:** Dai Do, South Vietnam

Born: Winslow, Arizona, July 29, 1940

In August 1964, Jay Vargas was a young lieutenant aboard ship in the South China Sea when word about the Tonkin Gulf incident came down. The gauntlet had been thrown down, the challenge made, and the United States responded.

The ammunition caches on board the patrolling American ship were opened, the lids of the ammo boxes cracked and the Marines locked and loaded their weapons. Oh, they had locked and loaded before, but this time they meant it.

"I'll never forget the first Mass after the Tonkin Gulf incident," Jay said with a smile as he remembered. "We had been afloat one hundred five days, and it had gotten to the point where hardly anybody went to church. There were other things to do.

"However, after we had locked and loaded all of our magazines, church call was sounded and it was really funny.

"Everybody came up with rosaries and prayer books, medals they wanted blessed, their last confessions to be heard. It was amazing that those Marines were able to get religion that quickly.

"Father McDonald—he's up here at Mercy Hospital—was amazed. 'I couldn't even get three guys to church last Sunday,' he said, 'and now I can't even see the end of them.'

"There was this mass of humanity in front of him. I sat there and had to laugh at this guy. He was tickled to death but totally unprepared. He didn't have enough Hosts, didn't have enough wine, didn't have enough anything. But it was great."

There was a feeling in the air that something significant was happening. This sense of anticipation wasn't restricted to the South China Sea.

Ten thousand miles away, at the Marine Corps Recruit Depot in San Diego, California, a Marine veteran of World War II and Korea told a drill instructor, "You better start kicking these maggots [recruits] in the ass, because in six months Marines will be fighting in Vietnam."

The drill instructor nodded and added, "Yeah, but it will be over in a year."

The Veteran was right, because in six months, the Marine Corps' 1st Light Antiaircraft Missile Battalion landed at Da Nang and a month later, 3rd Battalion, 9th Marines (Three-Nine) waded ashore. The drill instructor was wrong, however, because four years later, Americans were still fighting and dying in Vietnam.

By then, Jay Vargas had risen to the rank of captain and

was serving as a company commander with a special
landing force off the coast of South Vietnam. Wherever
there was a trouble spot, the Marines were put aboard helicopters and in they went.

"That's how we ended up fighting them at Dai Do,"
Vargas recalled.

"We" were an understrength Marine battalion landing
team, 2nd Battalion, 4th Marines; "they" were well-
equipped elements of the 320th North Vietnamese Army
Division; and the battle began at 4 A.M. on April 30th when
a Navy utility boat was ambushed on the Bo Dieu River
south of An Lac.

One sailor died in the ambush and further traffic on the
river was halted until the threat was eliminated. The problem area was in the 1st ARVN Division's area of responsi-
bility, but there were no ARVN units available to clear the
ambush site. Consequently, Two-Four was given the assignment to investigate and eliminate the ambush sight at An
Lac.[2]

BLT Two-Four's four rifle companies were widely dis-
persed north of the Cua Viet River when the Navy boat was
attacked:

G Company held the northernmost position at Lam
Xuan (West) and Nhi Ha;

F Company (less one platoon) was three kilometers
south on the east bank of Jones Creek across from
battalion headquarters at Mai Xa Chanh;

H Company (commanded by Captain Jim Williams)
had a patrol base about two kilometers southwest of Mai
Xa Chanh;

E Company under the command of Captain Jim Livingston was stationed at a bridge on Highway 1 six
kilometers west of the battalion headquarters and was
under the direct control of the 3rd Marine Division and
thus not immediately available to BLT Two-Four.[3]

"The ARVN held the position on our left.

"Now, I'm not knocking those guys, but it just seemed that every time we got into a firefight, the ARVN would peel off and go on a different mission. When we attacked, they really peeled off and left our flank wide open.

"In fact, the American advisor called on the radio and was apologizing. I heard him on the battalion TAC NET say, 'They're on their way, we are moving out in a different direction.'

"They just peeled off and left our left flank exposed. It really hurt us badly, but I'm not knocking the advisors.

"Our mission was to keep the river open, because supplies were coming from the ships down through the Cua Viet to Dong Ha. It was vital—keeping that supply line open—because that's how we got our ammunition, fuel, food, and all the other supplies.

"To accomplish that mission, it was necessary to control the sector from the ocean to Dong Ha. To the left of us was the ARVN force, supposedly. Golf Company occupied a patrol base in the northern portion of the sector in Lam Xuan and Nhi Ha.

"Lam Xuan was not right at the mouth of the Cua Viet River. It came a couple of miles inland and up Jones Creek—they named it Jones Creek, but I don't know why. At the first bow to the left in Jones Creek was Lam Xuan. We weren't that far from the DMZ.

"Since we weren't that far from the DMZ, we took incoming quite regularly and it always came in unannounced.

"At the time, BLT Two-Four was conducting company sweeps both north to the Gulf of Tonkin (about two miles) and down toward Khai Truc, Dai Do and Dinh To to the stream at Bac Vong where the 2nd ARVN Regiment TAOR [tactical area of responsibility] began. We could see Dong Ha from there (Bac Vong). Our job was to make sure nothing got in to Dong Ha.

"It was one of those places where you could take your

company out and within a matter of five hundred meters be in a firefight.

"I kept wondering, 'Where the hell are these guys coming from?'

"They were coming across the white sands under white parachutes, crawling a few feet at a time at night, coming between us and the ARVN force that was on our left flank. I believe that the only reason the NVA had that access between us and our boundary is because the ARVN peeled out every time we got into a firefight.

"That left the NVA an open trough to come right down, so they were coming right across the desert between us.

"We would send patrols out and get a bloody nose. It would become a nice fight, but then they would peel off. We would assume that we had won, and pull back to our base camp. Then we'd get a mission to do another company sweep and get into another fight.

"Several days earlier Jim Livingston [Echo Company Commander] and I were ordered to take our companies up Jones Creek to relieve another company that had taken a Sunday Punch. As that company pulled back, Jim and I split the river—I took the left, Jim took the right. We ended up almost to Lam Xaun West.

"We were set up in positions on both sides of the river.

"Livingston was heliborne out of the position he had on the right side of the river and down to a bridge near Dong Ha. That left me up north by myself along with all of the equipment Livingston had to leave behind on the other side of the river, including some eighty-one mortars.

"We swam across the river and got his stuff. We had barely made it back across the river and set up an outpost when we started taking a hell of a lot of incoming.

"The sun was beginning to go down, and at about 1730 [hours] I received orders to heliborne out of there back to Mai Xa Chanh. From there we would head out toward Dai Do the next morning, to reinforce F Company's assault."

F Company and H Company had swept toward An Lac

[to the site of the ambush of the Navy boat] and had met
heavy resistance from two hamlets just north of An Lac—
Dong Huan and seven hundred meters to the west, Dai Do.
H Company, after sustaining numerous casualties was able
to penetrate and hold Dong Huan. F Company had attacked
Dai Do and seized the southeastern edge of the hamlet.
However, because of its many casualties, Foxtrot was
ordered out of Dai Do to Dong Huan to combine forces with
Hotel Company.[4]

Bravo Company One-Three, atop amtracs, crossed the
Bo Dieu River and assaulted An Lac. It was reminiscent of
the Marine assault on Iwo Jima during World War II.[5]

As with Foxtrot and Hotel, Bravo Company suffered
many casualties in its fight to take An Lac. However, as
night fell, a reconnaissance patrol from Bravo reported that
the enemy had abandoned An Lac, and the rest of the company occupied the hamlet.[6]

"As the sun was going down, the choppers started
coming in to pick us up. When they [NVA] saw the birds
coming in, they shifted fire into my LZ, and we had to abort
the mission. The only thing I was able to get out was the 81s
and parts of two of my platoons.

"We had one bird knocked down, and the rest of them got
out. I got on the radio and said, 'The sun's going down. I'll
take everybody out on foot.'

"It was only about four kilometers, but it was probably
the darkest night I've ever been in.

"I moved my company down Jones Creek back to the
[battalion] base camp. At every move, though, they kept
adjusting artillery in on us. As a result, some of the guys in
one platoon peeled off and got lost. They went off into the
desert somewhere.

"Luckily, as I kept going up and down the column, my
radio operator kept these guys together and told me about it.
So I went out with him and found those guys and pulled
them back toward the creek.

"We hit the creek and everybody kept marching. We left

at about 1800, 1900 [hours]—I'm not sure, it was dark—
and got back at midnight.

"The reason it took so long is that we had to walk, dig in,
walk, dig in. I tried to keep everybody moving, but you
know what it's like when incoming is coming in. People
sometimes freeze; they don't want to move. So it was a
matter of keeping the discipline, keeping everybody moving.

"Enemy artillery followed us at least halfway back to the
base camp. I heard on the radio that we were making a night
attack down at Dai Do. Consequently, the North Vietnamese shifted their artillery and missiles back to those guys.
This was about six clicks from our position.

"When the NVA shifted their fire, it allowed me to get
back to the base camp. I lost a couple of guys [KIA], but we
got everybody out. I got hit once with shrapnel. I think
everybody got hit, couldn't help it.

"What amazed me more than anything is that how many
of us in that company—I'll say one hundred and twenty—
made it back with just minor shrapnel wounds, and we had
walked through an artillery barrage. It proved to me right
then and there—and I've passed it on to my younger officers
today—'You can walk through an artillery barrage and
survive.' It's tough to sell it though.

"People look at you like you are full of it, but it is true.

"One of the things that saved us during that barrage was
the soil. It was soft, and the water table was three feet below
you. So the round went down before it exploded. A lot of
times it absorbed the shrapnel, and as a result, it didn't
spread out that quickly.

"We got back into our base camp and were told to get a
little shut-eye. I had a leg wound and refused to be evacuated and said that I was staying with the company.

"I was told, 'Okay, here's your mission for tomorrow.
Three boats with two tanks are going to pick you up at four
in the morning and take you down the Cua Viet River.
You'll get your five paragraph order from General Weise

(who was on a gunboat in the middle of this river). You will have to brief your troops as to what to do while you are afloat.'

Golf Company boarded the landing boats at 0900 on May 1. General Weise had planned a predawn attack by Golf, but the boats arrived late, necessitating the daylight assault.[7]

"General Weise debarked his boat and boarded mine. He told me what was going on and gave me my orders. I, in turn, locked all three of my boats together and briefed my platoon commanders. Everything was done while we were moving toward the objective.

"I was told the NVA had a reinforced company in there. I landed where the river kind of made a turn. There were approximately seven hundred meters of rice paddies between us and Dai Do.

"When I was moving down the river, I thought I was going to fall in as the reserve element in the attack. However, when General Weise briefed me, he said, 'The minute you hit, you're going for broke. You are going to have to go right into the attack. The other two companies in there have been torn apart.'

"We landed, and the minute the ramps went down, we were under attack. Incoming was coming right in on top of us. I dropped off the 81s and the 60s and told them to establish a base of fire for us from this one beach line into Dai Do.

"To describe Dai Do for you: We landed where the big river, the Bo Dieu River, came around, and there was a little river to the left of us that went up to Dai Do and Dinh To. So I had a boundary and on that boundary over to my left was another company [Bravo, One-Three].[8]

"When I made that first landing, I could turn around and look at Dong Ha [The city of Dong Ha was two and a half kilometers from Dai Do, and the Dong Ha Combat Base was another kilometer south]. Just the river separated us. Apparently, the enemy's mission was to take Dong Ha.

"There were a lot of mines and barbed wire, but I think

they were going to go hell for broke. That was 3rd Marine Division headquarters, and I think that was what they were going to do.

"I immediately went into the assault with two up, one back [two platoons attacking, one platoon in reserve]. I probably had one hundred and twenty-two folks, which is small for a company because usually there are two hundred and five. I also had the two tanks that had come up on the boats with us providing support.

"We had to fight spider holes all the way across the open area. Halfway across is when things went to hell. The tanks had fired all their rounds, both their machine guns and their big guns. One of the tanks decided to turn around and head back without saying anything.

"I jumped on the tank while the fight was going on and banged on it, which didn't do any good. I went to the rear and got the phone and threatened the guy with a court-martial.

"I said, 'You can't leave me out here. I can use you for psychological effect. Just keep driving for the village.'

"I basically got a 'screw you' and he took off.

"The other tank stayed with me but started to go back and I got to that radio and said, 'No way. You're going in there with us, or I am personally going to shoot a three-five in your tail.'

"At that time General Weise came on the radio, the battalion TAC NET, and told that tank driver that if he came back, [he] would blow him out of the sand because 'I'm back here where I can see you.'

"So the tank did a wheelie and stayed with us.

"At this stage, NVA were popping up from spider holes. I remember shooting at one guy—whether I hit the poor son of a bitch or not, somebody did. There were about fifteen of these guys and they kept popping up out of the spider holes all the way across this seven hundred meters.

"What I had done was call in naval gunfire, artillery, I had gunships on station, I had air strikes going on; I had everything you could use as supporting arms going in on top of that position. I laid down a smoke screen. I went back and got the reserve element, and we came through in a frontal assault through the left platoon. This was only a matter of the length of this building.

"I remember taking three bunkers . . . [and according to subsequent battlefield reports] that got everybody back on their feet. They said, 'The hell with the bunkers and the machine guns,' and they hauled ass to the edge of the village. We must have taken ten or fifteen well-constructed bunkers.

"There were enemy troops running crazy in there. I had kept adjusting the [air and artillery] strikes, and my FOs did a beautiful job. The air officer and the artillery officer kept shifting fire and moving in air strikes.

"I was more or less saying, 'Shoot that over there. Bring in another air strike here.'

"It was almost like—I hate to say this because people sometimes don't believe it—I wasn't vulnerable. I didn't believe I was going to get shot. Oh, I got hit again and it spun me around. I took some shrapnel that ripped my knee-cap open in the assault. But I just didn't feel that I was going to die.

"I'm not saying I didn't give a damn. I still had control of everything. I didn't lose control of my thinking process. I was still adjusting artillery. I was still shooting. I was still throwing grenades in bunkers.

"But I think I became so involved with the troops and what was taking place, well, I had other things to think about. At that time everybody was being hit.

"Out of the one hundred and twenty-two troops I started with that morning, only about sixty of us got into the village. We had a couple of Otters [mini amtracs], that were following us, and we kept throwing wounded on them.

"I've never seen so much fire, or been shot at that much, and the amazing thing is that we only lost three guys in that

initial daytime assault; only three Marines got killed, a lot
of wounded.

"I really think, and I kind of curse myself for this, that we
had the North Vietnamese on the run at that time. The
enemy was running out of Dai Do into Dinh To and there
was another six-hundred-meter open gap to Thuong Do, and
they were running out of the back of the villages into the
open rice paddies.

"The pilots of the helicopter gunships and fixed-wing
aircraft were having a field day. Between the artillery and
the air strikes, it was devastating.

"When I got into Dai Do and looked around, it looked
like the moon to me. I couldn't believe how much damage
we had done to that village with supporting arms. It looked
like the frigging moon.

"I don't know how many dead NVA bodies were in there,
but there were hordes of them laying around. Chunks of
them were hanging in the trees; heads, arms, feet, you name
it, they were all over the place.

"Once we made it in there, the troops were so, well, they
felt so elated. I know exactly how they felt, because that's
how I felt. We felt victorious.

"I consolidated my remaining troops and held up everything because I knew I was running low on ammo. I also
wanted to take care of the wounded still with me. So I
decided to regroup and make sure I had as much firepower
as I could possibly muster. That was why I decided to hold
up.

"Right then and there, while we were reloading and
checking everything, troops were picking up AK-47s and
we were trying to get our wounded out, is when things
turned around.

"The NVA were running out of the back of Dai Do as fast
as they could. However, once they got into the open area
between Dai Do and Dinh To, they were getting peppered,
really creamed by the artillery and air strikes. They were
being chewed up badly.

"Somebody on the other side must have realized, 'Hey, this is bullshit; my chances of living are a lot better if I get out of this right away.'

"So they did a U-turn, which was their only way out, and back they came.

"At that time, three lines of them came on us. I still had the artillery coming in, and if it hadn't been for the artillery and the supporting arms, oh, they would have taken us right back. They could have taken us in a matter of seconds.

"I told everybody to pull back toward the edge of the village. There was a cemetery with a lot of freshly dug graves. The sun was going down; I had lost the whole day.

"When we made it back to the graveyard at the edge of the village, I told the troops to dig the fresh graves, take whoever was in it, and throw them out. And that's what we did.

"Lo and behold, here they came with a counterattack. It was, well, it's hard to believe. While the troopers were digging holes, digging up the bodies, they were engaged in hand-to-hand combat with the enemy.

"These guys were running at us, coming right through. I watched Marines who were completely out of ammo swinging their weapons like baseball bats, hitting them in the face. I watched them sticking bayonets into the enemy, throwing grenades, picking up the AK-47s and using them against the NVA, I watched Marines pound NVA soldiers with their helmets, I watched guys choking the enemy guy because there was nothing else to use. Throwing anything.

"It was crazy; people shooting, people stabbing, people biting, jumping on each other, kicking each other. Anything they had to defend themselves, they were using. The NVA were out of ammo, too, and they were doing the same thing we were doing. It was chaos.

"The funny thing is, I don't think anybody lost control. The first sergeant didn't, the troops didn't, they knew what they were doing. It was like an ice-hockey fight; it was that crazy and that close.

"I hope I didn't paint a bad picture of him, the NVA, wanting to get out of the battle. I respect the NVA, but he knew he was in trouble, and he was looking for a way to get out. In the opposite direction was the artillery and air strikes and he wasn't about to try to go out that end of that village anymore.

"He had only one way to go and that was through us.

"I think they were just as scared as we were; I really believe that. I don't think the NVA knew where to go. They felt safer among us than going out the back of that village. I remember shooting several of them—[later battlefield reports] said I knocked down eight of them that particular day—and some of them ran right through, on to the river.

"Some of them didn't even have weapons in their hands. They just wanted to live. That didn't dawn on me until years later, that they were just looking for a place to survive.

"They came through us. Christ! I don't know how many we killed. I swear there were a hundred of them that we killed in the initial burst of machine guns. And they still kept coming.

"Those [sixty-five] of us became like concrete; nobody was going to move us.

"Anyway, the sun went down again, and here there are [sixty-five] of us in this village. We were surrounded. They had gotten completely around us.

"It was at this time that Jim Livingston was moved north of the river. That's where he held that night.

"I had encircled us with, you name it, every piece of artillery available. They fired all night. We had artillery shooting from Dong Ha, Camp Carroll, from Cue Viet. They did a super job.

"I brought them within fifty meters of my lines, and they fired all night. And the Puffs, the 130s with the Gatling guns, came over us periodically when we were being assaulted.

"We were attacked all night, and my advice was, 'Everybody stay in your holes and shoot anything that walks.'

"We had one NVA—he had to have been on drugs—come through like he was delivering the *L.A. Times*: arms full of grenades just throwing them and walking around. I know personally, I hit him twice, and the troops got him six or seven times in the chest. He'd go down and he just kept bouncing back up and throwing grenades. Finally he went down and stayed down.

"The gunships did a marvelous job that night too. They came in, flipped on the spotlights one time, and we saw seventy of these guys fixing bayonets, getting ready to go for broke. Well, this gunship just wiped them out, made mince meat out of them.

"General Weise was always talking to me. 'Can you hold on? Can you just hold out until sunrise? Are you okay? Will you be able to make it?'

"Naturally we were going to make it there, because there was nowhere else to go.

"At one point, we were down to fourteen rounds between [sixty-five] of us. I got on the radio and called General Weise—'We need some ammo.'

"We had an S-4 by the name of Captain Lorraine [Lang] Forehand and he drove up in an Otter. The first batch of ammunition that came to us on the Otter was 90mm rounds for tanks.

"I got on the radio and said, 'What the hell am I going to do with these!?'

"It's funny now, but I must have sounded absurd. I talked to the General (Bill Weise) the other day and he said, 'I'll never forget that conversation.'

"I'd been hit in the mouth and my lips were split; nobody could understand what I was saying. I had skin flapping and basically I said, 'What the hell am I going to do with these 90-mm rounds? Hit them with a hammer? I can't shove them in a goddamn M16, sir. For Christ's sake! I need some ammo.'

"He said, 'Don't worry, don't worry, I'll get it to you.'

"So, [Forehand] jumped on the next batch of Otters,

came over, did a wheelie, and threw out all this ammunition. We got fat on grenades, we got fat on mortar rounds and we got fat on the M16 rounds. Then they drove off into the darkness.

"How the hell they ever got through there without getting shot, I'll never know, because at this stage the North Vietnamese had us completely surrounded.

"The next morning, the sun started coming up and we began looking around. Our jaws were touching the ground as to how many bodies were laying around us. Again the description of the trees, what was left of them, the description of anything that was standing around us, everything was 'blown to hell'.

"The numbers of enemy dead out in the rice paddies where the gunships and artillery had taken care of them, there were hundreds of them. The moaning, those who were in pain laying out there. Good warriors, I have to give them credit. They fought like hell.

"I guess simultaneously all of us started seeing the light come up. We weren't about to get out of our holes, but it must have looked funny, because we slowly stuck our heads up out of our holes, looked around, and slowly went back into our holes. All of us were doing the same thing, looking at each other, really bug-eyed. Several of us chuckled about it over a beer not too long ago.

"It's amazing how many of us got out of that. There were [sixty-five] and sixty-three of us made it through that night. Two got killed, two machine gunners early on. It's amazing how we lived through it.

"I had an old tree near me—I don't know what kind—but I can remember every time the artillery came in, I could hear the shrapnel hitting that tree above me while I was down in that hole. They were also firing 81s from the little gunboats on the river, and I could hear the shrapnel hit that tree.

"I'm sure you saw the movie *The Green Berets* with John

Wayne, and how the enemy came through in hordes; that's
how they came at us all night.

"When I think back about those three days, I just shake
my head. I don't even know why I'm here; I really don't
know. I look at it this way—I know it sounds corny—but I
think God has something for me to do. I don't know what it
is.

"I really believe that. I was severely injured, but to come
out of there alive was, well, it indicates to me that I still
have something to do. I don't know what it is. I wish I
knew.

"Anyway, when the sun started coming up, Livingston
started coming across the rice paddies to join up with us. He
took so much of the pressure off us, because at first light
they were coming on with a fresh frontal attack toward us.

"Livingston came across on their right flank and they
turned and had a helluva battle with him. He went through
the same type of fighting I had gone through the day before
coming across the rice paddies.

"Finally we joined forces at the edge of the village and
pushed the North Vietnamese back out into Dinh To toward
Thuong Do, and that's when the gunships had another field
day.

"Later, General Weise and Sergeant Major John Malnar
joined us. General Weise got hit, he was bleeding like a
stuck pig. Sergeant Malnar stood and was helping me grab
the general, and he [Malnar] took an RPG right in the back.
It didn't go off, but he was dead instantly.

"I had an M-79er and another kid out there probably from
here to that building—fifteen or twenty meters—out of
ammo. They were both screaming back and at this stage of
the game the counterattack was on big time; they were
coming at us with everything.

"At that time I called in artillery on our position.

"Our artillery officer talked to me on the radio and said,
'Are you sure you want this mission?'

" 'I want it.'

"I had told everybody what I had done, and the troopers were dug in. They weren't scared of artillery coming in on top of us, because we had it coming in all night on top of us.

"Thank God the maps were off, because those rounds landed forty meters in front of us, right in the middle of their organized frontal assault. I couldn't believe it. I saw fifty, sixty people disappear in a matter of seconds. It just annihilated those guys.

"This gave me time to grab the general and drag him back to this embankment. I had a .45 and was dragging him. All I wanted to do was get him back at least fifty meters and set him up against a tree, because we had some other troops back there.

"Remember me talking about this little creek on our left flank? Well, as we turned, it was on my right. I told everybody to start moving back, and I told the artillery officer to start adjusting the artillery fire behind us.

"Everything was going okay until I looked over and an NVA trooper came out of the paddy. There was this dike there, no higher than that table, and he came out of the river and saw us.

"I've got the general and I'm dragging him. I've got this .45 and I'm looking at this guy. I guess he was just as stunned as we were. Just as he started to raise up—to let us have it with whatever he was going to shoot us with—I fired my pistol.

"Swear to God, it went from here to the door, hit the ground, and ricocheted up. The kid just stood there, his eyes were this big. It hit him in the cartridge belt and blew him back in the creek. He could not believe this had happened.

"I don't know whether he was dead or not, but the next thing I noticed, he goes back over this embankment and disappears. Weise was bleeding like a pig and he is going into shock at this time, but he remembers this.

"I never could hit anything with a .45 anyway.

"So I got the general back and a couple of troops grabbed him.

"I can remember one of the guys who lost an arm and was holding it, begging me, 'Please come back for me.'

"I said, 'I'll be back.'

"This kid—he still sends me Christmas cards—had his arm severed by an artillery round. It wasn't bleeding, it was burned so badly; that's what blew my mind. [After returning] all he could say when I grabbed him and was carrying him out was, 'Skipper, my arm, I want my arm.'

"I felt like saying . . . well, I didn't.

"So, like an idiot, we turned around, went back about ten feet, and I found his arm. I had this arm and the kid, and I was hit again. We both went down.

"It was shrapnel; it was hot. I think it was an RPG that hit the tree. Anyway, I went down but I was able to get back up and carry that trooper back fifty meters. I don't know what made me drop him off and get back up, but I did.

"I just had to go back; I knew I had some Marines back there, at least five that I knew of, and I couldn't leave them, not after what they had gone through.

"[Subsequent battlefield reports] say I brought back a total of seven wounded Marines, but I thought it was six; I might have brought back an NVA, I don't know, I was at that stage.

"At this time the North Vietnamese were all over, they were everywhere. They were running around picking up our weapons, grabbing our rifles. So as I went back I grabbed some grenades off a couple of Marines and an AK-47. I remember firing and fighting my way in.

"I can remember shooting eight people and they went down. Whether or not I killed them, I don't know. I remember throwing the grenades, and I remember finding the five other Marines.

"One of my corpsman went with me each trip, and he wrote that particular part of the [battlefield] statement.

"F Company had regrouped with whatever they had left,

and they were in a bomb crater, and I guess, according to the corpsman, what I did inspired those guys, and they got back up on line and commenced another assault.

"At that time I think I had lost a lot of blood. I was bleeding and I passed out. After I got helilifted, a new battalion came across the river [Lieutenant Colonel Jarman's battalion, One-Three] and swept through our position.

"Our battalion in that three days lost eighty-one KIA and the enemy bodies left on the battlefield numbered about eight hundred.

"I've taken you through a lot, and I've skipped a lot, but that's kind of how I saw it.

"People have asked me to talk about it, but when I do, they look at me afterwards like: 'You're making it all up. We've never heard about Dai Do.'

"More people would have known about the Battle of Dai Do, but there are no records. Bill Dabney, Colonel Bill Dabney, who is still on active duty, told me at the National War College that he was in the bunker at 3rd Marine Division at Dong Ha which had all the messages, all of the OPs material pertaining to our particular battle.

"He was called to a meeting and as he went out of the bunker, direct hits came right on the bunker and destroyed everything.

"Those that were involved think that Dai Do was as significant as Khe Sanh.

"I've seen a lot of these guys in the past years.

"I saw one in Washington a week ago who I thought would never walk again. His brother is a gunnery sergeant in the public relations branch. I was sitting on a board across the hall, and right away the gunny saw me and said, 'Who is that guy?'

"When he found out, he called his brother and he later walked in the door, and it is amazing; after all these years, I recognized him. And he's walking too. He took some rounds right here in the upper left hip, and it blew most of the hip away. He took a shot right in the chest too. I don't know how he lived.

"He's doing very, very well. He's one of the aides in the Senate or House.

"I keep in touch with many of the troops who were with me, to see that they are all doing well. They went through hell and are so damned proud of being Marines."

8

Dai Do—Livingston

IN 1965 and 1966, Jim Livingston was a platoon commander assigned to Three-Three, which was stationed in the Gulf of Tonkin. He had operated in proximity to Vietnam, and by 1967, he had been promoted to captain and commanded Echo Company, Two-Four. His first task was to search out the elusive Vietcong.

"The VC were sometimes hard to find," the lean, intense Marine brigadier general said recently at Camp Lejeune, North Carolina, where he once commanded the 6th Marines. "But if you take a dirt farmer from Georgia like I am and put me in the sticks of Georgia, I can beat a handful from New York any day of the week. That's what I mean: The VC kids were fighting in their backyards.

"We fought the VC down at Quang Tri when I first joined Two-Four, and we beat him. I mean, we ambushed the hell out of them. One day we had six ambushes and cleaned out the whole VC cadre from this little village by the Quang Tri River.

"We hit them every way we could. We even captured two of their women who were swinging AK-47s.

"They never beat us. We learned their terrain and got

95

familiar with their area. That's where we got smart; don't go out there and fight him initially. The first move is to get familiar with the area you are fighting in. Learn what the hell he does for a living, learn his soldiering ability, means of operation, and then you go after him.

"Don't go out there and plunge into it. The way you beat him is to learn his game and then take away his advantage, which is understanding the terrain and the soldier. That's what I emphasize to my kids here at 6th Marines."

After successfully battling the guerrillas in Quang Tri, BLT Two-Four moved north and engaged the finest troops in North Vietnam in the spring of 1968.

"We fought the Palace Guard at Dai Do; the best they had. These were big guys with new uniforms, brand new weapons, close-cropped haircuts. They were good-looking soldiers.

"Granted, most of the ones I saw were dead, but they were big guys, quality troops.

"We didn't fight a ragtag outfit. These guys were the best they had. That's why I say we fought the Palace Guard, and I don't think the North Vietnamese would have committed his Palace Guard unless there was no one else left.

"We handed their asses to them. There was no mystique about beating those guys. Superhuman? Ah, bull."

JAMES E. LIVINGSTON

Rank: Brigadier General (then Captain)

Date: May 2, 1968

Unit: E Company, 2nd Battalion, 4th Marines

Place: Dai Do, South Vietnam

Born: Towns, Telfair County, Georgia, January 12, 1940

"Up from Dai Do there were some sand dunes, but it was primarily rice paddies. On the other side from Big John down to the ARVN camp, that was all sand. I won't say desert, but it was sand-dunish. We played games with the NVA out in that area a few times.

"It was almost like hide and seek, shooting at one another, particularly out on ambush patrols and recon patrols. That area was well within range of the weapon systems they had north of the Ben Hai [River]. You had to watch yourself. When you stopped out there, you dug.

"A couple of times up there, rocket fire literally covered me with sand; it was coming in that close. When I got my Silver Star, there were so many rockets that I was completely covered with sand.

"Fortunately, unless you take a direct hit out in the sand, that rocket has such velocity, it buries itself before it explodes.

"Rice paddies had a similar characteristic. The ground in some of them was pretty soggy. I remember one day we had a short round from a four-deuce [4.2 mortar]. The damn thing landed right between me and my gunny. Fortunately, it soaked itself right up in the mud and failed to explode.

"Another time I was sitting in an area just to the east of Dong Ha, and a 105-round hit the little building I was in. I was sitting at a table, which was ironic. The table had six holes in it and my utility jacket had thirteen holes in it.

"I guess the Master was with me. That was probably the luckiest call I had over there. I'll never forget that one. That was before Dai Do.

"Initially, my company was located north of Dong Ha, and I was in charge of protecting the bridge that was later blown up in 1972, when the NVA were piling down. There was a lot of enemy contact north of the bridge."

On May 1, Echo Company was released from the 3rd Marine Division and returned to the operational control of BLT Two-Four. Echo's return to the battalion boosted Bill Weise's spirits. "My morale went up several notches," he recalled.[1]

Captain Livingston moved overland from the bridge he

was protecting on Highway 1 to An Lac and met scattered resistance. General Weise: "Captain Jim Livingston knew he was badly needed at Dai Do. A natural fighter, he overcame his inclination to stomp on the enemy positions that harassed and tried to delay him. He returned fire when only absolutely necessary, skirted enemy strong points, and moved to An Lac as quickly as possible."[2]

As he neared his objective, Captain Livingston confronted a last obstacle—a nearly unfordable stream. The current was swift and deep, about five and a half feet. He overcame the problem by strategically placing a half dozen of his tallest Marines who had stripped to the waist in the deepest part of the stream. The taller Marines then passed their shorter, heavily laden comrades from one to another across the stream. The drenched Echo Marines under Jim Livingston moved into An Lac "itching for a fight."[3]

Jay Vargas and his Marines began the assault at about 10:40 A.M. They battled their way into Dai Do and were on their own until about five P.M. General Weise sent Bravo One-Three to help Golf late on 1 May, but it never made it. After a severe mauling, Bravo fell back and was pinned down short of Dai Do.

Jim Livingston: "Hotel Company under Jim Williams made the initial contact. Fox Company hadn't been committed, but Hotel had been beat up pretty good and they had been pulled back. Golf Company—Jay Vargas and his Marines—had gotten to the fringe of Dai Do, and they were holding on.

"When I pulled into An Lac, the Old Man [Bill Weise] had me help organize Bravo Company which just got the hell knocked out of it. They had KIAs all over the battlefield in front of us, and we were helping get those kids back. There was one young second lieutenant who was still alive, but they were in shambles.

"General Weise gave me the order to take Dai Do and I got my guys together. We were down by the Cua Viet River just south of Dai Do, and they [the NVA] were probing out in front of us that night and we hit them a couple of times. We were right in that little corner between [an unnamed creek] and the Bo Dieu River; the battalion CP [Command Post] was also in there.

"I kept talking to Vargas that evening, and he was getting hit pretty hard. The Old Man told me to go in and link up with Golf Company and take Dai Do.

"We had between five hundred and a thousand meters of open rice paddies between us to go through. I had two platoons up and one platoon back as the reserve.

"We kicked off about five o'clock in the morning after knocking the hell out of it with artillery, fixed-wing; we were piling it on there.

"One time they were thinking of doing away with bayonets down at Parris Island. I said, 'No, that is one thing that took us through Dai Do, bayonets.'

"We fixed bayonets and went for it.

"We passed by some bodies and a burning amtrac. The first thing we hit was about eighteen RPG positions. I knew that because I fell down behind a grave and it almost disappeared in front of me. They had me zeroed in because of all of the radio equipment with me.

"There was a little pocket where we initially penetrated and I lost about ten KIA in an area about the size of this room. We fixed bayonets and penetrated that first trench line, and we rolled up some NVA. I would hate to guess, but we are talking about a couple of hundred. One of my young machine gunners was stacking 'em up like cordwood.

"We fought all that morning and finally kicked them out of Dai Do and linked up with Golf Company. I lost probably half my company there. I went in there with about one hundred and fifty Marines, and we were down to, the exact numbers escape my mind now, seventy-five or less; the others were either KIAed or WIAed.

"After I had pushed through the town of Dai Do and we established a weak linkup with Golf Company, the remnants of Hotel Company were sent down. For some reason they got by the edge of me, I'm not sure today exactly what their mission was. I guess they were to link up with me.

"They were really starting to get hammered, and they screamed, 'Where is Echo Company?'

"I told General Weise, 'They are really fixing to get into trouble. I'll go get 'em.'

"I was probably down to fifty Marines or less, but we went out and linked up with Hotel Company. Then I decided to take the battle to the enemy again. We had about six or seven hedgerow arrangements, and we got after 'em again in Dinh To.

"We were killing them so fast up at Dinh To, we were running out of ammo. Our ammo got to the point we were shooting AK-47s. We were shooting anything that would shoot. That was the reason we had to pull back.

"We were calling in suppressing artillery fire on top of us; we are talking a matter of a few yards. There was shrapnel flying all over the area.

"We were also dropping fixed-wing. I always told my guys, 'Don't call in napalm unless you will feel the heat.' Well, we were feeling the heat that day; that's how close the combat was.

"Their guys were good fighters, yeah, they were good, but a lot of them were drugged. Also, their extremities— arms and legs—were bound with leather-like bindings. This kept them from losing a lot of blood when they were hit. Therefore they were able to continue fighting. You could blow off a leg, or blow his arm off, and if he was drugged up enough, he still kept coming.

"In each of my squads, we kept an M14 for a sniper weapon, and I picked up one of the sniper weapons. I dinged a couple with it, and I gave it to a kid [as] I moved to another position.

"We were doing pretty damn good, but what began to stop us was that the North Vietnamese were shooting artillery on us just as fast as we could shoot it on them. It was basically all landing in the same place, we were that close. Later I found I was on top of their regimental headquarters when I got shot.

"We were taking it to them and they tried to get around our flank and cut us off. We were taking some heavy casualties from both sides. The doggone South Vietnamese—who I thought were on my left side down toward Dong Ha—had pulled out and left that flank exposed. So we were getting shot at from two directions, plus they were swimming down the river.

"There were boocoo [beaucoup] of them bandits there. If I hadn't got shot, I think we could have held our position for a while.

"We were still fighting and were taking some KIAs and WIAs. We could see the whites of their eyes; the NVA were that close. What they did was level some heavy machine guns on us that they had been using for anti-aircraft, the old 12-7s. One of those suckers shot me in the leg before we could get to him.

"It knocked me down, but I managed to keep the outfit together and we were still rolling them up pretty good. We were holding, but I discerned that I couldn't afford to stay there. A couple of Marines, who were themselves shot, helped me keep mobile enough, and we were able to get the outfit back into Dai Do.

"Then the Old Man decided to pull me out because I was banged up pretty good.

"There were about thirty or thirty-five Marines left out of my company; that's a high estimate.

"The North Vietnamese had brand-new AKs; they had a variety of small machine guns, the old SKSs; we ran across sniper weapons. So they had the whole spectrum, plus they had us zeroed in with artillery. I don't recall them shooting that many rockets; they were shooting artillery. Pretty sizable stuff.

"The only thing we had that they didn't was air.

"At that time I had one lieutenant, and the other company

had one officer left. My XO, Dave Jones—he's over at Baltimore, he's a doctor of education—he got hit with a mortar. One of my other young lieutenants, Jim Sims, who is now an architect up in Atlanta, got shot in the stomach; he had just gotten back off leave, poor devil. It seems like my other lieutenant, a guy named Postdal, got shot too; he was medevaced.

"Dai Do was really conventional warfare—tanks, artillery, air support, the whole thing. It was tough, man, I tell you, it was tough. But Two-Four was about as ready as any battalion could be. We were a very seasoned outfit.

"I think that if we had hit Dai Do six months sooner, it would have been tougher. My company was very combat-ready. Those kids had a lot of confidence in themselves. They had never been beaten.

"But I tell you, those kids were ready at Dai Do. When I said, 'Fix bayonets and let's go for it,' they were ready. They went into Dai Do and were very successful.

"Marines have always been aggressive, which I think, is a product of boot camp. The greatest thing we have in the U.S. Marine Corps is Marine Corps boot camp, the basic training program. In it you acquire a common understanding about what the Corps' intent is.

"I think that is where we have it over the other services. We don't ever want to lose our boot camp, or our OCS [Officer Candidate School]. To me, that is the critical linch-pin in this business.

"I was a series commander at Parris Island in '66, I was a battalion commander there before I came here, I was at Quantico as a company commander with the Platoon Leadership Class at OCS. There is the critical issue.

"We don't ever want to think for a minute that the Marine Corps will be the same without that basic training. We want to protect Parris Island, San Diego, and Quantico with our life's blood as far as I am concerned.

"Marine Corps boot camp has got to be tough. It teaches a kid how to deal with pressure. It subjects him to pressure

with the intent of identifying the individuals who can't hack
it when the rubber really meets the road.

"That's what makes a Marine trustworthy to another
Marine, that common background. One guy's dad may be a
Ph.D. and another's might be a dirt farmer, but they come
from that same common point of departure as Marines.
They both have proven themselves in the same sort of cir-
cumstance. There is a unique brotherhood, a unique bond.

"Old combat guys know: The more adverse the combat
situation the unit has been through, the more that basic bond
is developed.

"I think you can go back and see the units that have the
close bond are the guys who really went through hard
combat. I know Two-Four is that way.

"Combat makes people have a lot in common very
quickly."

"I hope the next mission we are assigned is clearly
defined. I don't have any problem going down and doing
what is necessary, but I hope whatever it is, we clearly
define our intent.

"I think that's what killed us in Vietnam; we never clearly
defined what our intent was. Hell, the Marines could have
whipped the hell out of any NVA outfit any day of the
week. We did that. Two-Four is a prime example of that.

"We took on an NVA division, and we walked away with
our heads held high, even though we suffered substantial
losses.

"To me there isn't [a fighting] unit in the world—and I've
seen them all to some degree—that can beat a U.S. Marine
unit. In the same regard, you don't want to go out and lose
people just for the sake of 'being there.'

"We've got to clearly define our intent and then stick
with it. We don't want to waffle it up front and then waffle
it when it doesn't feel good. That's what we did in Vietnam.

"If we are going to war, then let's go or not go at all.

There is no such thing as a clean war. There is not a clean way to kill a guy. Everything we do is oriented toward that intent.

"My attitude about it is, and I tell my regiment, 'I want you to kill him better and faster.' You want to go in there with the objective of kill the bastard, get it over with, and get home.

"That's what I look for in these kids. Otherwise, the taxpayers shouldn't be paying us."

"Dai Do was quick; there wasn't any media. It was not extensive like Khe Sanh or Hue. It wasn't something you could focus on for any length of time.

"It was quick and dirty.

"The media guys who were there got out as soon as the bullets started flying. They didn't stay around. After I got shot and medevaced, I was going back through Big John and these newspaper guys who, when the bullets started flying got the hell out of the area, were back with the bodies.

"They were taking off the ponchos from the heads of some of the kids, exposing their faces and taking photographs. One of them happened to be a young kid who worked for me, very close. In two days he was going to Hawaii to see his parents; his folks were already there waiting for him.

"And here he was laying on a stretcher with a poncho over him. He had been shot in the head by the NVA. These reporters were sitting there with a camera taking pictures of him. That really jerked my jaws. I've never been so jacked in my entire life!

"That was the real press we had there. To me that does not speak of a quality effort. My two or three exposures with the press over there was very, uh, very, I'm searching for a nice word, I was very unimpressed.

"I think that the media business is too competitive and, as a result, has lost much of its credibility.

"We need to get back, in my mind, to the very ethical journalism. I think Ernie Pyle is certainly a good point of departure. We don't have that point of departure from Vietnam, we don't have an Ernie Pyle from Vietnam.

"Who is going to remember some of the reporters we've got now? Everybody can recount what Ernie Pyle did, and those types of individuals, good role models. I'm sure there are some out there, but as a group, collectively, I don't see that many good role models in American journalism anymore.

"Where were they in Afghanistan? Where were they in Kenya? Where were they in Angola? If it's not going to get out on the national boob tube, it's not worth reporting.

"We've got to get away from what I call splash journalism—sensationalism. 'If it doesn't make a good picture, it isn't worth a damn.'

"I see so much of this staged journalism on television. You don't have to be a Ph.D. to see that it has been staged for the benefit of the evening news.

"However, I think the American people are astute enough to pick up on it."

Two years after the little-heralded battle at Dai Do, newspaper and television coverage focused on campuses across the United States when several exploded with violence. On May 4, 1970, young people, protesting the presence of ROTC on campus, rioted at Kent State University, and Ohio National Guardsmen shot and killed four students.

A few days later, at the Jackson State campus in Mississippi, local and state law-enforcement officers opened fire on a dormitory at night, killing two more students. Numerous demonstrations resulted, and fearing additional campus violence, most of the nation's schools closed until the fall term.

The media covered the demonstrations and closures like battles.

In Washington, D.C., ten days after the killings at Kent State, in an untelevised ceremony at the White House, President Richard Nixon presented Jay Vargas and Jim Livingston, commanders of Golf and Echo Companies from BLT Two-Four, Medals of Honor for heroism at Dai Do.

9

Orders

COLONEL William Barber (Ret.) is a Marine legend. He has seen it all, from Iwo Jima to Vietnam.

He completed boot camp at Parris Island in 1940 and then went on to parachute training, after which he was designated a paramarine. In 1943, he became an officer.

He joined the 26th Marines and landed on Iwo Jima in 1945. This bloody battle was the most costly in Marine Corps history—almost twenty-five thousand casualties—and then-Second Lieutenant Barber earned a Silver Star for dashing into enemy fire to save two comrades. He was wounded in that action and evacuated.

In 1950 during the Korean War, five to seven Chinese divisions swarmed across the Yalu River in an attempt to trap the 1st Marine Division at the Chosin Reservoir. Then-Captain Barber was in command of F Company, Two-Seven, and assigned to defend a three-mile mountain pass along the division's main supply line.

On November 28, an enemy force of regimental size attacked the battle-weary Marines and after a seven-hour fight had F Company surrounded. After two units sent to reinforce Barber's troops had been driven back, he was ordered to fight his way down to the reinforcements.

Aware that if he abandoned this pass, it would result in eight thousand Marines being trapped, Captain Barber requested permission to hold his ground. He chose to risk the loss of his command to the numerically superior enemy force rather than let his fellow Marines in the division be trapped.

On the next day he was severely wounded in the legs and had to be carried up and down his lines on a stretcher so that he could encourage and lead his men.

After five days of bitter fighting in subzero weather only 82 of the 220 Marines in his company were able to walk away when relieved. In front of F Company's lines were approximately a thousand dead Chinese soldiers.

For that action Bill Barber was awarded the Medal of Honor. Following the Korean War, he continued his Marine Corps career. After the Marines landed at Da Nang in 1965, he was assigned as a media liaison officer.

The Vietcong, in order to be successful, had to alienate the local populous from the government of Vietnam. To do that the VC needed their support. Sometimes this support was freely given, but more often than not it derived from terrorism and extortion.

The Marines in the populated regions of I Corps searched for the elusive guerrillas, and when they were located, the VC were punished militarily. However, it soon became apparent that defeating the enemy on the battlefield wasn't all that was going to be needed if the war was to be won.

Since local support was critical for the VC, the Marines launched the Civic Action Program to undercut that support. The Marines, when not out fighting the VC, began to provide medical assistance; build schools, orphanages, and hospitals; repair damaged roads; and launch other constructive programs.

A television reporter was assigned to do a story on the Civic Action Program and Bill Barber was there to provide assistance.

"I helped the reporter with his story as much as I could,"

Colonel Barber recalled at his home in Southern California recently, "and after I saw the final product, he asked me what I thought. I told him I thought it was pretty good, but I didn't understand the ending. It didn't fit with the rest of the story."

The reporter told Barber that he was under instructions to film three different endings to the stories he filed from Vietnam: Pro-war and positive; antiwar and negative; and neutral. The newsman told Barber that he thought the story deserved the positive ending, but his Stateside editor decided on the antiwar ending.

"There were two other newsmen present when he said that," Bill added, "so I think he was telling the truth."

The veteran Marine was neither angry nor critical. He seemed more puzzled than anything else. He returned to the United States and in 1970 retired from the Marine Corps.

Colonel Barber served thirty years in the Marine Corps, during some of its finest hours. When he retired a journalist asked him, "What was your most difficult order?"

It was an intriguing question. His reply said a lot about being a serviceman during the Sixties.

"When I was commander of 2nd Marines in 1968," he said, "an order came in—it might have originated in the White House—which said that Washington, D.C. was off limits to the Marines."

Marines not being able to visit their nation's capital. Why?

There was a peace demonstration scheduled that weekend and the Powers That Be apparently didn't want Marines there at the same time. It might create problems.

Some of these Marines had slugged it out with the Japanese on Iwo Jima, the Chinese at the Chosin Reservoir, and the Vietnamese at Khe Sanh and Dai Do.

"That really bothered me," the colonel said, "but I couldn't let my young officers and staff NCOs see that it bothered me. They were the ones who were going to have to carry it out."

And the order went out: "Washington, D.C., is off limits to U.S. Marines."

He paused for a second and said; "Yes, without a doubt, that was the most difficult order I ever had to give. I told that to the reporter, but it never made the news. I guess he didn't think it was newsworthy."

> "I went into a public 'ouse to get a pint of beer,
> The publican 'e up and sez, 'We serve no redcoats 'ere.'
> The girls be'ind the bar, they laughed and giggled fit to die,
> So out into the street I go, and to myself says I,
>
> "It's Tommy this and Tommy that and chuck him out, the brute,
> But it's thin red lines of 'eroes when the guns begin to shoot
> Yes, it's Tommy this and Tommy that, and anything you please,
> But Tommy ain't a bloomin' fool, you bet that Tommy sees."
>
> —Adapted from "Tommy" by Rudyard Kipling

Lang Vei

EUGENE ASHLEY, JR.

Rank: Sergeant First Class   **Date:** February 6-7, 1968
Unit: Company C, Fifth   **Place:** Lang Vei, west of
Special Forces Group   Khe Sanh
  Born: Wilmington, North Carolina, October 12, 1931

ON February 6, 1968, the North Vietnamese massed and attacked a Special Forces camp located at Lang Vei, which was located several clicks west of Khe Sanh. The enemy launched the attack with a ground assault and nine Soviet PT-76 tanks. The North Vietnamese also employed tear gas in the attack.

This use of tear gas by the enemy revealed a bizarre double standard that was indicative of the complexities of the Vietnam War. When it was learned that some American units had used nonlethal tear gas against the Vietcong to minimize civilian casualties, some protesters shrieked. They called it "inhumane," "against the Geneva Convention," and "barbaric." But when the North Vietnamese used tear gas, there were no protests. Was it because this was to be expected of our enemies? Or was it because there were no headlines saying "NVA Using Gas Warfare in Vietnam"?

Whatever the reason, the Americans who were serving in Vietnam knew about it, and when they came home and were confronted with protests, their response was often silence. How could one thing be wrong for the Americans and right for their enemy?

It was a political question, and the Americans who served in Vietnam were not politicians; they were just soldiers like Special Forces First Sergeant Eugene Ashley, Jr. who was a brave man trying to do his best. But bravery was never the question.

The attack against Lang Vei began at 10:45 in the morning with a mortar attack, and shortly after midnight an American advisor serving with the Lang Vei defenders reported that the installation was under heavy attack.

A battalion from the 66th Regiment, 304th NVA Division—equipped with satchel charges, tear gas and flame throwers—launched the infantry attack in coordination with the tanks. Within thirteen minutes the nine Soviet tanks had rolled through the defensive wire around the Special Forces compound, rumbled over the antipersonnel mines and were in the heart of the compound.

Back at Khe Sanh, Colonel David E. Lownds called in immediate artillery and air support for the garrison, but it had little effect, because the compound had been overrun so quickly.

At 2:40 A.M., Camp Lang Vei reported that there was a Communist tank sitting on top of the bunker that housed the Tactical Operations Center (TAC).

During the initial phases of the NVA attack a senior U.S. Army Special Forces advisor, First Sergeant Eugene Ashley, Jr., supported the defenders with high-explosive and illumination mortar fire from a former camp position nine hundred meters to the east of the present campsite.

When communication was lost with the personnel inside

the bunker, Sergeant Ashley requested and began adjusting air strikes and artillery support against the enemy positions.

At 6:30 A.M., the Marines at the KSCB reported that Sergeant Ashley had radio contact with the men still inside the TAC Center.

He then organized and equipped a reaction force of Montagnard, South Vietnamese, and American Special Forces advisors to reinforce the friendly troops still trapped on the hill.

With complete disregard for his own safety and the rescue of his trapped comrades uppermost in his mind, Sergeant Ashley led the small band into assault positions.

An hour later a report was received saying that there were fifteen men still alive inside the TAC Center, including the commanding officer of Company C, 5th Special Forces Group, Lieutenant Colonel Daniel F. Schungel.

At 8:30 A.M., Sergeant Ashley and two other Special Forces members took a small company of local personnel and assaulted the enemy-held position where his comrades were located.

After they had moved one hundred meters, the small band came under intense automatic, semiautomatic, and tank fire from the North Vietnamese in the camp. Realizing the perilous position to his men, Sergeant Ashley moved his force back and again brought air strikes against the NVA.

When the last plane swooped in and dropped its ordnance, Sergeant Ashley again led his troops against the North Vietnamese position in an attempt to free the trapped members of the Special Forces camp.

He led the assault through booby-trapped areas and the intense fire of the determined enemy force, which began hurling all of its firepower against the approaching Allied force. Again the small band was forced back while Sergeant Ashley provided covering fire.

When his men reached a safer position down the hill, the sergeant fell back to reorganize the company before advancing up the hill alone, so he could more effectively direct additional air strikes at the enemy. He was receiving direct fire from the enemy, yet he remained in position, directing the air strikes.

Returning to his forces, he launched a third attack against the enemy stronghold, advancing through bunkers that now had been booby-trapped by the enemy, through the automatic-weapons fire and through the bomb craters with one goal in mind—to rescue his buddies from certain death.

He displayed unbounded heroism with the highest degree of intrepidity as he encouraged his forces forward until, again, the volume of enemy fire became too great, forcing another withdrawal where he again reorganized for another attack.

Once again, Sergeant Ashley rallied the gallant force forward to free his trapped comrades but was turned back again with more casualties, more bravery, and more honor. The company had sustained numerous casualties and was weary from its continual engagement in combat. Many were exhausted to the point of unconsciousness.

Sergeant Ashley, evaluating the condition of his force and his desire to rescue his commanding officer and comrades from certain death, displayed a raw courage and a tactical brilliance.

Again he mounted up his men for a fifth assault and called the forward air observer to coordinate the assault with the air cover. He then asked the FO to contact the men in the bunker to relay his plan of attack.

One more time he rallied his battle-weary forces forward. As they moved through the booby-trapped satchel charges and small-arms fire, Sergeant Ashley directed the FO to have air strikes escort his unit to the top of the hill. Bombs were exploding around him, booby-traps were tripped, and the enemy small-arms and automatic-weapons fire was placed on the advancing force.

Simultaneously, the enemy was trying to gain entrance to the TAC Center with explosive charges. Sergeant Ashley knew that this was his last chance to get his comrades out alive.

When his force was again falling back, Sergeant Ashley ran from man to man, encouraging them forward through the blaze of enemy fire. Twice during this assault he saved members of his company as he engaged the enemy infantry within five meters.

The air strikes rained down bombs near the summit, effectively silencing the enemy fire from that area. Sergeant Ashley rallied his forces onward to the TAC Center, although they were receiving voluminous fire from other enemy positions.

When all else failed, Sergeant Ashley charged forward with his weapon on full automatic and engaged the enemy.

Then he was caught in the chest with a burst of automatic weapons fire. He was wounded twice more and was carried from the summit by his comrades. In the end it wasn't small-arms fire, or automatic-weapons fire, or grenades, or RPGs, or even tanks that killed Gene Ashley. As he lay wounded on the hillside, an artillery round landed on him.

Although his severe wounds forced his removal from the hill before the survivors could escape, the four-hour battle had kept diversionary pressure on the enemy and eventually allowed his comrades in the TAC Center to escape.

The courage and audacity he displayed in the five charges up the hill toward the TAC Center went unreported. There were other things to report: The Marines at Khe Sanh were still "trapped"; Hue was being pounded into rubble; Saigon was picking up the pieces, as were dozens of other cities that were attacked during the Tet Offensive.

There wasn't room for Gene Ashley's name in the papers, but that was okay, because he had carved his name in the hearts and minds of the Marines and soldiers who watched him going up that hill.

11

Force Recon

TERRENCE C. GRAVES

Rank: Second Lieutenant
Unit: 3rd Force Recon
Company, 3rd Recon
Battalion

Date: February 16, 1968
Place: Near Con Thien,
Quang Tri Province

Born: Corpus Christi, Texas, July 6, 1945

As a result of the enemy's well-coordinated Tet Offensive in January 1968 the North Vietnamese and Vietcong forces were able to capture several major cities and province capitals throughout South Vietnam.

Although the surprise attack achieved initial gains, a determined effort by Allied Forces was successful in driving the enemy back into the jungle. By February 11, the Saigon command reported that thirty-two thousand enemy soldiers had been killed in the two-week offensive.

However, the enemy still held the ancient capital of Hue in the northernmost province of Thua Thien. The North Vietnamese Army's 325th(C) Division and 304th Division were besieging the 26th Marine Regiment at the Khe Sanh

Combat Base to the west. Propagandists in Hanoi were claiming to the world press that they would hold Hue and that the rest of Vietnam would rise up and defeat the U.S.-backed Saigon government. They were also predicting that Khe Sanh would fall like Dien Bien Phu, the battle where the Vietminh defeated the French colonial forces. Ultimately, the battle drove France out of Indochina.

It was imperative that the Allied forces retake Hue and relieve the pressure on Khe Sanh. Before this could be accomplished, however, G-2 had to find out the enemy's plans, where he was massing, and his supply routes. Then the Marines would go after the enemy.

On February 16, fifty miles north of Hue, nine Marines of Team 2-1 from the Third Force Recon Company went on a long range patrol deep inside enemy-held territory southwest of Con Thien during Operation Kentucky. Second Lieutenant Terrence Graves was leading the patrol on an intelligence-gathering mission.

The patrol had been breaking brush most of the day when it came upon a trail. The lieutenant decided to follow it, searching for a good spot to set up a snare (differing from an ambush in that the main purpose was to capture a prisoner). It was a typical Force Recon mission.

The American patrol followed the trail until it came to a bomb crater. It looked like a good place to make the snatch, so Lieutenant Graves positioned his men in a 360 around the rim of the crater and waited. It was a game of Hide and Watch. It was an old cliche yet true: "Combat is prolonged periods of boredom punctuated by moments of sheer terror."

A brief time after the Marines had established their perimeter, two North Vietnamese soldiers came strolling up the trail from the south like it was Sunday morning. They were about one hundred and fifty meters away when they were first detected moving toward the American position.

"We heard them talking down near the streambed," Corporal Danny Slocum stated later.

Lieutenant Graves decided to wait for them to come up to his position where he could pull off the snare and evacuate the area. He didn't want to fight; he wanted to grab the two enemy soldiers and get out before anyone noticed.

However, as the Marines waited for the enemy to saunter into the trap from the south, Lance Corporal Michael Nation (the patrol's rear guard) observed seven more NVA moving across a ridge line to the north from the opposite direction. The young officer reassessed the situation and decided to ambush the seven NVA coming in from the north rather than trying to snare the two enemy soldiers below. The seven all had packs and weapons.

If the Marines tried to snare the two NVA, the others coming from the north would probably hear the commotion and come to investigate. Quietly Lieutenant Graves led three team members up the hill to set up an ambush site.

In addition to Slocum and Lieutenant Graves, Lance Corporal Nation and a PFC named Lopez set up the ambush just above and parallel to the trail the NVA soldiers were coming down. The Marines waited patiently for the enemy to enter the killing zone.

"We were sitting up there waiting to ambush them, and Nation opened up on them," Slocum recalled. "He started it."

The other Marines opened fire with their small arms and automatic weapons. They also threw grenades while Corporal R. B. Thomson started firing his M-79 on the enemy soldiers.

It was brief, vicious, and noisy. Slocum noted that enemy body parts were being scattered around the area. However, because the trail was cut into the hillside below them and out of view, the Marines were unable to see if all of the enemy had been killed.

After waiting motionless for ten minutes, Lieutenant Graves led his three men into the killing zone. He went in one direction and the other three Marines moved in from the opposite direction from where the NVA had come. However, as they approached the ambush site, the Americans were greeted by intense small-arms and automatic weapons fire.

That's when Slocum was hit; just as he was going into the ambush site. Despite the intense fire, Graves crawled to his wounded corporal to render aid.

"Doc," Lieutenant Graves called back to Corpsman Stephen Thompson, "come patch up Slocum. He's been hit."

When the corpsman moved up and began working on Slocum, Graves and Thomson continued to the ambush site together. When the two Marines began receiving fire from the ambush site, they assaulted the position. After another brief firefight, Graves and Thomson returned and reported that all of the NVA were now dead.

Lieutenant Graves then maneuvered unprotected through twenty meters of knee-high grass to the crater where the radio was located. He called in a medevac for Slocum and repositioned the men with him into a tight 360-degree perimeter. When he was confident of his team's positioning, he radioed for air support from Huey gunships, and called in and began adjusting artillery fire.

Lieutenant Graves ordered his team to move to the crest of the hill to the evacuation site. He and two other Marines provided rear security as the team moved to the hilltop.

"When we started moving," Lance Corporal Nation remembered, "Lieutenant Graves was on the radio. When we got to that twenty meter stretch, we were pinned down by heavy fire and everyone had to stay down." The team was now being attacked by an estimated enemy force of two companies.

Despite the heavy volume of fire, Lieutenant Graves continued to observe for the Marine artillery units. After calling in an adjustment, he would sit up, see where the round hit, and readjust the fire as needed.

"The rest of us were firing back at the North Vietnamese soldiers," Nation recalled, "but they could have kept us pinned down if it hadn't been for Lieutenant Graves encouraging us. 'Come on!' he would say. 'Let's get up there! We can't do any good here!' "

The Marines moved out again as the lieutenant continued to call in his artillery. When the Huey gunships arrived, Graves calmly assumed the role of close air-support observer in addition to his other duties.

As the Huey gunships began attacking NVA positions, Lieutenant Graves radioed the locations of the enemy gunners who were firing on the choppers. The Hueys were successful in suppressing the enemy fire and Graves told his men that an evacuation helicopter was coming to extract them.

Because of this dual role as artillery–air support observer, Lieutenant Graves was able to subject the larger NVA force to continuous assault. Using his supporting arms to the best possible advantage, Graves was able to move the team to the landing zone.

"Once we got there, we regrouped and got into a tight 360-degree defensive position again," Nation said, "and were told to shoot at anything that moved."

His Marines were excited and they were peppering the area with gunfire.

"Take it easy, don't waste ammo because we don't know when the choppers will be coming to pick us up," Graves told his men. "Squeeze them off just like you did at the rifle range in boot camp."

The Marines settled down and their fire discipline returned. They stopped shooting their weapons on full automatic and began taking good shots.

A CH-46 Sea Knight arrived and attempted to land on top of the hill. However, Lieutenant Graves was forced to wave the chopper off when enemy automatic-weapons fire became too intense. He was concerned for the safety of the chopper crew.

"This is when the lieutenant, Emerick, and R.B. [Thomson] were all sitting down there about a meter apart,"

Slocum reported. "A machine gun opened up and got all three of them. The lieutenant was the first one to get hit, and he caught two rounds . . . as I understand it, and then R. B. was hit, and he was hit pretty bad. Emerick was just starting to crawl up the hill. He was hit and just slumped over."

Doc Thompson moved over and started to treat Graves' wounds, but the lieutenant told him to look after Thomson. "He's in worse shape than I am," he said.

Meanwhile Emerick had stopped breathing and didn't have a pulse. Slocum and Nation took off his pack and feverishly began giving him artificial respiration.

"Slow down!" Graves yelled to Nation. "Don't go so fast or you'll get too dizzy to do any good!" Nation slowed down; Emerick's pulse returned and he started breathing again.

After he was sure his men were being properly cared for, Graves selected another landing zone for extraction. Lieutenant Graves got back on the radio and continued calling in artillery missions and air strikes while firing his M16 at the NVA. Despite heavy return fire, he was able to maneuver his team to a new landing zone without sustaining additional casualties.

However, when the pickup helicopter landed, it again came under increased automatic weapons fire, which critically wounded another member of the team. Lieutenant Graves stood erect by the side of the helicopter directing his men as they scrambled on board.

Finally the lieutenant jumped aboard the helicopter himself, but when he realized that Slocum was missing and had not made it on board, Graves grabbed a radio and leaped from the helicopter. A PFC followed him out and the two went and found the wounded man.

Aware that the helicopter was sustaining numerous hits, jeopardizing the other patrol members as well as the chopper crew, Graves signaled for the pilot to lift off. The pilot indicated that he would wait, but Graves continued to signal for the pilot to lift off, which he did.

Lieutenant Graves continued to direct air support against the enemy positions until another helicopter was able to land. The second chopper made it in and hovered long enough for the three Marines to scramble on board. However, as it was lifting off, the rescue chopper sustained numerous hits and crashed shortly after takeoff.

"It hit and landed on its side," Slocum reported, "and I think the lieutenant got hit again."

Slocum climbed out of the aircraft and found the copilot on the ground. Twenty NVA soldiers were approaching, and one was shouting orders, not paying much attention to the downed chopper. Slocum asked the copilot if he had his pistol and the officer said no, but he had a carbine inside the chopper.

Slocum climbed back inside but was unable to locate the weapon. He climbed back out and went to the side of the aircraft to where there was an M-60 machine gun. But just as he put his hand on the gun, the NVA opened up on him. Two enemy grenades exploded nearby, knocking out the young Marine.

The NVA must have believed Slocum was dead, because they moved around the chopper and began firing randomly.

"I think they were killing what people were left," Slocum reported when another Marine patrol reached the crash site the next day. Except for Slocum, all of the other Marines had been killed, including Second Lieutenant Terry Graves.

12

Where the Rubber Meets the Road

IT seemed like everyone he knew either had been in World War II or Korea and he'd heard all of the war stories. He was working at a food plant and he had two choices: He could either spend the rest of his life in the factory, or he could go out and make memories.

He decided to make memories.

On November 6, 1964, six months out of high school and long before the war started cooking, Al Lynch was drafted. "When my draft notice came," he said over a cup of coffee in Wheaton, Illinois, "I just enlisted. It's kind of funny, because I was afraid to tell my folks that I had had my number moved up. Why, I don't know."

After basic training at "beautiful Fort Knox, Kentucky," he went to Fort Gordon and Fort Benning in Georgia, overseas to Germany, and in December 1966, he volunteered for duty in Vietnam with the 1st Cavalry Division (Airmobile).

"I'd been running all of my life," he confided to his guest. "I was always being picked on in school and I was afraid to fight. I wasn't a jock, I didn't want to fight. I was kind of a wuss, I guess."

Because of that, there was always a doubt in his mind. "What kind of stuff am I made of?" he wondered. He didn't know, but he knew that one way to find out was to go where the rubber meets the road—combat duty in Vietnam.

ALLEN JAMES LYNCH

Rank: Specialist Fourth Class   **Date:** December 15, 1967

Unit: Company D, 12th Cavalry, 1st Cavalry Division (Airmobile)   **Place:** Binh Dinh Province

Born: Chicago, Illinois, October 28, 1945

"We got off the plane at Cam Ranh Bay. It was funny, because on the plane it was a very comfortable seventy degrees. Everybody was scared flying into a combat situation.

"Well, we got off the plane and there were no rockets or gunfire. Instead, there were cars and buses just like back home. Golly-wompers!

"I remember going through the doorway, and I got hammered by the heat! We all were in khakis, and after we got off the plane, I don't think there was one of us who wasn't drenched with sweat.

"They put us on this black tarmac and the heat was probably triple what it was everywhere else. One guy who stayed drunk all the time we were at Fort Ord passed out. He went real quick.

"Then they put us on buses—they had screens on the windows to keep the friendlies from throwing grenades in on us—and took us over to our reception station. We spent two days at Cam Ranh and flew up to An Khe for jungle school, where we learned what not to do in Vietnam. That lasted three days.

"We went up to LZ English in the morning, and that afternoon we went out.

"When I got there, they gave me a LAW, a Claymore, and 150 M60 rounds, on top of all the stuff I had. We humped about two clicks up the beach. I was put on perimeter guard, and everybody else went swimming. If you were a cherry, that was the price you paid.

"Most of the guys had been in the Second Battle of the Ia Drang and when we [the new guys] went in, they didn't want to hang around with us. The new guys stuck with the new guys, and the old guys stuck with the old guys. They didn't treat us bad, but they didn't treat us like good buddies, either. Before doing that, they had to see how we reacted in our first couple of firefights.

"Cherries always had somebody old with them in the foxholes, so that when we heard a new sound, somebody could explain it—like the lizard.

"If a new guy was on watch and heard the lizard, he'd turn and wake the old guy and say, 'What's that? Do you hear that?'

'Awwww, it's just a lizard.'

'Naw, that's not a lizard. He just said, fuck you.'

"The old guy would probably groan and say, 'It's a lizard who says, "Fuck you." That's why we call it the fuck-you-lizard, now lemme get some sleep.'

"Or while on post you would see bushes move toward you. If you thought you saw something move, you'd wake up the guy behind you to make him look. Cherries did a lot of waking up of the guys behind them. But that's how we learned; we learned it by doing it.

"Prior to my Medal of Honor action, we had been engaged on and off—mostly on—for about two months with the 22nd NVA and the 19th VC. We had been chasing them—literally chasing them—all over Bong Song, mostly along the coast: a lot of little firefights, a lot of little ambushes, a lot of little stuff.

"It was starting to get heavy because they [the NVA and

VC] were being compressed into the area where we were going. We had just pulled back to English the night before to stand down, because we had been engaged so much, but that same day A Company had their butts kicked, so they pulled us off English and air-assaulted us in.

"We were maneuvering in one village looking for the stuff. We had just had chow, probably eleven o'clock [A.M.], and they told us, 'Do a sweep in this other village,' and we walked into a big ambush. They waited until we got into the middle of the village before they opened up, and then all hell broke loose.

"As best I can remember, we were advancing platoons in columns: the first platoon on the left, the second on the right. The third and fourth platoons were reserve, I guess.

"Anyway, we had a two-man point leading the second platoon and they walked into an AK. Quesarus went down first; he got both legs shot up—shin bones broke—and he couldn't move. Well, Duck came running back and he got about halfway and he got hit in the shoulder. I went out and got him and the medic came out.

"It was funny, 'cause Duck was happy. He was in pain, but he was so happy. 'I'm going home!' he said. 'I'm out of here, I'm going home. Oh, boy! Just don't get me killed.'

"We came back in and Duck started to realize, 'Hey, I'm hit. This is real shit.' Then he told me that Quesarus was out there and had been hit real bad. So I dropped my radio and ran straight across to a ditch and then crawled left down the ditch to Quesarus.

"He was wounded real bad, both shins were messed up, and I used his aid kit to bandage one leg and my kit to bandage the other, just like they taught us.

"Well, me and Sergeant Quesarus were there for quite some time and I think we killed a few while we were there. There was a real thick, heavy bamboo hedgerow and we couldn't see who we were killing, but we knew we were killing 'em because, well, you know when you hit them and somebody dies.

"We were some scared puppies. Then Esparza came over.

"When Esparza came running across he came diagonally instead of charging straight ahead to the ditch and then crawling over like I had done. He made it about half way across, and he got shot in the leg. I went out and pulled him back to the ditch.

"We could hear the dinks on the other side of the line [hedgerow] rustling, talking and setting up positions. Right down from us in the ditch, there was a heavy machine gun. From what I understand, it was a .51 on wheels—a big sucker—and we got that, the whole crew.

"We couldn't see them [the enemy], because we were firing through the hedgerow, which was really nice.

"We'd stick our 16s through, put it on boogey and waste them. We could hear their check-out cries. We did a lot of firing. Later, after the ambush, our guys went out and found a lot of bodies.

"After we did the machine gun, I tried to move Quesarus but couldn't, because there were snipers in the trees and there was a lot of fire coming down. By that time, my unit had come up and knew we were out there. I stuck my head up and hollered, 'Hey, I need some help to move him.' I was going to carry him, but I needed somebody to help carry his weapon and help get him across.

"It seemed like they were a million miles away. It is really weird, because the part that I ran across seemed a lot wider looking over than looking back. When I ran across the open area, it seemed like, Wow! a long way to run. Once I made it, I crawled down the ditch to Quesarus and looked out to see the other guys; it didn't look that far.

"I'd pop up, look and pop back down, so I don't know how far it really was. I don't think it was a hundred meters. I've never been a good judge of distance, but I'd guess between fifty and seventy-five meters, probably more to the fifty side.

"Now there were three of us there—two wounded guys

and myself—and our guys got confused. 'How many are
you?'

"I yelled, 'There are three of us.'

'And you?'

"I said, 'No, there are three of us, one-two-three, three.'

"They yelled for me to come back, and well, you don't
leave your wounded. That's what you're taught: Don't leave
your wounded. So I told them what they could do with
leaving, so we stayed there.

"They tried to get to us three or four times. They tried to
back a track up to us, but it got blown away. Another time
my platoon leader was going to come over, but he got shot
in the back of the head. He was brand-new, brand spanking
new.

"He was our new platoon leader—we had just lost our old
one—and I was his RTO. My first impression of him was,
'He is really sharp.' He had been there [in Vietnam] a
while, but he got killed trying to get to us.

"Our guys tried to get to us again, but every time they
would get up to do something, the tempo would pick up,
and each time they kind of pulled back. We were mortared,
rocketed, and two or three times they called in artillery on
our position.

"After we had been there a while, Sergeant Quesarus
threw a hand grenade up over the hedgerow. Well, it went
about halfway up and rolled back down. The hand grenade
stopped like right here [two feet away] and nobody touched
it.

"We just looked at it and nobody made an attempt to dive
on it.

"It was like: 'You jump on it;' 'You first;' 'Uh uh, I ain't
gonna.'

"It didn't go off.

"'Well, that's it; we're going to get out of here. If the
frag ain't going off, then we are out of here.'

"After that the planes came in. We were in the ditch, and
when the planes flew over and strafed the road, we could

look up and count the rivets on the belly of the plane. He
dropped a big bomb, a big damn bomb. I want to say
750-pound bomb.

"All I know for sure is that we got lifted up; I got a
bloody nose and one of the guys got a bloody ear; little
trickles of blood everywhere.

"Another plane came in and he dropped some napalm. I
remember that because we tried to light our cigarettes off it.
I had a bandolier of cigarettes but we didn't have any
matches. Quesarus had bled all over my matches, and I had
one match left with a little bit of blood on it. I figured, I'll
light it, stick it to the cigarette, and puff real hard. I lit it and
it went *Pppsssttt*.

"We were going mad! You know how weird your mind
gets. We were thinking, we can't die because we haven't
had our last cigarette yet. We really wanted a cigarette bad,
and nobody had a damned lighter. I had a Vietnamese one
that didn't work.

"A big piece of shrapnel landed on my fatigues. I picked
it up and burned my fingers trying to light my cigarette with
it. After that the jets came in and strafed us.

"I had dropped the radio when I went out to get Duck.
Had I not dropped the radio, I could have called back and
explained what was going on. I should have brought the
radio with me; I should have brought more frags. I only had
two, one in each [thigh] pocket.

"After the air strikes, it got real, real quiet. It was stone
quiet. I said, 'Well, I'm going to get up and see what is
going on.' Both of the other guys were wounded and
couldn't.

"So I went out and checked out a couple of bunkers. It is
funny, because we had caught a Vietcong suspect earlier.
Well, I found him and he was blindfolded, hands tied
behind his back and squatting in one of the hootches.

"Nobody else was around. Our guys had pulled back; we
were the only ones there.

"I went back and got Quesaraus and carried him to a

more secure area; it looked more secure. Esparza tried to make it on his own and he passed out. I went back and got him.

"I found a lighter, took it off my lieutenant. His body was there and so were a number of other bodies. I checked to see if he was . . . dead. There was nothing I could do for him, and we needed some nicotine. I got the lighter out of his pocket and I lit up a cigarette.

"I told Quesarus and Esparza that I was going out to try and find our lines. I ran out a little, because I figured that they wouldn't pull back that far. I went about seventy meters and I heard somebody yell, 'We're over here! We're over here!'

"I looked over and there was this big tank sitting there with all of our guys. They asked, 'Where are they?'

"I said, 'Right back where we first got hit. They're right over there.'

"A chopper went over and one of our guys popped smoke, and I said, 'Right by the smoke.'

"Then I cracked up. I had maintained until then, but when everything was over, I cracked. All of a sudden it hit me. It was like, Wow! I was trying real hard to maintain.

" 'Here is where the rubber met the road, buddy. Your whole life has pointed to this one thing. This is why you came here.'

"It is easy twenty years later to sit back and psychoanalyze what was going on. During that whole time I was scared absolutely out of my mind. But I was more scared of running away than anything else. The one thing I wanted to do was run like hell, but I couldn't.

"The one time I was getting ready to, I think it was Esparza who said, 'Don't leave us out here.' Wow! I don't think so, not after that. What idiot would run? Not this idiot.

"So I hung in there until it was over, and then they sent me back to the rear with Quesarus and Esparza. They went into one tent and I went into another. They gave me some medication, I stayed back in the rear for about a day, and then I went back to my unit. When I got there, they said, 'We're putting you in for the Medal of Honor.'

"I said, 'Yeah. Right.'

"Jeez, I really didn't do that much. There were three of us in the ditch. We all helped each other survive. They went out after the ambush and found almost twenty bodies right where we had been.

"Anyway, when I got back to my unit, I was right back pulling patrols. I think I ran patrols all of the way up through February. We were standing down on LZ Two Bits. We had been out in the woods quite a bit.

"I wasn't scared after that, not terrified, not at all. As a matter of fact, it was like a changing point in my life. If there has been anything in my life that has changed me inside, it was that incident.

"That's where I felt, right or wrong, good or bad, that's where my rubber met the road. I went out there, I did what I had to do, I did the best I could. I can look back to that point and say, 'I've got guts. I don't have to prove it to anyone.' I proved to myself—in here—that I am brave. I've got balls.

"I passed the test."

13

Cam Lo

GROWING up as a young boy in Southern California, Larry Maxam enjoyed the outdoors. He had joined the Scouts when he was in the first grade and advanced to earn the Eagle Award and Order of the Arrow.

Math and science were his two best subjects at Burbank High School, but by his senior year he became restless and bored with his studies. As with many other seventeen-year-olds in the turbulent Sixties, he seemed to be searching for something—excitement, adventure—something he was unable to find in school. In his senior year, he dropped out and began his odyssey.

When elements of the 3rd Marine Division landed on the beaches north of Da Nang on March 8, 1965, newspaper headlines around the world announced the event. Larry Maxam must have thought, in the vernacular of the times, "This is where it's at" because, on the same day the Marines waded ashore north of Monkey Mountain, he enlisted in the Corps.

Maxam's propensity for math and science landed him at the Naval Air Technical Training Center in Jacksonville, Florida, with the Student Unit, Marine Aviation Detach-

ment. By the end of the year, the war in Vietnam was
escalating and in February 1966, Maxam was dropped from
his student status and he became a rifleman with the 2nd
Marine Division at Camp Lejeune, North Carolina.

In the next fifteen months, he had seven different assignments with the East Coast–based Marines and had been
promoted to the rank of Lance Corporal. The war in Southeast Asia was heating up, yet it seemed to be passing him
by.

When a young private asked what his chances of getting
sent to Vietnam were, a Marine general had said, "There are
only two types of Marines; them that's been and them that's
goin'."

Finally, in July 1967, Larry Maxam was assigned to D
Company, 1st Battalion, 4th Marine regiment, 3rd Marine
Division (REIN), Fleet Marine Force (Pacific).

For the next three months he served as a rifleman,
radioman, and squad leader, and on October 1, 1967, was
promoted to corporal. He continued to serve with Delta
Company until February 1968. At last, after twelve different duty assignments, he seemed to have found a home in
the Marine Corps.

He would spent the rest of his life with Company D.

LARRY LEONARD MAXAM

Rank: Corporal   **Date:** February 2, 1968
Unit: Company D, 1st Bat-   **Place:** Cam Lo
talion, 4th Marines
     Born: Glendale, California, January 9, 1948

When the North Vietnamese and the Viet Cong launched
the Tet Offensive, their targets were not restricted to military installations. In fact, the enemy seemed more interested
in populous civilian areas. By disrupting the cities and

provincial capitals, the NVA and VC hoped to undermine the South Vietnamese government and cause a general uprising.

Two days after they commenced their attack, seven hundred and fifty North Vietnamese regulars were massed in attack position against the Cam Lo District Headquarters near the DMZ. North Vietnam's 320th Division had committed a battalion from the 52nd Regiment and a battalion from the 48th Regiment.

In addition to the two battalions, there were five support companies from the 320th that provided recoilless rifles, heavy machine guns, RPGs, satchel charges, mortars, and bangalore torpedoes.

Opposing the NVA were two squads from Delta Company One-Four, and a squad from Echo Company Two-Nine, (forty Marines in all) in addition to approximately eighty South Vietnamese popular and regional forces.

The friendly forces had established a box perimeter around the district headquarters with several strands of concertina wire strung around the outer edge. The barbed wire couldn't stop an enemy assault, but it would slow it down. That's why it was there.

The new moon and overcast skies shielded the North Vietnamese regulars as they silently snaked their way forward to the northeast corner of the perimeter. Once in position, a couple of sappers crawled forward and inserted bangalore torpedoes under the concertina. The attack began at 2:10 A.M. on February 2 when the bangalores exploded, blowing gaping holes in the outer strands of wire.

The NVA then opened up with 82-mm mortars, recoilless rifles, RPGs and small arms as the assault element of approximately two hundred NVA regulars moved to the northeast corner of the compound. All but the inner strand of wire had been breached, endangering the Allied forces.

The friendly forces responded with .50- and .30-caliber machine gun and small-arms fire, and the battle was on.

At this point, the NVA began throwing satchel charges

inside the perimeter. The noise was deafening and proved too much for the popular forces holding the east side of the compound. The South Vietnamese forces panicked and fled to the interior of the perimeter where they took cover behind some brick walls. They left their weapons on the perimeter.

As a result, approximately two hundred North Vietnamese regulars began massing along the abandoned section of the perimeter. The other three sides of the perimeter were under equally heavy pressure, but they were holding.

Platoon Commander Second Lieutenant Michael Stick tried to shift some men to the abandoned sector, but casualties were the only result. In response to this, the two-hundred-man enemy assault force stood up and began to work its way through the concertina wire.

Corporal Larry Maxam was in position on the northwest corner of the perimeter with his fire team when he saw the enemy troops slipping through the wire on the northeast corner.

If the enemy soldiers could get inside the perimeter, they could systematically eliminate each Allied position as their comrades on the outside provided covering fire with mortars, rockets and RPGs.

Corporal Maxam immediately took stock of the situation and realized the extreme danger. He turned his fire team over to his assistant fire-team leader, picked up his rifle and began sprinting across the compound to the abandoned sector.

"From the moment he exposed himself and started his run," Lieutenant Stick stated later, "he became the target of every enemy soldier."

One of the weapons left by the fleeing South Vietnamese forces was a .30-caliber machine gun that would provide a field of fire covering most of the abandoned line. This was Corporal Maxam's destination.

As he darted across the compound, small-arms and machine gun fire poured in. Just as he reached the abandoned section and began moving up to the .30 cal, an RPG or Chi-Com grenade—nobody was sure which—exploded. Corporal Maxam was peppered with shrapnel, but he remained on his feet and kept running. Despite the enemy barrage, Maxam was able to reach the machine gun.

He quickly spun it around toward the advancing soldiers in the concertina wire. Although outnumbered two hundred to one, he cocked the .30-cal and cut loose.

Lieutenant Stick: "Realizing that he was their only remaining threat on the otherwise completely abandoned line, the advancing NVA poured all of their fire into his position."

Not only was Maxam under small-arms and machine gun fire, but the enemy also lobbed mortar and RPG fire at the lone defender. As the battle roared on, an RPG scored a direct hit on Maxam's sandbagged position.

The young Marine fell back, clutching his face.

Dazed and in extreme pain—his right eye had been gouged out by the blast—Maxam crawled back to his gun. He resumed firing at the advancing NVA with belt after belt of ammunition.

With his deadly fire pounding them, the North Vietnamese began to waver.

As Corporal Maxam continued his fight, he was hit again by small-arms fire and still he refused to fall. Weak from loss of blood, he hunched himself over the machine gun and kept firing. His bunker had been blown away, and he received seven bullets through the abdomen and groin, more into his flak jacket and helmet, and shrapnel wounds everywhere.

By now the NVA attack had stalled and the enemy began retreating back out of the concertina wire to safety. Nevertheless, the enemy continued to fire RPG, recoilless rifle, machine gun and small-arms fire into Maxam's position in a frantic effort to silence his lethal fire on the retreating NVA.

The rockets, artillery shells, and bullets pounded the young Marine's position, and he was hit again and again, yet he kept firing. Finally Corporal Maxam was too weak to maintain the .30-caliber machine gun, but he still wouldn't yield.

"Half blinded, stunned, coughing blood, and knowing he was dying, Corporal Maxam refused to cry for medical aid which might have saved him," the lieutenant stated.

Instead he picked up his rifle and slid off the machine gun onto the ground and assumed a prone position. He would rely on the training he had received at the rifle range at Camp Pendleton—"All ready on the right, all ready on the left, all ready on the firing line. Watch your targets—Targets!"

Corporal Maxam rested his battle-scarred head on his rifle's rear sight rib and continued to fire on the enemy.

Finally, at 5:30 A.M.—after standing alone for over an hour and a half against two hundred enemy soldiers and three hours after the battle started—Larry Maxam's head fell from the rifle stock to the ground.

Lieutenant Michael Stick:
"He had insisted on giving his life so that forty of his fellow Marines might live and triumph. He had freely chosen loyalty above life; he had acted above and beyond the call of duty."

14

The Trench

DAMN choppers!

The young soldier—his buddies called him Stumpy—was sitting on an LZ as Hueys took off and landed, making a terrible racket. He had just spent a month in the hospital with a case of malaria, and while he waited for a chopper to fly him back to his unit, he was writing his mom to let her know he was okay.

As he awaited the chopper that would take him to the field, he wrote: "I'm all right now. I'm out of the hospital and I'm going back to my unit."

But those damn choppers kept landing and taking off, and he was having a hard time concentrating on the letter. After about half an hour, he finally turned around to glare the choppers into silence, but he froze when he saw what the choppers had been hauling.

Before him were rows and rows of dead Americans in body bags. Chaplains from various denominations were moving between the rows and attending to the dead. Stumpy had to look twice in order for his mind to comprehend what his eyes had revealed.

It scared him, really scared him, and he wrote: "Mom,

you won't believe what is happening. The choppers are bringing in all of these bodies from the field, people who were killed in action. These guys are all dead. I'm very scared, Mom. Where they just came from is where I am going. My knees are shaking because I'm looking at all of these bodies."

In an attempt to boost his mother's morale (his, too) he added, "But don't worry, Mom, Charlie isn't going to get me."

His sister wrote that his mom cried after she read the letter. He later regretted making his mom cry, but he had been so scared and he had to tell someone.

KENNETH STUMPF

Rank: Sergeant Major (then   **Place:** Near Duc Pho
Specialist Fourth Class)
Unit: 25th Infantry Division   **Date:** April 25th, 1967
    Born: Menasha, Wisconsin, September 28, 1944

"I was almost twenty-one years old, and I knew the draft was going to get me. I was working in a printing company in Wisconsin at the time, and I knew it was coming. My two brothers had already been in the U.S. Army, and I was proud of their service to our country. I was looking forward to going.

"When I got to Vietnam, I was assigned to the 3rd Brigade of the 25th Division up in Pleiku. My first trip to the field was along the Cambodian border just west of Pleiku in September of '66. I was taking my [malaria] pills and everything, and I'll be damned if I didn't come down with malaria in only two weeks. I thought I was going to die.

"The medical people kept doing blood smears, but they

kept coming up negative. I was getting sicker and sicker. Finally it came up positive and I was in the hospital at Vung Tau for about a month.

"My temperature was maybe 106, 107, and so they packed me in ice and put a fan on me to get it down. I thought, 'Holy Christ! I can't believe how this is going.'

"I was so sick, so miserable. Finally, when I was feeling better, I could leave my bed and eat. I was so hungry but every time I'd eat, I'd throw it right back up. I went down to 114 pounds.

"After about thirty days I got to feeling better, but they said I would be in recovery for between sixty and ninety days. I was laying there recovering, feeling a little stronger, and one of the nurses told one of the doctors, 'They are bringing in a lot of casualties from the field and we don't have enough bed space for them.'

"I sat up in my bed and said, 'You can discharge me.' I was so weak, but I thought that these guys needed the bed space more than I did. So off I go, back to my unit.

"When I got back, the guys in my unit thought I was a newby; they didn't know who I was because my face was so sunken in. But I started to recover after some of those good ol' C rations.

"After about a month or so, my platoon leader, Lieutenant Murphy, asked me if I wanted to be his RTO—radio-telephone operator. I said sure and was his RTO for a while.

"I really liked being an RTO, because I got to know everything that was going on before the rest of the troops. I knew if we were getting hot food, I knew where we were going, I knew if we were staying in an area for the night, if we were going to hump a couple of more clicks [kilometers], or whatever.

"Before the Medal of Honor action, we were walking down a trail, my squad was the second squad in the element. The trail turned and I noticed that everybody ahead of us had stopped. There was a VC rucksack on the trail and our guys were standing around it.

"I was standing there and three or four feet away there was a guy standing. He was looking toward the lead element, and I was thinking, 'Is there anybody in our platoon with a blue jacket?'

"Then I realized that it was a goddamn VC! I could have reached out and choked him! He was that close. The trail turned and I wasn't sure if some of the guys were in my line of fire and I didn't want to shoot the guy and risk hitting one of our guys.

"The VC was standing there with his rifle and for some reason I guess he decided, 'I better see if there is anybody else around.'

"Well, he turned around and looked, and all of a sudden his eyes got that big! Mine got this big! Sergeant Noel was standing next to me and we were both looking at the guy and we were getting ready to shoot him.

"As we got ready to fire, the VC took off. Since we were walking in the second squad back, I had a round in the chamber, but my rifle was on safety. Sergeant Noel didn't have a round in his chamber and his rifle was off safety.

"When I pulled the trigger, it didn't do anything, and when he pulled the trigger, it went, 'Click.'

"I could have reached out and grabbed him, but I was so startled. I was just standing there and thinking about what was going on up front.

"I could have choked the son of a bitch.

"After a couple of months, we had a lot of newbies rotate in, because we had a lot of people who were killed and wounded. I was a PFC at the time and the lieutenant asked if I wanted to be a squad leader.

"I said, 'Sir, I'll be a squad leader, and I'll do the best I can do.' That was about January.

"Then I got promoted to E-4 in March, and my action happened in April.

"On April 21, 1967, just before my action, one of our platoons was hit coming across a bridge, and we lost a lot of people that day. When it finished up, we were so short of people in the company that we ended up with only fourteen guys in my platoon. I had seven and Sergeant John Madonich had seven. Normally a platoon operates with around forty-two.

"We patrolled in platoons all of the time, but for the first time since I had been in Vietnam, we patrolled as a company. Well, I was walking in front of my company commander, Captain Caudillo. He was one of the guys who recommended me for the Medal of Honor, but unfortunately, he was killed about three weeks later.

"Anyway, we were walking in a rice paddy up near Duc Pho in Quang Ngai Province around ten o'clock in the morning and we get a call that a helicopter had wounded a North Vietnamese and he had crawled into a spider hole.

"The captain said, 'Specialist Stumpf, take your squad and see if you can find him. Sergeant Madonich, take your squad too.'

"Sergeant Madonich had a radio; I didn't. So off we go. It was open terrain, so it didn't take long to get to the area where the North Vietnamese had been seen.

"We got over there and his squad and my squad were about one hundred and fifty meters apart and the rest of the company was about five hundred meters to the rear and holding.

"In my squad were two brand-new guys who had just gotten to Vietnam. Of the three guys I later pulled out from in front of the bunker, two were brand-new guys, and one of them was a big black guy. He was six-eight.

"When he came in and they said this was one of my new squad members, I looked up at him and said to myself, 'Man, you ain't going to make it, you'll never make it through three hundred and sixty-five days. You don't belong out here.' I couldn't tell him that, I couldn't destroy his morale right away. He made it two days when he got hit. His name was Bush.

"I always walked point before I was a squad leader, and after I became a squad leader, especially when I felt that something was going to happen. I had married people in my squad and I felt those people had more to lose. If something happened to me . . . they had a family and I was single. Being a squad leader, I also felt responsible to set the example.

"In this particular case, I was walking point to set the example.

"So I'm walking point and we searched the area and didn't find anything. I told the guy in back of me, 'Now you stay here. I'm going back down the trail and call back in on Sergeant Madonich's radio and tell them that we searched the area but couldn't find anything, and see what they want us to do.'

"I got back to the last man in the squad, and all of a sudden the whole goddamn world opens up! What my squad had done was walk around a corner in the trail, and in front of them was a company of North Vietnamese in bunkers.

"So I went running back up to where I had left them. The trail turned to the left and became hedgerows. One of the guys came running out and said, 'There are three of the guys laying in the trail next to a bunker complex and they are wounded really bad. They are all fucked up and can't get out.'

"I tried running around the corner of the trail to get to them, but there was so much fire and heavy vegetation that I had to swing back and get into the trench and go from there.

"There were four of us and we fell into a trench that was right in front of the bunkers. It was bushy and camouflaged—you know how they camouflaged things so much—and I didn't know where the three guys were, but I knew I was pretty damn close to being straight across from them.

"I didn't know it at the time, but there were three trenches running all around the area, and after we had gotten in the first trench, the North Vietnamese had cut off the rest of the perimeter, boxing us in. So I told the guys, 'You look this way, you look that way, you look in this direction, and I'll cover this way.'

"What was on my mind were the guys that were wounded out in front of me. I kept going up and down the trench thinking, 'How am I going to get those guys out of there?' I ran here, I ran there, and every time I tried something, the North Vietnamese would pop up and start firing and throwing grenades. Some of the North Vietnamese were trying to sneak into the trench with us. Every time they tried at my end, I'd shoot them.

"I looked down to the other end and saw somebody shoot a dink who was trying to get into the trench over there. The four of us probably killed ten or fifteen North Vietnamese who tried to get into the trench with us.

"We did this for about two hours, trying to get out of this trench to get those three guys, and I can't get out of this goddamn trench because every time I try to come out, the North Vietnamese would come down on me.

"So I run down over here and I try to get up, but there's a bunker and I don't even know it's there. And they open up. And somebody jumps in the trench over there, and my guys kill him. It goes back and forth, and I'm throwing grenades, and I don't even know what the fuck I'm throwing grenades at.

"I had a sand bag full of grenades—probably twenty or thirty—strapped on to the back of my harness. Some people didn't like grenades; I loved them. I threw those grenades all over the place trying to do something.

"I tell you what, I was scared, but I think I was more scared that I wouldn't be able to get those three guys out than I was of the North Vietnamese. The North Vietnamese were something standing in my way.

"It kept going through my mind, 'You've got to get in there and get those guys back here.' But everything was breaking loose.

"Then I'd think, 'What the hell is going on?' I was indecisive about what to do, because I still didn't know exactly where the three guys were. I was getting frustrated, because I couldn't get out to my wounded soldiers.

"Finally I said, 'That's it, I've got to do something. I've got to make an attempt. If you are going to stop me, then stop me, but I'm going to make an attempt. I'm coming out of this goddamn trench.'

"I wasn't looking to kill anybody, not at that particular point. I'm not caring about those North Vietnamese. I'm caring about my people out there, wherever they were. My main concern was going in there and getting my people back to the trench.

"I knew that when I ran in there, I had to find them right away. So I ran right straight in toward the bunker. When you go in like that and are getting fired on, everything is kind of blurry, but I saw them there and they were looking up at me. I'm thinking, 'Aw, man, they're all full of holes.' White was probably wounded the worst. He must have had seven, eight, nine holes in him but he was alive.

"I said to him, 'Crawl on my back,' and I crawled all of the way back with him on my back. Bush and Hernandez, my two new guys, I dragged back. Hernandez had seven or eight holes in him, too.

"I got the three guys back to the trench, but we were still cut off inside there. Once the North Vietnamese sealed off the perimeter, our company couldn't get in to us, because they were fighting bunkers on the outside area too. It was another hour or two before someone was able to break through to us.

"When I think this thing over—and I've thought it over in my head about a million times over the years—they could have wiped us all out. Once the North Vietnamese had us isolated from the rest of the company, I believe their plan was 'Don't kill them all, because the rest of the Americans will come and try to get them out, and we can get more.'

"I know for sure that they could have killed the three on the trail, without a doubt. They were immobile; they were just lying there. I heard one of them moaning because he hurt so bad. I think it was Hernandez.

"At the same time, my other three guys who were lying in the trench had been wounded and were firing. It wasn't that I was strolling out there and nobody was returning the NVA fire. These three guys were returning fire.

"That's what I mean. The action where I was awarded the Medal of Honor was a team effort. These guys were keeping some of the North Vietnamese off of me. I know they were, they had to be. I wear the Medal of Honor for all my squad. They earned it as much as I did.

"Everything was noise; the snaps of the AK-47, the crack of the M16s, whatever other weapons they had. I know they had machine guns, Browning automatics, SKSs, RPGs. They fired some RPGs into us that I don't even know where they came from. It was thud, boom.

"I was way inside that bunker complex, and I went out and got some more bunkers. In fact, I was so far inside that I was just running around in there; that's what Lieutenant Murphy said.

"He and his men were on the other side from where we were assaulting and they stayed there. We were over here and the relief force that broke through to our position was back here.

"There were trenches here and here and here, and they went all around the complex. In the area in between Lieutenant Murphy's men and Captain Caudillo and the relief force was where I was running around by myself.

"I had lost my whole squad and I was thinking, 'Well, let's do something. We've got to wipe these goddamn people out.' I was running here, running there, throwing grenades here, throwing grenades there.

"Lieutenant Murphy told me later, 'Jesus Christ! We almost shot you I don't know how many times. "Goddamnit!" I was yelling at my people, "Don't shoot him! That's Stumpy out there!"'

"Well, I didn't know they were over there. There were people running down in these other trenches. I jumped in the trench and tried to shoot those people in the trench. I didn't realize that Lieutenant Murphy and his people were shooting at these people too. (When Lieutenant Murphy went back to Vietnam in '68, he was Rocky Blier's company commander. Heck, Rocky Blier and I played American Legion baseball against each other.)

"Once they broke through, we were able to medevac the rest of my squad. The funny thing about this chopper run was that when I was loading one of the guys on board, the bullets were hitting the chopper and it took off so fast it left the door gunner on the ground with us.

"I said, 'Hey, you're infantry now!'

"Anyway, once the company opened the gap to us, other [American] soldiers were able to come in and fill the trench. The trench that we were in ran a long way, but all of these bunkers were all along there too.

"My squad had knocked out a couple of those bunkers earlier when we were fighting back and forth. All of a sudden there would be nothing coming from a particular bunker, especially when we bombed. When we came back they were filled with NVA replacements again.

"We stayed in the trench for another two or three hours and Captain Caudillo said we were going to pull back and bomb the area.

"After the final bombing run, I told Captain Caudillo, 'I think we should make a charge, sir. It is getting dark and if we call in one more air strike, it will take too long. It will be totally dark and the NVA will disappear into the jungle.' It wasn't the American style to fight at night.

"He said, 'Okay.'

"We closed in on the enemy in the trench and that is when I started going out into the bunkers again. There was one bunker—the one they talked about in my [Medal of Honor] citation—that was causing us a lot of problems, and I said to Captain Caudillo, 'Sir, I'll get that bunker.'

"I had run out of hand grenades, so Captain Caudillo gave me some grenades and I went out and got it.

"One of our platoons—I don't remember which one— went too far down one of the trenches after we attacked. When it started getting too dark, the captain made the decision to pull back, and these guys were still out there.

"After we pulled back, I was laying on the ground smoking a cigarette. After so many hours of the heat and the excitement, I was just drained. My mind was blank and I heard someone say, 'The company commander is looking for Specialist Stumpf.'

"I got up and went over to the captain and he said, 'We've got a platoon that is lost in that bunker-complex area. Can you go find them?'

"Of course, I was the one who had to go out there, because I knew that complex and the layout of the trenches. But it was dark out there! That was the first time since ten o'clock in the morning that I understood the situation. Most of it was react, react, react. This was the first time since I had been told, 'Go find this wounded NVA that has crawled into a spider hole,' that I understood what I was being told.

"I thought, 'Whoa! Jesus Christ!' Now, you talk about a guy who was scared, I mean I was scared, scared, scared stiff, because nothing was happening and I began anticipating what might happen.

"Well, Captain Caudillo didn't know which direction these guys had gone.

"When he said that they were in a trench, I didn't know which one, but I knew they were on the south end of the village.

"I called them on the radio and said, 'I am going to come toward you. Put your point man up front, somebody who is not going to hear something and all of a sudden start firing.'

"I knew deep down in my heart I was never going to kill an American, no matter what. He is going to have to shoot me first. I am not going to get into a firefight with an American.

"So I'm walking along. Nothing really happened. All of a sudden I heard something, and I see these guys in the trench. I said, 'Are you American?' That was the only thing I could think of.

"He said, 'Yeah, it's me.'

"What a relief! I said, 'Okay, we're going back.'

"I was really scared that we were going to get into a firefight with that platoon if we were in opposite trenches. It was my luck I picked the same trench they were in, and we met head-on.

"We went back to our unit, and it was over.

"We had forty-four casualties that day, and six of them were from my squad.

"We ended up killing eighty-eight."

[Ken Stumpf served two more tours as an infantry soldier in Vietnam and is now a sergeant major assigned to Fort Sheridan, Illinois.]

"Lieutenant Carl Stout was our forward observer. I ran into him at the Chicago parade—his wife is now the President of the VVA (Vietnam Veterans of America)—and he asked, 'Whatever happened to Latimer?'

"I said, 'You don't know what happened to Latimer?'

"He said, 'No.'

"I sat there and told him the story.

"Latimer was the artillery forward observer for our company.

"At the time—December 15th of '66—Latimer and I were PFCs. We were about five-six and neither of us weighed more than 120 pounds, both little boys.

"We came in from the field to Pleiku for the Bob Hope Christmas show. They gave us all of the beer and all of the steaks we wanted for a week.

"One night we were sitting there, talking and drinking beer. All of a sudden Latimer said, 'Aw, you infantry guys aren't worth a shit,' or something to that effect. I sat there and drank some more and drank some more, and he kept going on, arguing with someone else: 'Artillery is the king of battle.'

"It was one of those, 'I'm better than you are; the Twins are better than the Yankees.'

"I wasn't even in the conversation, just sitting there drinking beer, but it got to the point that it was pissing me off and I was thinking, 'Now goddamnit! I'm infantry.' It is the infantry soldier, for the most part, who dies on the battlefield. I have just as much pride wearing my Combat Infantryman's Badge as I do wearing the Medal of Honor.

"Finally I had enough and I said, 'Artillery is what?' Neither one of us could talk straight, we were both drunk, and I'm not sure what came out of my mouth and I'm not sure what came out of his mouth.

It got to where we were standing and saying, 'Now I'm telling you to keep your fucking mouth shut!' Neither of us little shitheads could beat up anybody sober. Anyway, he swung at me and missed. Heck, the wind when he swung almost knocked me over. I swung at him and hit him, and knocked him out cold.

"We went back to the field and didn't speak to each other. He hated me and I hated him. A couple of months later the platoon was setting up for the night, and a couple of guys got into a card game by their position. Latimer was with our platoon at the time and he was one of them.

"He was playing with some of the guys I knew, so I sat down—I liked to play poker—and got into the card game. We hadn't talked to each other for a couple of months. We hated, I mean hated, each other. We avoided each other with a passion.

"Well, in a card game you have to talk. 'How many do you want? You want three?'

" 'Yeah, give me three.'

"We played cards there for about an hour or so and gradually eased into talking to each other. And then we became very good friends. Everything worked itself out, and a really deep respect for each other developed. We could sense it, and he really liked me and I really liked him.

"But I still liked the infantry and he liked the artillery. I didn't blame him for that; he was proud of his profession and I was proud of mine. We got to be real chums.

"On the day of the Medal of Honor action, Latimer happened to be with the guys who broke through to help my squad out.

"He and I were laying in the same trench firing at a bunker here, something over there, a guy running across back there, somebody jumping in the trench over here.

"All of a sudden Latimer stands up, getting ready to fire, and bam! he got shot right through the heart. He was on my right and he fell right into my arms.

"I reached out to catch him, and as he fell he said, 'Stumpy, I'm dead.'

"And he was.

"I didn't know at the time he had been shot right through the heart. I was looking around and his face wasn't smashed in or anything and I'm thinking, 'For crying out loud! How can this guy be dead?'

"I was hurt, really hurt. I was probably crying.

"Suddenly it was, 'Fuck it, time out, I don't care, go ahead and shoot me if you want. I'm taking Latimer back to be medevaced and he's dead.' At that point I stopped firing. I took Latimer in my arms and I carried him out of the trench to where I had loaded out my squad at the LZ.

"I got up very slowly, just about the same way he had stood, and I carried him to the LZ. Normally you don't do this, you medevac your wounded; they are the first priority. But this guy was special to me. We became so close.

"I laid him down on the ground, and then I went back to the trench.

"I can't remember his first name, but I'll never forget him."

William Royce Latimer was from Chicago, and his name can be found on Panel 18E, Line 86, of The Vietnam War Memorial.

15

Dewey Canyon

PRIMARILY because of his age and maturity—he had been a Marine enlisted man for sixteen years—Wes Fox was assigned as an advisor to the South Vietnamese Marines. However, Fox became dissatisfied with how they were fighting the war; they weren't gung ho enough. The South Vietnamese version of "Search and Destroy" seemed more like "Search and Avoid".

As he neared the end of his tour of duty with the South Vietnamese, he contemplated extending for six months to go north to be with the U.S. Marines in Quang Tri. The fighting in this region was, for the most part, conventional warfare instead of the unconventional VC fighting in the southern provinces. It was where Wes Fox wanted to be.

However, it was not a decision he could make unilaterally; he had to consult his wife, Dotti Lu, and he met her in Hawaii for a four-day R & R.

"My wife flew to Hawaii with my oldest daughter," Wes recalled recently. "But my baby, the one that was born a month after I left the States, stayed home with my parents. I was wanting to extend in-country, and I hadn't even seen her.

"I wasn't a warmonger, but that was my profession. I wanted to be a Marine and do what I'd been trained to do, but how was I going to square that with Dotti Lu?" It was a question that nagged him for three days.

"I saved it until the last day and then I dropped the bomb shell. 'I really want to extend.'"

Wes Fox had been a first sergeant until 1967, when he received his commission. Consequently his commission was temporary, and he believed that his chances of becoming a regular officer would improve if he extended an additional six months in Vietnam; it would look good on his record.

Dotti Lu agreed. "If that's what you really want to do, I'll go along with it."

"I really asked a lot of that girl," Fox said, "and she came through beautifully—a perfect Marine wife. Even today, if it is possible, she is more gung ho than I am."

WESLEY L. FOX

Rank: Colonel (Then 1st   **Date:** February 22, 1969
Lieutenant)
Unit: Company A, 1st Bat-   **Place:** Quang Tri Province
talion, 9th Marines
        Born: Herndon, Virginia, September 30, 1931

Wes Fox wanted to command a U.S. Marine rifle company, but he was a lieutenant and the billet called for a captain. If he couldn't get a rifle company, then he hoped he could return to Force Recon, where he had served earlier. He had already been slated to go to the 3rd Marine Division, though.

"I was glad I got the 3rd, because the 1st Division was fighting the Vietcong, whereas the 3rd Division was up in the northern part of I Corps. That whole area was occupied only by North Vietnamese Army or U.S. Marines. Good guys, bad guys and each easily identified.

"I checked into division and the adjutant asked, 'What do you want?'

" 'I want a rifle company if I can get one as a lieutenant.'

"He looked over some papers. 'Well, One-Nine is short of company commanders. I think you've got a good chance of getting a company in One-Nine.'

" 'I'll take it.' It didn't matter to me.

"After he made it official, he laughed and said, 'You haven't heard of the Walking Dead?'

" 'Naw, I haven't heard of the Walking Dead, and it doesn't really matter. It'll be Walking Death after I get there.'

"This nickname—the Walking Dead—indicated to me that I was going to get what I wanted; to find somebody to get this war on with. I don't know where One-Nine got the tag the Walking Dead, but it turns out that One-Nine was one of the best battalions, if not the best battalion, with which I have had the privilege of serving.

"During the two times the company was back at Vandergrift Combat Base saluting was required because, it was the situation there. I had my company salute with the greeting "Alpha One-Nine, sir."

"Being combat Marines, they didn't take to it too well. But I wanted to instill a little company spirit, and that was one of my ways of doing it.

"The battalion commander asked me once, 'What did that Marine say to me this morning when I met him?'

"That made me feel good, because I realized that some of my Marines were catching on.

" 'That Marine just wanted to make sure you knew who he was and what unit he was with, sir—Alpha One-Nine, sir.'

"The battalion commander was George W. Smith who is tops; he retired as a major general; Bob Barrow was the regimental commander, who retired as the commandant of the Marine Corps and Ray Davis was the division commander. Shoot, you don't need to say much about him; Medal of Honor in Korea and he retired as the assistant commandant of the Marine Corps.

"With those three guys as my leaders, I was in a no-lose situation. You couldn't do anything but win in anything you wanted to do. My whole six months with One-Nine was just that way.

"Those three Marines were the epitome of leadership. They would give you a mission and leave you alone to do it, but they were always there with all of the support you needed. Operation Dewey Canyon was a great success just because of those three individual leaders. It made things easier, and the company commander just couldn't do anything wrong."

In the later part of 1968, One-Nine was heli-assaulted into Khe Sanh to investigate the region from the former KSCB to the Laotian border. There were no signs of any enemy activity in the area.

"The rest of the 3rd Marine Division was doing pretty much the same thing, going out and looking over the TAOR for any sign of the enemy and not finding anybody. This was north of the A Shau Valley where the 1st Cav had first battled the North Vietnamese in November 1965. It was an NVA supply point.

"Until then, the area of the A Shau that we were going into was virgin territory; U.S. forces had never been in there because there was no way to support an operation easily by air, artillery or supplies.

"So Colonel Barrow came up with the idea of advancing fire-support bases in leapfrog fashion where we would have ridge top artillery fire bases with helicopter support for everything from C rations, water, and ammo, to include the guns being lifted into position.

"That gave birth to the Dewey Canyon idea of launching an assault into the upper A Shau Valley, terminating on the

Laotian border, which was where the Ho Chi Minh Trail was located.

"In January of '69, my company lifted off by chopper and opened up an old fire-support base, Shiloh, to kick off the operation. Barney Barnum's battery of 105s came in and set up. That was the first time I met Captain Barnum, who had already been awarded the Medal of Honor during his earlier tour in Vietnam.

"Shiloh plays an important part in Alpha One-Nine's Dewey Canyon workup. During Christmas of '68, the whole battalion was back at Vandergrift, but Christmas for combat Marines isn't all that great.

"Right after Christmas the rest of the regiment was getting ready to go into Dewey Canyon, and Alpha Company lifted out to Shiloh. For three weeks we sat there—fun and frolic in the sun. All we had to do was provide security for that fire base until we rejoined our battalion.

"I would send out two security patrols—squad patrols for the most part—each day, and then send out one platoon a day down to the river for swim-and-fish call. The XO and I would take turns going along.

"The river had a nice sandbar, so we would swim, lie on that sandbar, and get beautifully tanned. Before we would leave to head back up the hill, we would throw a few grenades into the big pools of water and pick up all of the fish we needed to supplement our C rations. I still don't know my fish all that well, but they were good eating, and big fish.

"It was really nice lying away from the worries of war, knowing that we had security out so we didn't have to worry about getting hit. Using a little imagination, I was almost able to put myself on Miami Beach.

"We did that for three weeks.

"I have often thought about all of the Marines that got hurt and didn't go beyond Dewey Canyon. Our time on Shiloh was so fitting. At least they had a moment when they could get some pleasure out of combat.

"A side effect of our stay at Shiloh was that we had two groups of people who came into the fire base—Montagnards, I guess—who had managed to miss all of the relocation sweeps up to that point. The South Vietnamese government's aim was to relocate all Montagnards in safe havens. We liked this idea because everybody out there was either one of us or bad guys.

"The families that came in while we were on Shiloh were probably Communist sympathizers, or maybe even working for the North Vietnamese. These people came in and gave themselves up.

"The reason they did was because of our swim-and-fish call. This was [affecting] their food crop, killing fish in the stream, and they knew they couldn't survive without the fish.

"We kept them under security—handled them like prisoners, really—until we could helicopter them out. Of course, we didn't mistreat them, but we kept an eye on them.

"We wrapped up Shiloh with Barney's battery being lifted out one afternoon. My company was to follow when the choppers returned.

"But they couldn't get back that day, because of other commitments. Then the weather really set in bad that night. For four days no choppers flew, and we had no water except for the river down below. We didn't need any C rations because we had—I don't know how many—pallets of C rations on the hill; they had been stockpiled for further movement forward.

"We were stuck there but were not all that bothered about it until the wee hours of the morning, when a freight train went right over my little hootch. *Wwwwhhhhhrrrrroooommmmm!*

"Then a big explosion. Then three more rounds hit on Shiloh. One round had hit right in one of my machine gun positions and blew four Marines away.

"That turned out to be one of our batteries—not

Barney's—firing H & I [Harassment & Interdiction] three clicks north of us. One gun put in the wrong data which, as fate would have it, put it right on Shiloh.

"As I was working directly for regiment, I was immediately on the radio to get a cease fire. No more rounds followed, but this incident really shook up Alpha.

"I understand that heads rolled, and rightly so. The gun commander had put in the wrong data, and of course he was court-martialed. The battery commander was relieved of command.

"Those dead Marines stayed on the hill with us for several days, poncho-covered humps there on the hill. This tends to, well, grate on you, because it was a constant reminder of somebody's mistake. It was such a waste.

"When the choppers were able to come in and get the bodies out, then we were ready to move out. We moved on down to Fire Base Erskine where the rest of the battalion was gathering for the 'jump-off.'

"Heck, we lifted in and there already was a helicopter burning off the side of the fire base. I'm thinking, 'We're getting into some good heavy stuff. We're going to war.' Alpha One-Nine was ready and willing. My platoon commanders, down to my privates—you couldn't ask for anything better—were ready. I had damn good Marines.

"For about three weeks all Alpha did was provide security for that fire base. Meanwhile, the 2nd and 3rd Battalions of the 9th Marines were maneuvering into position and opening up other fire bases. The first battalion was in the center, Two-Nine was on the left, and Three-Nine was on the right.

"As far as One-Nine was concerned, we had two companies attacking down each of two ridge lines; Alpha and Charlie were on the left ridge, and on the right ridge were Bravo and Delta. H & S Company and the battalion commander were with Alpha and Charlie. We had one company in the attack and the other company trailing. When we got to Laos, we would then move parallel along the Ho Chi Minh Trail.

"Colonel Barrow moved out to Fire Base Cunningham and set up the 9th Marines CP. It wasn't strictly a 9th Marines operation, however. The operation concluded with some Army involvement and some South Vietnamese Army units participating.

"Their involvement was to free the 9th Marines' battalions with four rifle companies for the assault. All of the fire bases had to be defended by a rifle company. Therefore the Vietnamese and [U.S.] Army units were used for fire base security so all of the Marines could be where they ought to be—in the assault.

"I mentioned earlier about Charlie and Alpha attacking down the ridge line leapfrogging one ahead of the other. On the 19th of February, we heard what we thought were tank engines. 'The NVA are attacking us with tanks down the ridge line,' I thought. Well, let them come with tanks, because in that jungle they would have to come in single file, and we would kill them, one by one.

"But that gave us some apprehensive moments, hearing those diesel engines and thinking we were under tank attack. It never materialized, and the next day Charlie Company jumps off in the attack.

"They ran into a little opposition. It turned out to be two 122-mm guns, and what we had heard the night before was the diesels from the half-tracks the NVA were using to get the guns off the ridge to keep us from capturing them.

"Captain Jack Kelly's Charlie Company captured both of them in firing condition and immediately formed a perimeter with the idea of getting them lifted out. One of them is over at Officers Candidate School here at Quantico. When the weather cleared we got some big choppers in and lifted the two 122 guns out.

"Colonel Smith kept H & S Company inside Charlie Company's perimeter with the guns, and I continued the attack for [the Laotian border]. The NVA guns were located within a couple of clicks of the Laotian border—our objective—and that became mine to get and I got it by the end of the day.

"We found some goodies on that hill, also: 122-mm ammo, antiaircraft guns, and a lot of good stuff. I stayed on the border and Charlie remained back on the ridge behind me. The next day I sent out patrols around my base.

"Battalion called me to send one platoon back down to them, because Charlie Company had been probed from the east and they had determined that there was an enemy force off to the side. I sent Lieutenant Bill Christman and my 3rd Platoon back to Battalion, who in turn sent them down to find out what this force was doing in the valley. This is on the 21st of February 1969.

"By dark Bill was locked into a fight and he couldn't break contact, because he had two Marines dead under NVA machine guns. Of course, he was not coming out of there until he could get his two Marines. Every time he tried to go in and recover his two Marines, the NVA would open up. He couldn't overcome the NVA force and he couldn't get his two Marines out.

"So Lieutenant Colonel Smith is on the hook with me: 'Bring the rest of your company back down to this position.' The feeling was that this enemy force was going to try and recapture its two guns.

"While I was sitting on the Laotian border, Delta and Bravo had attacked down the other ridge line and had arrived at the Ho Chi Minh Trail. Bravo held up there, and Delta came down the trail and joined me. So Delta Company was already in my position as I went back to join Charlie Company and the battalion CP.

"It was dark when we got in and Charlie Company opened up a section of the perimeter. They didn't let us sit in the middle and get a good night's sleep, though; they wanted to share the perimeter, much to my Marines' disappointment.

"After dark the NVA let Bill's people come forward and

get the bodies. That was one thing I noticed about the NVA. There was nothing vindictive about them. They didn't have a hate-kill attitude. I feel that they knew the U.S. Marines were not going to leave until they could get their two Marines out from under the guns. It wasn't that the NVA had pulled out—I think they were still there and they let Bill's people come up, pick up the two dead ones and get them out.

"Battalion's plan was that if we didn't get hit that night, Alpha would go back down and do something about that force the following day. The concept has always been that the bad guys never stay in the same place very long, especially after they had been located. That night Battalion targeted the area and our A-6s came in and bombed the position where Bill had made contact. Throughout the night we had artillery batteries firing on it. If they didn't attack us, the next morning I was to go down there and see if they were still there.

"As the NVA and VC never stayed in one area once you found them, I really didn't expect them to be there, and neither did Battalion. Colonel Smith said, 'If they aren't there, go on down to the creek bed for Checkpoint I. Go up the creek bed to Checkpoint II to see where they have gone.' That was as far as I was to go and then back up on the ridge for return to the perimeter.

"We left in the morning, but there was a holdup in leaving the ridge. I guess it had something to do with getting artillery fire onto the suspected position. I wanted to leave at daylight, but it was something like nine or ten o'clock when we started down the ridge.

"Because we had had bad weather—no flying—Battalion was out of water. If I was to get to Checkpoint I and not make contact, Battalion was going to send a water detail from Charlie Company down to carry water back up for H & S and Charlie Company.

"That all sounded pretty good.

"Daylight came and I finally moved Alpha out. Because

Bill had been in the fight the day before, I naturally put Bill's platoon in the rear. However, I put Bill himself at the head of the company to make sure we went down the same trail to get in to where he was the day before.

"Bill had said that there was a fork in the trail and we needed to make sure to take the right path. We are moving down the trail—I am behind the lead platoon, which was the 1st Platoon—and we come to a fork in the trail with Bill standing off to the side.

"'All right, sir, this is it. I am going to rejoin my platoon.'

"We move on down, and all of a sudden our point opens up, M16s and a North Vietnamese machine gun. It turns out there was a bunker down on the streambed with three NVA in it. My point didn't see it; he never did see it because they killed him with the opening volley. The next Marine was wounded.

"But then the first squad overran that bunker position. So we were in the creek bed. I start forming a perimeter around that creek bed and figured, 'Well, it's just this one isolated bunker.' There was no other contact.

"Finally, 3rd Platoon gets down and Bill Christman tells me that we had missed the trail going into the NVA position that he was in the day before. He said he wasn't aware there were that many forks in the trail. He had stopped at the first fork, and the wrong one.

"'We bypassed the enemy position,' he said.

"They didn't do anything on our way down, so I concluded that they had pulled out during the night. I asked Bill, 'How far over is the bunker position?'

"'It is really not that far,' he said. 'They must have left. This bunker we just got must be all that's left.'

"So I formed a perimeter and sent out fire teams to check out the area. I called Battalion and gave a Sit Rep of what happened and told them, 'Send down your water detail.'

"We sat there half an hour before the water detail got down. It was about noon when they came down, and were in the creek bed filling their canteens when we started getting light mortars in the treetops. No problem, they were detonating in triple-canopy jungle treetops.

"I could hear the tubes popping off to my right rear where Bill Christman had said the NVA complex was located. The tubes were popping real clear. At about the same time a machine gun opened up in our direction. We could see the spent tracer rounds fall among the trees.

"Again no threat, no casualties due to machine guns. There were a couple of shrapnel cases from the mortars in the water detail. I had Corporal Parnell, third squad leader of the 2nd Platoon (about seven men) escort the fifteen-man water detail back to Battalion, because their sergeant had been wounded from a mortar round and asked for an escort. I also had Parnell take out one KIA and one WIA from the bunker contact up the hill.

"The water detail got back up the hill and the mortar tubes were still popping, the machine gun was still rattling, and it was vectoring me in on their position. Because Bill was on that side of the creek and in position, I put him in the attack toward that gun despite his platoon being in the fight the day before. Before the fight was over, all platoons would be committed.

"I put the 1st Platoon on his left, so I had the 1st and 3rd Platoons in the attack on that position.

"Some of my Marines refer to that situation as 'when we were ambushed.' It sure wasn't an ambush. It can't be an ambush when you are deployed, ready and looking for a fight. You're as guilty as he is when the fighting starts.

"And we were guilty; Alpha really wanted to fight.

"At the time I didn't know that the enemy force was as big as it was. Later, intelligence said it was a battalion and [that] I had gone down the hill with seventy Marines. I had left my mortar section weapons platoon up on the ridge, because I didn't need them in triple-canopy jungle. So I had three very light rifle platoons and guns.

"But they moved as good Marines; the sound of the

enemy guns was the direction of attack. They didn't have to be told, they didn't have to be kicked, and they didn't have to have their nose pushed into it. They all moved smartly to the enemy.

"The next thing I know, the two platoons are locked in, we are in good solid contact with the machine guns and bunkers. We were hitting the bunker position from the reverse, but it really wasn't an envelopment, because I had lost the element of surprise. They knew I had gotten behind them, and they had a chance to reorganize.

"My two platoons stopped moving and I moved up to get a feel of what was going on. That was when I was wounded the first time. An RPG round hit a bush three feet from me, which caused me to lose respect for that RPG. Unless it actually hits you, it sure isn't going to hurt you much. It makes a hell of a noise, but it doesn't blow much shrapnel. I was hit in the leg and in the side with small pieces of twisted, tinlike metal.

"As the RPG exploded, I was talking to Colonel Smith for the first time since moving out from the streambed. I don't know how time figures in this, but my Marines had been in contact for some time by the time our attack began to stall.

"After the brief interruption I continued to talk with Colonel Smith and he wanted to know my situation and what he could do to help. Well in that situation, once we were in the streambed with Battalion on the ridge top and the enemy in between, I had to pass on artillery help.

"There were low clouds, kind of a misty rain, and no air support. It was a perfect rifleman's war. We were up against the enemy and on equal terms—what you see is what you get, a gunfighter's war.

"My attack had stopped, and I saw I had two choices. One, I could say, 'I'm sorry,' and get the hell out. Or, two, commit my reserve and go for it.

"I decided that if I tried to break contact and withdraw, I'd have the same problem that Christman had the day before. I thought I was hurt [Marine casualties] worse than I was. I figured I would lose more Marines trying to get my dead and wounded out from under the guns.

"So I made the decision to commit my reserve platoon. I moved forward to get a better view of what was happening. I called Lieutenant Davis (2nd Platoon commander) forward and gave him the order to go into the attack. A mortar round or an RPG landed among us, and Davis was hit pretty seriously in the back.

"The Medal of Honor citation states that I issued orders to my platoon commanders there. Shoot, in that kind of fight you don't get all of your platoon commanders together. I already had two platoon commanders in the fight; they already knew what was going on.

"It was only Lieutenant Davis, my XO Lieutenant Lee Herron, and me in that group. But that was too many, because somebody saw us and did something about it. Davis was seriously wounded and was out of the fight. I told Herron to take the second platoon into the attack.

"He gave me a strange look like he didn't know exactly what to do. (He had spent a year at language school learning Vietnamese, a year that was useless in this situation.) I think he had forgotten the basic infantry tactics.

"I thought, 'Oh, no, I'm going to have to hold class right here.'

"But Lee said, 'Aye, aye, sir,' and moved out smartly.

"He picked up Davis' platoon and took them forward with the old 'follow-me' tactics. The machine gun fire was pretty heavy at that point. Almost immediately I am getting a radio call from Sergeant David Beyerlein, who was the 2nd Platoon sergeant, that Lieutenant Herron had been killed, cut down by machine gun fire.

"I think about Lee sometimes. He must have been scared to death for those last two or three minutes of his life. I feel that he was not comfortable with what he had to do, but he knew the objective and he never wavered.

"Colonel Smith was always great about saying, 'Stick up

for your Marines because they are good. They'll charge right up the enemy's gun barrel for you without asking why.' Lieutenant Lee Herron was one of those Marines.

"Anyway, Sergeant Beyerlein had the 2nd Platoon as the platoon commander. And just the way it always seems to happen; you get one piece of bad news and then you get more. Immediately I got word that my other platoon commanders were down; Christman had been brought down by a machine gun; and my 1st Platoon leader was seriously wounded and out of the fight.

"Lieutenant George Malone had the 1st Platoon. (He is still in the Marine Corps today. All these Marines were awarded Navy Crosses for that action.)

"I did some movement between my other two platoons, but really didn't have to. My platoon sergeants, Staff Sergeants Michael Lane and Robert Jensen, and Sergeant David Beyerlein did a fabulous job. Again, I don't think they had too much to do because each Marine knew his role: Attack!

"In that situation it didn't take any kicking or shouting. They knew where the enemy was located, and they were closing on him.

"Herron was dead and Beyerlein had my reserve in the attack through the middle of my force.

"There was a machine gun across a draw from us that was plain murder. We had gotten all of the other machine guns. I was wondering, 'Who am I going to have to send after it—either the 1st or the 2nd Platoon.'

"I really didn't want to put anybody across that open ground to get to it, because it was obvious that whoever went across was going to get torn up.

"At that time—unbelievable, but it was an unbelievable day to begin with—the sun came out. It was like something magic: 'Let there be sun.' The clouds had parted, leaving a big hole above us.

"Battalion got on the hook and said, 'There are two OV-10s up if you can use them.'

" 'I sure as hell can.'

"I got them in the hole above me, identified the gun position, and those two OV-10s ran on that machine gun. Their rocket runs silenced that gun and we got across and took the gun.

"Just about the same time, Battalion is saying that Delta Company is coming off the Ho Chi Minh Trail down to my assistance. Earlier, I had talked to the battalion commander before I committed the 2nd Platoon. Colonel Smith wanted to know if I needed help.

"I realized that Delta was the only one who could come to my assistance, and by the time they got down there it would all be over. But thinking that my company was hurt worse that it was, I would need Delta to help me carry out my dead and wounded. So for that reason, I agreed that the colonel should send Delta down.

"In all of the fighting, I had forgotten about Delta. We knocked out that machine gun with the OV-10s, and Battalion was on the hook [saying], 'Delta is on its way down the trail, keep a lookout for them. Put somebody at that fork so they can get down to you and come into your rear. We don't want you running into each other and shooting each other up.'

"Battalion realized that I had been attacking up the hill from the streambed and Delta was coming down from the ridge line. It was a catastrophe in the making.

"So I had my gunny send a detail and backtrack around to bring Delta in behind me. After we knocked out that machine gun, there was no other fire coming in on us.

"I figured, 'If Delta is getting in the fight (again, not knowing how bad my company was hurt) just hold what you got. We don't want anybody shooting up Delta. We'll let Delta get a little bit of the action.'

"So everyone was lying behind trees, bushes, in holes and depressions. It was deathly quiet. Because of the thick jungle and my Marines not wanting to be seen, it was difficult to account for my squads, let alone individual riflemen. At this stage no one really wanted to move. Dead enemy snipers were hanging out of trees and guts were in the banana leaves. The area was really torn up. I was feeling low because I felt that Alpha had really been chewed up.

"I kept wondering, 'What is going to happen next?' I still had no idea how strong the enemy was, or what Delta was going to have to do once they moved through me.

"All of a sudden we all see movement coming through the trees directly to our front. The first thought everyone had was, 'The NVA are out of their holes and are in a counterattack on our position.' At the same moment, though, there was a flash of fear; we realized that we were looking at U.S. Marines.

"My guides going back up the trail had either not gone far enough or had not been quick enough, and Delta Company had taken Bill Christman's path of the day before. They ended up coming right into our front with no NVA in between us.

"Alpha had already attacked through the whole complex, destroyed all the NVA, and all Delta had to do was come down and say, 'Hi!'

"Captain Ed Riley walked up to me and said, 'Alpha Six, what are you doing down here.'

"'Semper Fi! I'm glad to have you around, my friend. Let's go see how bad I'm hurt.'

"It was getting dark and my 3rd Platoon corpsman passed over the radio net that Christman was going to die unless we could get him some IVs. We didn't have any more blood down there with us. I guess we had used all of Delta's, too, because there was a crisis of getting IVs for Christman.

"I had him on a stretcher, and some Marines were racing to the top of the ridge with him. The battalion surgeon—I can't remember his name; but for a Navy guy [he] was a gung ho sonofagun—charged down from the Battalion CP with IVs to try to save Christman's life.

"Bill didn't make it.

"I picked up my dead and wounded, as much as we could

carry, Delta was helping us out with this chore and immediately started moving Alpha back up to the perimeter. Captain Riley stayed down there with what was left of his company, to collect all of the NVA equipment and to blow it.

"We got back up on the ridge and took our position on the perimeter, what was left of us. I remember lying in my hole, really shaking, I guess kind of in shock, waiting for Riley to blow the NVA gear, wanting him to get out of that valley.

"I thought he would never blow that thing. Finally this big explosion was heard and he came back up on the ridge. We never had any more problems.

"The toughest time of that whole twenty-four-hour period was back up on that ridge. I have never experienced anything like it as far as shock and the aftereffects go. That's when fear really came in on me.

"It wasn't so much of what I had been through as it was that I was worried about Riley still being down in that valley.

"In all of that action, I had ten Marines killed. Almost everybody else was wounded, some pretty seriously. A couple of my Marines are still in VA hospitals today.

"Some totals say eleven Marines were killed in that action, but only ten of them belonged to Alpha. The other KIA was Delta's while moving down to Alpha's position.

"There were something like one hundred and twenty dead NVA."

"There was another operation called Apache Snow in May of '69. I was close to leaving One-Nine and we had jumped off for Apache Snow. I was expecting a flight out back to the World any day.

"That was a tough situation. Number one, we had a new battalion commander who had asked me to extend through Apache Snow. I was already completing a six-month extension and Dewey Canyon had given me what I had extended for.

"I wanted to find 'em [the enemy]. I had a chance to find 'em, and I found all I wanted. I was now ready for a change of duty and some family time.

"By that time I had made captain, and my commander wanted me to stay with Alpha Company. He asked me to remain in command, but I really couldn't do it.

"I had a wife and two daughters in the States, and Dotti Lu had really been great about my one extension. I thought it was asking too much of my family [for me] to stay over there any longer. The more you flirt with that sort of thing, the more chances you literally have of staying over there forever.

"I told him, 'No, sir, I'm going home.'

"Finally one morning—you never get the word that it's going to be tomorrow; you get the word right now—'Catch the next bird out; you've got to be at Da Nang like right now.'

"At that time it was really hard, because I loved that company and the Marines who made it what it was. It really was—you read it all of the time—like a desertion. It's leaving those who have meant everything to you, who have been your life, and you really feel . . . well, it's not easy.

"I was caught between two things: my family back in the States and that family I was leaving on that hill. It wasn't the moment I was looking forward to; it just wasn't what leaving was supposed to be.

"As I passed my Marines in their holes on my way down the hill to the LZ for my heli-flight, they stood, saluted, and said, 'Alpha One-Nine, sir.'"

16

Happy Valley

LARRY E. SMEDLEY

Rank: Corporal
Unit: Company D, 1st Battalion, 7th Marines
Born: Front Royal, Virginia, March 4, 1949

Date: December 21, 1967
Place: Quang Nam Province

HAPPY Valley—how deceiving a name for so deadly a place; it just didn't fit, but that's how the Marine Corps had referred to it from the beginning.

The valley controlled the approaches to Da Nang and the huge American air base to the east. If the North Vietnamese and Vietcong were going to hit the Da Nang Air Base, then the attack would probably originate from these broad, sweeping lowlands.

Just as the name Happy Valley didn't seem to belong, likewise neither did Larry Smedley. He was from a broken home and had moved back and forth from Virginia to Florida with a stop in Georgia. His last public school was Howard Junior High School in Orlando.

A month and three days after he turned seventeen, on

April 7, 1966, Larry enlisted in the Marine Corps at Orlando, Florida. He received his recruit training at Parris Island, South Carolina, and the individual combat training that each Marine from typist to tanker receives at Camp Lejeune, North Carolina.

After a year with the 2nd Marine Division on the East Coast, Larry transferred to the 1st Marine Division in Vietnam.

Larry Smedley was a hard charger. You could tell by his service record book—five months after he enlisted, he was promoted to private first class; three months after that he was a lance corporal; and nine months later he made corporal. In his five months in Vietnam he had risen from a rifleman/squad radioman to squad leader.

He was a good Marine.

Five days before Christmas 1967, D Company, One-Seven, was using Hill 41 east of Da Nang as its combat base. Company Commander Captain Joseph Blichfeldt had sent out the 1st Platoon to seal off the approaches to Happy Valley's "rocket belt," a thin area from where the enemy could launch rocket attacks against the American air base.

Originally Captain Blichfeldt had planned to position a squad on each of the two ridges that formed the valley. However, because the moon wouldn't rise until eleven P.M., the captain explained to Second Lieutenant Michael Neil that it might be necessary to have a unit on the valley floor itself to detect enemy movement.

The lieutenant was cautioned about the possible danger should this become necessary. Before departing, Corporal Larry Smedley requested that his squad be given the southern ridge, where he would have access to the valley floor should it be necessary to leave the hilltop.

Smedley and his men were given the southern ridge, less than 200 meters from where 125 enemy soldiers had been spotted a month earlier. If there was going to be contact, it would be here.

When Corporal Smedley arrived on the southern ridge,

he discovered that it was too dark to observe the valley floor from the high ground. He requested permission to move his men down to the low ground.

He was given the okay.

Several minutes later, after setting up a linear ambush on the valley floor with his squad, he radioed back and said, "Sir, I can get some VC from here."

The Marines were in position, and the deadly hide-and-watch game began.

First the Marines had to get their night vision. This could take, depending on the available light, up to thirty minutes. After their eyes were adjusted to the pitch-black night, the Americans began fine-tuning their ears. They would probably hear the enemy before they saw him.

Better than that, though, the Marines would probably smell their adversaries long before they could hear or see him. After spending several weeks or months in the jungles, the North Vietnamese and Vietcong would develop their own aroma. You could, quite literally, smell 'em.

Likewise, the enemy was often able to discover the Americans by their smell. In the early days of the war, a patrol was mounting up for an S & D south of Da Nang. As they waited for the early-morning formation, the veteran platoon sergeant began sniffing the air; there was a strange, out-of-place smell.

Finally, he sniffed out the source.

"Whatcha got on there?" he asked a young private.

"Hai Karate cologne, sarge," the private replied.

The staff sergeant swatted the young Marine's helmet and it flew to the deck. "You're not going on a date!" The veteran noncom bellowed. "You're going out to find and kill the enemy!"

The way the young private smelled, though, the VC would be able to detect the Americans long before they would be able to see them. At best, the enemy would merely slip away; at worst, they would arrange their own ambush.

The staff sergeant "urged" the young Marine to the road that lead up to the platoon area. "Now get in that binjo ditch and wipe off that smell."

When the private emerged from the primitive sewer line, he no longer smelled like Saturday night in Denver; he smelled, instead, like Death in Vietnam.

Larry Smedley had been in Vietnam long enough to understand this and the other intricacies of war; that's why he was a squad leader—that and his initiative.

Smedley and his six Marines had waited for more than two hours until they finally observed enemy troop movement.

"At approximately 2130 the patrol radio operator whispered into the radio that they were completely surrounded by over one hundred enemy carrying large objects [rockets and mortars]," Captain Blichfeldt reported later. The enemy was too close to the Marines to call in artillery.

"I told Corporal Smedley that I had a blocking force to the west and a reaction force was on its way from the east," the captain stated. "The men were surrounded for about fifteen minutes before they were able to open fire."

When the end of the VC column proceeded past, Corporal Smedley opened fire and a vicious firefight developed.

With surprise his ally, Corporal Smedley leaped to his feet and yelled to his men, "Follow me!" He charged the confused enemy shouting orders and screaming as he fired from the hip with his M16.

This exchange of fire could be seen from the company base on Hill 41. The enemy broke contact and ran in the direction of the approaching Marines in the reaction force. Corporal Smedley employed pursuit by fire as he set up a 360-degree defense perimeter to await the link up with other friendly units in the area.

The enemy broke contact and the Marine units were able to link up.

With the combined force, the Marines began sweeping the area looking for dead and wounded enemy soldiers and their gear. After moving a couple of hundred meters, a VC machine gun opened fire wounding several Marines.

"At that time," Captain Blichfeldt stated, "Lance Corporal [Michael] Storey came up on the radio calling for more corpsmen and illumination. He said that three Marines had been wounded and Corporal Smedley was going after the gun that got them."

Disregarding the intense fire, Corporal Smedley charged the enemy machine gun position, yelling instructions to his squad while firing his rifle and throwing grenades. An enemy rifle grenade exploded, which blew off part of his right foot, and knocked Smedley to the ground.

Despite the painful wound, the young Marine struggled to an upright position, got what few men were left and led the assault against the enemy gun emplacement.

"Then Corporal Smedley was hit again, this time in the shoulder," Lance Corporal Storey recalled. "He went down but again got to his feet and advanced toward the machine gun. Still our men were being shot, and Corporal Smedley knew in his own mind that the machine gun would have to be knocked out before a medevac could be called in."

"The last transmission I received over the radio," Captain Blichfeldt stated, "was that Corporal Smedley had gotten up a final time and disappeared into the thick brush, screaming and throwing hand grenades."

Finally there was silence; the gun had been put out of action, but Corporal Smedley did not return to his men. The first Marines to get to the VC position reported later that Corporal Smedley died about fifteen meters from the machine gun with two bullet holes in the shoulder and his right foot blown away.

"The enemy and all his equipment," the captain stated, "were riddled with grenade fragments."

17

Dust-off

WHEN Major Pat Brady commanded the 54th Medical Detachment in 1967 and 1968, he and his crew were always able to get the patients out and back to the hospital. Neither rain, nor sleet, nor gloom of night stopped the 54th from getting the wounded out. Gunfire didn't stop them, either.

They were flying Dust-offs, medical extraction missions.

These missions were extremely hazardous, but Major Brady and his men were always successful, and that was what mattered. However, because he was at the controls of the Huey, Brady often got the credit. A newspaper headline once said he saved sixteen soldiers, but Major Brady didn't quite see it that way.

"It takes four people to fly a mission," Brady, now a major general in Washington, D.C., told a visitor recently, "all equally important. I insisted (where I could influence it) that all crew members be recommended for the same medal regardless of rank or who was in charge. On two instances I got a different award than my crew (the CMH and DSC); and in both cases I used more than one crew for the award action."

PATRICK HENRY BRADY

Rank: Major General   **Date:** January 6, 1968
(then Major)
Unit: 54th Medical Detach-   **Place:** Near Chu Lai
ment, 67th Medical Group
        Born: Philip, South Dakota, October 1, 1936

"They were truly a remarkable bunch of guys.

"Of the forty men in our detachment, twenty-two of them
were hit, and received Purple Hearts.* Some of them were
wounded a couple of times before they were finally evacuated.

"My medic, one of the finest soldiers I have ever known,
was hit three times while he was in Vietnam. His name is
Steve Hook. The first time he was hit, he wasn't injured that
badly. The second time he was with me.

"We went in on a pickup after a hell of an operation. It
was supposed to have been a secure area. I was coming in
and, bang, these two guys jumped out of spider traps beside
my aircraft and shot both my crewmen.

"I jammed the aircraft up into a keyhole in the trees to get
some protection, and the guys on the ground killed the two
Charlies. My crew chief was hanging in his harness and I
thought he was dead.

"Hook was bleeding from the back, and of course, like
always, there was tremendous confusion as they were

---

*"I got hit my first tour, not bad.

"There was a crash, I guess it was an A1E. As we were going in to get it, another
one crashed in front of us. We went in to the fire and we were silhouetted. Charlie
must have been sitting right under the crash site with a .50-caliber, and he blew the
roof off the helicopter and the shrapnel cut above my eye.

"It was the easiest medal I ever got. But I had to go see a doctor, and in those days
if you went to see a doctor, you got a Purple Heart."

cramming patients onto the aircraft. They loaded about twelve patients—all Americans—onto the aircraft.

"I came up out of the trees and looked back and there was Hook going through the bodies, starting IVs and trying to help the wounded. But he's been shot in the back and is bleeding. The guy beside me is having problems and I'm trying to fly the aircraft.

"Finally I got hold of one of the patients and pointed to Hook's back. So he got a handkerchief and he was treating Hook while Hook was treating the other patients. He went to the hospital and came back to us. That was the second time.

"The third time I was in the float ship working the area. It was a very quiet day, nothing going on, just routine pickups here and there. I hadn't heard from one of our birds, and it was bothering me. Hook was on that aircraft.

"I can't tell you to this day why it bothered me. There was no reason for me to be upset. I called in and said, 'Where's Dust-off 54?'

"They called back and said, 'No sweat, Fifty-five.' Fifty-five or Double Nickel was my call sign; we had all set numbers for our call signs. 'They (54) made a pickup and should be back pretty soon. We lost communications with them, but they went down into the valley. Everything is all right.'

"I got mad at the guy on the radio for not being excited, although I don't know what made me excited. I said, 'I'm going to refuel and go take a look.'

"I refueled and headed out, and as soon as I got above the crest, they were screaming on the radio for help.

"What had happened, they had gone in and had been mortared. Hook had taken some shrapnel in the head and it kind of ruined one of his arms while he was standing on the pad. The aircraft had been destroyed.

"My timing was such that I got over the top just after this had all happened. So I was able to get in and get him to the hospital real quick. That was a miracle. The timing was just phenomenal.

"Another miracle was that we had a neurosurgeon in the area. So they operated on him that afternoon and they were able to save him.

"He had severe problems for a long time, but now he plays golf and can use his arm pretty good, and his head is all right. He got a Silver Star, I think, for that action. He went out into the mortar fire to drag in patients. That's when he was hit.

"He's a mailman in Iowa and is doing great. A lousy golfer, but otherwise just great. I go see him when I can. My maintenance guy, Sergeant John Hodgdon, was the greatest maintenance guy, and one of the finest people I have ever known. He's a cop in Minnesota. We've got a bus driver in San Francisco.

"They all were great, phenomenal Americans, an incredible group of soldiers. I think of them often and we get together occasionally. Sergeant Rocky, the Blob, KIA, Wayne, the Wopas, Batman—they saved a lot of lives.

"I think one of the reasons the Dust-off personnel were so good was that these guys had a mission and it was beyond criticism, in a war with much criticism. They were a cross section and the dominant element of the unit was good. The leadership of the unit was good whether it was NCO or officer.

"The whole thing was a challenge, they never wanted to fail on a mission. We never wanted to come out of the field without the patient. And we were saving lives.

"To save a life, if you have ever been through it, is an incredible, exhilarating experience. It's the greatest feeling in life. These guys were into that, and we had a tremendous reputation. They were very proud of what they were doing.

"They were doing tremendous good for the Vietnamese people and the American soldiers, for everybody. It was a great team.

"I'm not sure how many patients Dust-off carried in

Vietnam, probably in the hundreds of thousands. My first tour we carried South Vietnamese soldiers, American soldiers, civilians, and we also carried VC and NVA, but mostly Vietnamese.

"In my second tour, we hardly noticed the Tet Offensive; it was that bad where we were. Our area [near Chu Lai] was very hot most of the time. We had six aircraft and on an average had seven shot up every month, or 116 percent.

"We averaged 50 percent aircraft availability due to battle damage and maintenance. A lot of time we had to fly float ships, the spare maintenance ship.

"We covered a tremendous area with those six aircraft; from north of Da Nang to Quang Ngai in the south. In a ten-month period we carried more patients than were carried by chopper in the entire Korean War, just in our one six-aircraft detachment.

"I can remember reading about an operation the Marines were in up at Khe Sanh, and there were a lot of headlines about them losing three aircraft in one day. Shoot, we lost twelve on the same day.

"We had some months when we carried over three thousand patients with only three aircraft available. One day I carried over one hundred and twenty-five patients, over five thousand patients in two tours. A lot of casualties were generated in our AO [area of operation].

"We had a lot of problems with the enemy trying to lure us in on my first tour. In fact, I could talk all day about our early experiences. All of the people we were dealing with then were Vietnamese. We would get a mission and a set of coordinates, and that was it; you couldn't talk to anyone on the radio.

"We would go out to a set of coordinates and if we were to say to them on the ground, 'Pop smoke,' or 'Show me your signal,'—it's the only thing in Vietnamese I can say—you'd see four or five different smoke bombs down there.

"So we developed a technique where we would make a

low, fast pass over the area, just dive through to see who was there. If they were friendlies, then we would turn around and come in.

"You could never say, 'Pop red smoke.' The guy on the ground would never say to you, 'I'm throwing out red smoke,' because then you would get two or three different red smoke bombs down there. He would pop smoke and we'd identify the color.

"Charlie was always somewhere in the area and a lot of the times he was listening. Charlie would talk to us sometimes, 'Dust-off, we kill you.' Stuff like that.

"On my second tour, the majority of patients I carried were U.S. soldiers, although we continued to carry enemy wounded, not only for humanitarian reasons but in hopes it would cut down on enemy damage to our aircraft.

"Flying was especially tricky at night. In fact, we landed right in the middle of the VC several times.

"One time we landed in the middle of this village and the guys were hanging out the doors saying, 'There's something strange going on here, a lot of guys running around in black pajamas.'

"So I flipped on my spotlight to see what was there. Sure as hell, we were right in the middle of the VC. You could always tell they were VC by the black pajamas and the weapons they carried.

"We scared them as bad as they scared us, because I flipped off the light and got out of there just about the time they started shooting at us. As a result, we used flares when possible.

"The things we did in the 54th that may have set us apart were the flare missions and the weather missions—we found a way to get in at night in weather [with flares] and in daytime in weather [sidewards]. I remember one night mission. It was the second tour. I was in the mountains making a pickup and clouds had covered half the mountain peak. Someone popped a flare and it silhouetted the mountain and I could actually see it. It stuck in my mind.

"I had never seen a flare up close, and I once asked what would happen if one of them came through my rotor blades.

"I was told, 'Don't worry about it. They are made of cardboard and it probably wouldn't knock you out of the sky.'

"One night I was circling down and one [a flare] was getting closer and closer. I was busy as hell and having a real rough time. I looked up and saw that the flare was coming toward my rotor blade. I said, ' The heck with it, I'll let it hit.'

"I looked away, and when I looked back, it was so close that I could see that the damn thing was metal with holes in it. 'Jesus! If that thing hits, it will knock us out of the sky!'

"I broke away just in time for the flare to miss us.

"The procedure [using flares] itself is not complicated. You make the approach out of the open side window circling around the flare. If all the flares burn out, you stop, go back inside on the instruments, and then slowly start to climb straight up. If you try to go out laterally, then you are in trouble.

"When another flare pops, you start back down. Once you get under the ceiling, you've got it made. On some nights with the moon above and no rain, you would be in good shape when you got under the stuff, because once you broke through you had exceptional visibility. You'd be surprised how well you could see on the blackest of nights.

"However, if it is dark and a guy does what he is supposed to do—we learned this our first tour—he can land a helicopter almost on top of your head before you see it. You can hear it, but you don't know where it is coming from. That's the truth.

"If you turn off your overhead lights and your console lights and have all of your other lights completely dim, almost out—you can't have any red glow, which can be seen in a bank—then you can get in. We made most of our approaches at night blacked out.

"I would come down to a hundred feet or so, as long as

I was above the highest obstacle. The crew would hang out the side door and guide me down into the area, once again with my head out the window.

"In those days I wasn't sure what units were operating in the region west of Chu Lai. I can't recall the names, but I remember their calls signs—Ghost Rider, Assassin, Barbarian, Zorba.

"We supported the Americal Division; a brigade from the 101st came through, and elements of the 1st Cav came through. They would come in, work the AO, and move on. It was a tremendously active area, the hottest part was called Death Valley."

"Death Valley was located west of Chu Lai and had been an enemy stronghold for years. Parker's Freeway, part of the Ho Chi Minh Trail, was just on the western side of the valley, and as a result, there was a tremendous amount of enemy traffic.

"The terrain was rough, with numerous terraced rice paddies from where enemy gunners could shoot down incoming choppers. Which, in my judgment, made this approach among the most dangerous."

In November 1967, a unit from the 101st Airborne made contact with an NVA force and sustained several serious casualties. In *The Screaming Eagle*, the 1st Brigade, 101st Airborne newsletter, dated November 22, 1967, Sp-5 William P. Singley reported that a platoon leader called in a Dust-off for immediate helicopter evacuation. An enemy rocket launcher and machine guns were hammering away at the American position.

Even when he made the call, the lieutenant thought, "No one can make it. Not in this storm. The weather is too bad." Of course, there was the enemy gunfire pouring in.

As the troops on the ground waited amid the rattling gunfire and the natural and man-made thunder, they heard Pat Brady and his crew circling above. It was about eight P.M.; clouds and a torrential downpour shrouded the landing zone. Major Brady peered down through the darkness and the clouds but could see nothing.

"I can't find you right now," he radioed, "but I'll be back."

"I couldn't blame him if he didn't come back," the lieutenant remembered.

Pat Brady: "We took off in a tropical storm. The winds were up to seventy knots [near hurricane strength] with tremendous rain and a very low ceiling.

"Initially we tried to get into the location under the stuff by following a trail when all of a sudden we came up against a mountain and it just went ink, completely black.

"So we backed out and went around. We found a river and tried to follow it, but when I turned on the searchlight, the reflection of the rain almost blinded me.

"I just couldn't find a way in there, and the guys out there were in really bad shape."

On the ground, Army medics worked feverishly to keep the wounded Americans alive, but they needed to get the soldiers out of there immediately or those guys wouldn't make it.

"I had a float ship, and it wasn't very well equipped electronically. I had remembered the flares which silhouetted the clouded mountain on an earlier mission and I went back and got another ship equipped for IFR flight. I called and asked the guys on the ground if they had any flares and they said yes.

"So I said, 'Here is what we'll do. We'll come out over the stuff and I want you to pop your flares. I am going to try to follow the flares down through the clouds until I come out under it.'

"We went up to about seven thousand feet to clear the mountains and tried to get a vector; actually, I was using my FM homer when we finally got in close. They started popping flares when we got overhead, and we started circling down through the mountains with those flares.

"The first time I tried this, the flare burned out at about

three thousand feet. That made you switch from visual to instruments very quickly. I brought the aircraft to a halt and froze it. Then we started to climb up slowly until another flare popped.

"Eventually we broke out under the stuff, and the flares then provided good visibility. I broke out right over the casualties the first time.

"We got the most seriously wounded guys on board and went straight up into the clouds and flew on instruments out over the ocean there at Chu Lai. When I saw the coastal lights under the clouds, we took the casualties in. We did this three or four times that night.

"Once we flew right into a thunder cell. We lost all control of the aircraft and were being bounced up and down a thousand feet at a time.

"But we got out of it, and were able to get everybody out.

"General Abrams flew up and gave me a DSC for that action. We continued to refine the procedure until we were doing it routinely. [Some people called them Brady Missions, but they were flare missions.]

"That's how we got Webster [Anderson, Medal of Honor recipient]. Of course, I didn't know it was Webster at the time, but it was the same deal with the flares. We went into a fire-support base that time.

"It was a cloudy night, his base was in the clouds when he got hurt; he came in with two legs and an arm gone. The reason I know it was Webster was that the people in the hospital followed it.

"They came to me and said, 'Remember that guy you picked up? He is going to get the Medal of Honor.'

"In addition to the night flare mission, there was the day weather mission. Weather was a killer; it killed a lot of pilots. I think we lost more to weather than anything.

"In Vietnam there was often low valley fog in the morning, and in the afternoon clouds covered the tops of the mountains. The fog and the clouds could really hamper flying.

"One day we got a call for a guy who was snake-bit on top of a mountain. When I got there, the mountain-top was covered with clouds. So I started up into the clouds. I knew I could break out into the valley if I got into trouble.

"So I'm going straight into the stuff and went white-out, and had zero-zero visibility. We went IFR and couldn't see a thing. I don't know if you know it, but you can be flying upside down in a white-out condition and not know it. If you are close to the ground, you are probably going to die.

"As soon as I went IFR, I'd fall off into the valley. I knew I was safe doing that. But they were screaming on the radio that the guy was going into convulsions, and I am wondering, 'How in the hell am I going to get in there?'

"I started back up the mountain the third or fourth time, and the wind hit me and turned me sideways. I'm in the stuff and looking out my side window to find a place to set it down and see if I am right side up, or whatever. As I was looking out my side window I saw my rotor tip and the tree-tops.

"So I knew I was right side up, and I could see thirty feet in the zero-zero stuff. That's all I needed. So I went straight up the mountain sideways, watching the rotor blades and the tree-tops right into the area, and we got that guy out.

"Those were the conditions on some of the missions we were flying the day we earned the Medal.

"It was not an unusual day—the Medal of Honor day—but it happened that a lot of people saw the action and wrote it up. I guess it was unusual to the people who saw us coming up through the ground fog. I guess it impressed them."

There were four evacuation missions flown by Major Brady that day in January 1968. According to official records, flying and landing conditions were hazardous—"thick cloud layer, zero-zero, mountainous terrain, minefield in open."

"Of course, they [the enemy] were getting after us too."

The first evacuation site was being repeatedly mortared from VC strongholds that surrounded the entire area.

"The first mission was low valley fog. A guy went out and said, 'I can't get in,' so I said, 'All right, we will give it a try.'

"We went out and found a trail at the edge of the fog, got under the stuff, and followed the trail into the outpost. We made the pickup. It was a piece of cake."

According to recently declassified Department of the Army documents about the battle:

"The fog at that time was so dense that Major Brady was unable to see the tip of the rotor blades through his cockpit window. To gain better visibility he turned his aircraft sideward, then looking out his open window, hovered in this unorthodox manner toward his destination. Blowing fog from it's [sic] path, Dust-off '55' hovered only a few feet above the road at an airspeed so slow as not to register on the airspeed indicator. Traveling at the speed of a walking man, Major Brady was extremely vulnerable to hostile fire at almost point blank range. Major Brady landed his aircraft in an area so tiny it would have been considered hazardous in good weather. He knew the pad had been mortared repeatedly just prior to his arrival and was still receiving sniper fire, yet he continued without hesitation."

"That was a Vietnamese mission, that was the first mission.

"Then I got a call that there was a bunch of American casualties out in the valley. We had been trying to get in but couldn't, and they asked me for help. I said, 'Okay, we'll be right out.'

"The valley was full of fog, about five hundred feet thick, and we were engaged in a tremendous battle. The whole area was alive with fights; they were going on all around us.

"The brigade commander didn't want me to go in. What

happened, as I recall, [was that] he wouldn't give me the
radio frequency of the guy on the ground, and that was all
I needed to get in. If he'd just give me the radio frequency
of the guy on the ground with the patients, I was pretty sure
we could get in and get the casualties out. We had just
completed a mission under identical conditions; we had
done it many times in the past.

"But he [the commander] was concerned. He said he
wasn't going to lift artillery fire for me to go in. He didn't
think I could do it. Two other ships had already been shot
down in that area.

"So I went and talked to the brigade commander at his
mountaintop outpost. I said, 'Just give me the frequency
and don't worry about the artillery, because I'm not worried
about it. Let me go. I just made a pickup in this stuff not far
from here. I think I know a way in.'

"I found out later that the commander went to my copilot
and asked him, 'Is this guy telling me the truth? Can you
guys really do it?'

"My copilot said, 'Hell, yes!'

"So we got in the helicopter, went out to the edge of the
stuff, found a trail, and went in sideways right over the VC.
We got into the pickup site, got some of the patients on, and
went straight up through the stuff.

"After we flew in, the medics over on the mountaintop
were watching for us to come up through the fog.

"All of a sudden our aircraft came up through the fog and
I guess they were on the fire-support base cheering for us as
we broke through. So we brought the patients in.

"There were sixty or seventy patients in the valley who
needed to get out, thirty or forty of them serious. I went
back and explained the technique. Several aircraft got in
line to follow me, and that was kind of scary, because we
somehow ended up on the wrong frequency.

"Anyway, we went in first and they were to follow us in,
but they couldn't get in and they had to go back.

"I don't know how many trips we made, but we went in

until we got them all out. We brought them all up on top of the mountain where the medics were.

"We got them to the medics for emergency treatment, and there were other aircraft up there to haul them back to the hospital for surgery. The bird I was flying on that mission got shot up pretty bad, the controls were shot up. When we were trying to load the patients, they opened up on us and tore up the aircraft pretty bad. That was the third mission.

"The fourth mission that they wrote about for the Medal of Honor citation was in a mine field. Another aircraft had gone in there and a mine went off. I'm not sure if he set it off, or somebody else did, but it killed a couple of Americans. These guys were laying all over down there.

"I was there and saw where he had set down, so when he pulled out, I put my skids right where he had set down. Our aircraft was damaged by an exploding mine, but it was flyable. As the two medics were carrying patients to the aircraft, one of them stepped on a mine and it blew them both up.

"I was looking out the side door, and boom, they both went up in the air. Shrapnel came through the aircraft, but the body they were carrying absorbed most of the fragments. I don't know if he was already dead, but that guy probably saved the lives of my medic and crew chief and never knew it."

Truly, a remarkable bunch of guys.

18

Long Time Coming

WHEN the Vietnam War ended, Americans wanted to move on and put it behind them, but in the process the Vietnam veterans were either vilified or, worse, ignored. That was one of the things that struck Jim Stockdale when he returned home in 1973 after his eight-year absence.

"The prisoners of war were kind of outsiders," the retired Navy vice admiral said, "and people lavished praise on us that was excessive. I think it was the beginning of a conscious reaction to what happened when you guys came out and how you were treated.

"As the years have gone by, I have been in conferences with Vietnam veterans and I have really been horrified by the stories of their abuse after coming home."

A Vietnam draft dodger reflected on the war and his actions recently. It was 1968, and Tet, Hue, Khe Sanh, Dak To, Dai Do—names alien to the generation of today—were bloody battles being waged. When his number came up in the draft, his father arranged for a psychiatrist to have him declared unfit for military duty. It was expensive, but it was done.

"You know," he reflected, "I'm kind of ashamed of that today."

There were those, though, who went, and felt no shame. Unlike the stereotypical Vietnam veterans of television and the movies, they didn't do drugs, or kill their leaders, or murder innocent civilians. Instead, they fought enemy soldiers, suffered terrible wounds, and returned to a confused America. Their pride was unspoken, but some interpreted this silence as an admission of guilt for uncommitted offenses.

Most kids want to believe that their fathers are heroes, and Michael Butt, an eighteen-year-old living in Rockville, Maryland, is no exception. The teenager knew his dad, Thomas, had served in Vietnam with the Marines in 1967, and was still carrying a North Vietnamese bullet in his leg.

"I asked him about what he did in Vietnam," Michael said over a Coke at a fast-food restaurant, "and he'd answer my questions."

However, Michael—like so many other Americans—didn't know exactly what questions to ask, and his dad would volunteer little. As a result, Michael was reluctant to press the issue; it had happened a long time ago and why bring back bad memories?

It was a time when cowards were praised and heroes cursed, and maybe his dad didn't want to be reminded. After he had been wounded, Thomas was transported to Camp Pendleton, California, and heard protesters shout, "Baby killers!" and throw cans of dog food at the wounded Marines.

After Pendleton, Thomas proceeded to Bethesda Naval Hospital in Maryland where he spent over a year recovering from his numerous wounds. Yeah, his son thought, maybe he just doesn't want to be reminded.

Still, Michael wanted to do something to show his dad how proud he was of him. The medals his dad had earned symbolized his bravery, but over the years they had been lost. So, the young son decided to see if he could get the government to replace them.

Michael's grandfather was skeptical and told him. "The

government isn't going to give you anything, but while you're at it, why don't you check on the medal your father was supposed to get?" Michael knew nothing about this.

When Thomas, then a lance corporal, was recovering from his wounds, a buddy told him that he had been put up for a Navy Cross, the Marine Corps' second highest medal for heroism. His platoon commander—Lieutenant John Bobo—had been awarded the Medal of Honor posthumously for the same action, but that was the last he heard about his own medal, and Thomas blew it off.

But that was all Michael needed, and he began an odyssey that lasted thirteen months (the same as a Marine combat tour in Vietnam) and ended on a parade field in Washington, D.C. "I wanted to get my dad the medal he earned but never got," Michael said, "and I wanted it to be a surprise."

At first he thought it was going to be easy: Just write Headquarters Marine Corps and have them send over the medal. It didn't happen.

The Marine Corps sent replacement medals for the ones lost but said that it could find no evidence of his father's heroism in Vietnam. If there had been a recommendation for a Navy Cross, it had long since been lost. Now what?

Michael started calling government officials, writing historical societies and placing ads in military publications trying to track down other survivors of the battle. As the months passed, the costs escalated, and Michael was finally forced to tell his dad what he was up to.

Thomas was at first reluctant to talk about it, but when he learned of his son's quest, he opened up and gave him the names of some of the guys he had served with in Vietnam. Thomas told of one buddy who had been shot in the same battle, and Michael said maybe he would help.

"No, son," Thomas said quietly. "He's dead."

"Are you sure?"

"He caught a bullet in the forehead and the back of his

head was blown off," Thomas said as he remembered a battle that had happened before Michael was born.

This startled Michael, to hear his father speak so bluntly. Nevertheless, Michael pressed on and got another name, a kid from Chicago.

Michael went to the phone book. There were thirteen people with the same last name in the Chicago phone book, and Michael started calling. One guy said he wasn't the one, but his barber knew the guy Michael was looking for.

Bingo! He had something to go on now, and other things started falling into place for him.

Because Lieutenant Bobo had been awarded the Medal of Honor for the same action, the detective in Michael began to surface.

"I figured whoever recommended Lieutenant Bobo for his Medal of Honor," Michael said, "would have been the one to recommend a medal for my father."

The man was Colonel George Navadel, who not only remembered submitting the medal recommendation for Thomas but also what it said. Michael was closing and the medal for his dad was in sight.

Other veterans and military people agreed with Michael that his dad should have been recommended for a high medal; a Navy Cross seemed in order. Three other Navy Crosses had been awarded for heroism during the battle, and the courage of Thomas Butt certainly warranted consideration. However, before he knew it, the paperwork that had begun nineteen years earlier was completed, and his father had been awarded a Silver Star.

The odyssey ended on the parade field of the Marine Barracks in Washington, D.C., in the summer of 1986. Standing at attention while the citation was read, Thomas received the Silver Star before a crowd of four thousand people and one proud son.

Michael's persistence had paid off when the medal was pinned on his father, but he received something else, an understanding that the country is only beginning to appreciate—that Vietnam produced more brave men than it did draft dodgers.

JOHN P. BOBO

Rank: Second Lieutenant **Date:** March 30, 1967
Unit: I Company, 3rd Bat- **Place:** Near Dong Ha,
talion, 9th Marines Quang Tri Province
  Born: Niagara Falls, New York, February 14, 1943

It was hot and muggy.

It seems that the guys in Vietnam were either swimming in sweat or shivering cold. A lot of people in the Real World didn't know that, but yeah, it got cold in Vietnam. Not the stinging cold of a Colorado winter, but the dull, penetrating, damp cold that jungle fighters know.

But it wasn't cold that afternoon in March in 1967. At least, not in northern I Corps near Hill 70 west of Dong Ha. Nope, it was flat-out hot and humid as the Marines from India Company Three-Nine awaited the return of their platoon commanders from the afternoon briefing.

Up near the DMZ (Demilitarized Zone), the Marines were fighting the North Vietnamese Army regulars. It was a different type of war than the one being waged to the south against the Vietcong guerrilla forces. Down there, the enemy was often hard to identify, but not in northern I Corps.

The enemy here was well equipped and well trained, and there was no mistaking him. Although the North Vietnamese didn't publicize the fact that their army was engaged in combat in the south, the Marines knew better. About the only thing the North Vietnamese didn't have in their arsenal was air support.

It was conventional warfare in every other aspect; it was good guys and bad guys going after each other.

And that's what I Company was waiting to do.

The platoon commanders returned from the briefing and began to move their platoons into ambush positions. It was getting late in the afternoon, but the heat hung over the Marines like a blanket as they saddled up and moved out. The low hills were covered by dense, waist-high brush that concealed the waiting NVA.

The 1st Platoon moved north along a trail to a junction and then west. The first squad of the 2nd Platoon moved northwest about nine hundred meters to establish a possible ambush site. The other squads of the 2nd Platoon established a perimeter around the company command group (CP) on Hill 70 and the 3rd Platoon remained in the position it held the day before.

Lance Corporal Thomas Butt settled his machine gun team near the CP and set up a night ambush position. At about six P.M., two NVA soldiers stood up in an open area in front of the Marine CP and waved toward the Marines. The Marines opened fire.

Immediately, a reinforced NVA company launched its surprise attack and opened fire on the Marines. In addition to the intense small-arms and automatic-weapons fire, the enemy was lobbing in 60-mm mortars. Although caught by surprise, Second Lieutenant John Bobo, the Weapons Platoon commander, organized a hasty defense, and began moving from position to position consolidating and encouraging the outnumbered Marines.

The initial enemy attack had resulted in numerous Marine casualties, and when the enemy attempted to overrun the position, Lance Corporal Butt rushed his machine gun team forward through heavy automatic-weapons fire. After he set up a forward slope defense, Butt began delivering devastating fire on the advancing NVA.

The battle was in full swing now, not the sanitized Hollywood version, but real combat. Explosions from grenades and mortars rocked the hillside as the wounded groaned with pain.

The enemy was closing on Butt's machine gun position now, and he was forced to relocate to a more tenable position. As the battle raged on, Butt was forced to move again and again, but each time, he redeployed and delivered a deadly barrage on the enemy.

Despite the overwhelming odds, the Marines on Hill 70 were cutting the NVA to pieces. However, due to their odd behavior, the Marines seemed to think that the NVA riflemen were heavily doped. The enemy soldiers seemed to be walking in a daze, muttering to themselves. A great many of them were killed while they wandered around.

However, even in this dazed state, the enemy swarmed over the hillside and Lance Corporal Butt was forced to move his gun team back inside the CP perimeter where Lieutenant Bobo had organized his defenses. The lieutenant was continually exposing himself to enemy fire as he moved from position to position, encouraging his men. One of his 3.5 rocket launchers came under heavy fire, and its team leader was killed.

The lieutenant ordered Butt to leave his machine gun and man the rocket launcher. Butt unhesitatingly rushed to the rocket launcher and, despite being shot in the right forearm, fired rocket after rocket on the advancing enemy.

Lieutenant Bobo was continuing to lead his Marines when an exploding mortar round severed his right leg below the knee. Despite the terrible wound, Lieutenant Bobo killed several enemy soldiers as they approached.

When he saw an enemy soldier standing over First Sergeant Raymond Rogers who had been shot in the leg, the lieutenant killed the NVA, saving the first sergeant's life.

Meanwhile, Lance Corporal Butt had been shot two more times, and due to a paralyzed right arm was unable to continue to fire the rocket launcher. He returned to his machine gun team and continued to direct its fire on the enemy. Repeatedly, the young lance corporal refused to leave his team.

He'd traded his weapon for Bobo's .45 and Lance

Corporal Butt killed several NVA soldiers left-handed with the pistol. As other Marines fell, Butt began pulling them to safety.

Lieutenant Bobo's leg was bleeding badly. Sergeant Rogers stated later, "I pleaded with Lieutenant Bobo to crawl to the rear and try to stop the bleeding. He refused and asked me to tie his leg off [with a web belt]."

The enemy continued to press the attack, and because of the overwhelming odds, the CP was forced to withdraw to a covered position. The lieutenant refused to be evacuated and told the wounded first sergeant to give him more ammunition for his shotgun and to help him get back on line so he could cover the withdrawal.

Once back in position on the ridge line, Lieutenant Bobo jammed the stump of his leg into the dirt to help curtail the bleeding. He assumed a semi-sitting position and continued to fire on the main enemy force that was advancing.

Noticing that Rogers had been wounded, Butt rushed to his aide and provided first aid. Then, as the CP moved back, Butt pulled First Sergeant Rogers to safety.

Shortly after moving Rogers, Lance Corporal Butt was disabled after being shot for the fourth time, the bullet going into his right leg, ricochetting across his abdomen, and lodging in his left leg. He was out of action, but his lieutenant continued the fight.

"The last time I saw Lieutenant Bobo alive," First Sergeant Rogers recalled, "he was in a half-sitting position, firing his shotgun.

"By his raw courage, dogged determination, and unselfish devotion to duty, he was a tremendous inspiration to the Marines fighting with him. I have never witnessed a more heroic act in my twenty years of service in the United States Marine Corps."

Chaplain

OFFICE OF THE DIVISION CHAPLAIN
1ST MARINE DIVISION (REIN), FMF
FPO, SAN FRANCISCO 96602

5 September 1967

FROM: Division Chaplain
TO: Force Chaplain, Fleet Marine Force (Pacific)
SUBJECT: Report of death; case of Lt. Vincent R. Capodanno, CHC, USN

1. At 0200 on 5 September 1967, this chaplain received an unofficial report that Lieutenant Vincent R. Capodanno, CHC, USN, had been killed in action late Monday 4 September 1967. Colonel Sam Davis, Regimental Commander of the 5th Marines, confirmed this officially at 0730 this date.

IT was terse, abrupt, and empty of emotion. It was a preliminary battlefield report noting that a man had been killed in combat. It said little about the man and nothing about the circumstances of his death; just that he was a chaplain and his death had been officially confirmed.

VINCENT R. CAPODANNO

Rank: Lieutenant (U.S. Navy)   **Date:** September 4, 1967

Unit: 3rd Battalion, 5th Marines   **Place:** South of Da Nang

Born: Staten Island, New York, February 13, 1929

Vincent Capodanno graduated from Curtis High School in New York City, and from there he went to Fordham University and Maryknoll Seminary, where he was ordained in June 1957. Father Capodanno belonged to the Catholic Foreign Missionary Society and served as a missionary in Taiwan and Hong Kong from 1958 to 1965.

When the war in Vietnam began to escalate in 1965, he volunteered to serve as a Navy chaplain with the Marines in Vietnam. He had served one tour with the 1st Battalion, 7th Marines. "Father C." went where the grunts went, and they liked having him around; he understood them.

"Father," a reporter said jokingly to him once, "that's not a very good advertisement for your faith, that flak jacket."

"I know," the priest replied, "but it's protective coloration so I blend in with the men. In addition, I understand their trials better if I accept the same burdens they do, such as wearing the jacket and carrying a pack."

"Do you go on operations, Father?"

"I make all battalion-sized operations."

"Have you ever been ambushed?"

"No, just exposed to general fire. And believe me, I was frightened. You have no idea where it's coming from or who it's aimed at. And like everybody else, I dread the possibility of stepping on a booby trap."

Despite his fears, Father C. remained with the Marines. In May 1967 he was recommended for a Bronze Star by Major E. F. Fitzgerald, who wrote:

"Few men have seen more combat action than their chaplain. Invariably he sought out that unit which was most likely to encounter the heaviest contact. He would then go out with that unit and continually circulate along the route of march. During breaks, never resting, he moved among the men.

"When his first tour of duty was over, he requested and was granted a 6-month extension. With his rotation approaching, he wrote to his regimental commander— 'I am due to go home in late November or early December. I humbly request that I stay over Christmas and New Year's with my men. I am willing to relinquish my thirty days leave.'"

He didn't make it to Christmas.

Massed elements of North Vietnamese and Vietcong units had been eluding Allied Forces in the Que Son Valley of Quang Tin Province for several weeks. The 1st and 3rd Battalions of the 5th Marine Regiment were deployed on Operation Swift in the area looking for three enemy regiments, their reinforcements, and service-supply elements.

Friendly fire support limited the enemy to local superiority at close range. As a result, savage hand-to-hand combat and fighting infiltrators characterized the operation. On the morning of September 4, 1967, M Company, 3rd Battalion, 5th Marines was being heli-lifted to participate in the operation. However, heavy enemy ground fire forced the company to land short of its destination in the valley, and the Marines were walking the rest of the way. The company was in attack formation, scouring the countryside. There was strong evidence that the enemy had been in control of the region for some time. There had been a dozen successful engagements with the enemy in the area since April, and it looked like this operation wouldn't be any different.

Chaplain Capodanno was moving up a small hill with the Command Group of M Company when enemy snipers opened up with sporadic small-arms fire on the lead elements of the 1st Platoon as it reached the base of another hill. The Command Group halted at the crest of the hill it was traversing as the 2nd Platoon moved into a blocking force on the right flank to support the lead element.

However, as the 2nd Platoon advanced to the forward base of one hill, it was pinned down by intense mortar and machine gun fire. The incoming fire was deadly and the 2nd Platoon reported over the radio that it was in danger of being overrun.

"We can't hold out here!" the frantic radioman reported. "We are being wiped out! There are wounded and dying all around!"

Upon hearing this report, Father Capodanno left the relative safety of the Command Group, and ran between seventy-five and one hundred meters to the 2nd Platoon's position. Because of the savage fire, the 2nd Platoon was ordered to fall back to a new defensive position.

"I was operating my radio," Lance Corporal Stephen Lovejoy later reported, "and received word to pull back and form a defensive position."

However, because of the additional weight of the radio, Lovejoy was slowed. He hit the deck to avoid being cut down by an NVA machine gunner. He had to get out of there and up the hill with his buddies. Every second counted, but the enemy fire was vicious.

Lovejoy looked up and saw Father Capodanno scrambling down the hill to his position. The two men lay facedown in the dirt, waiting for the enemy fire to slacken. When it stopped, Father Capodanno and Lance Corporal Lovejoy each grabbed a strap to the heavy radio and dragged it up the hill. Twice they had to dive for cover as the automatic-weapons fire resumed, but with courage and determination the priest and the radioman got the radio up to the new perimeter.

"Without his help," Lovejoy reported later, "I am sure I would have lost my life."

When they reached the top of the hill, the priest moved to a fallen Marine and began to administer last rites when tear gas was deployed and the Marines hurriedly donned their gas masks. The fumes from the tear gas swept over the Marines inside the new perimeter.

In his haste to get back to the perimeter, one Marine had left his mask down the hill. Father Capodanno quickly took his off and handed it to the youngster. "You need it for fighting," the priest said. "I'm all right."

When the other Marines noticed he was without a gas mask, they offered him theirs, but he said, "No, you keep it, you need it more than I do."

When he finished ministering to those inside the perimeter, Father Capodanno moved to a more exposed area where Sergeant Lawrence Peters lay dying. While running to the sergeant's side, a mortar round exploded and peppered the chaplain's arms, hands and legs with shrapnel.

He said the Our Father with Peters just before he died, and then the chaplain moved to a half dozen other wounded Marines, continually exposing himself to the deadly automatic-weapons fire. "Jesus said, 'Have Faith,' " he told them.

Sergeant Howard Manfra had been caught in a crossfire of two enemy automatic weapons on the exposed part of the hill. He had been shot five times and was dazed and unaware of where he was as he lay on the exposed slope.

Father Capodanno ran through the enemy barrage and administered to Sergeant Manfra. Lance Corporal Keith Rounseville noticed that the Chaplain was in the direct line of fire of an enemy machine gun. Rounseville told Father

Capodanno to take cover, but the priest continued to take care of Sergeant Manfra.

When his M16 malfunctioned, Rounseville yelled, "Father, my rifle doesn't work!"

Father Capodanno temporarily halted his task and reached across a hedgerow that was open to additional fire. "Here," Father Capodanno said after he secured Manfra's weapon, "take the sergeant's rifle," and he returned to the NCO. After he bandaged the sergeant's wounds, Father Capodanno said to him, "I have to go to others now."

At that time the North Vietnamese launched an infantry assault up the hill. The NVA charged as Lance Corporal Frederick Tancke was tending Corpsman Armando Leal, who had been shot in the leg and groin. He was trying to stop the bleeding when he saw an enemy soldier set up a machine gun fifteen meters away.

Tancke was shot in the finger by the machine gunner, and he dove into a depression to return fire. Chaplain Capodanno was moving down the hill ministering to more wounded and Tencke shouted to him, "Watch out! There's a Vietcong with a machine gun!" Father Capodanno dove for cover.

When Tancke tried to fire his M16 at the enemy machine gunner, it jammed too. He later stated, "The Vietcong laughed at me, squatted down with his machine gun, and stayed there."

Father Capodanno had reached relative safe cover, but when he saw the wounded corpsman, he leaped up and ran twenty feet and used his body to shield Leal from the enemy machine gun fire. Twenty-seven bullets hit the priest in the head, neck, and back, and Father C. died immediately.

Private First Class Julio Rodriguez later wrote to Father Capodanno's family: "Five of us went to get Father; three Marines were hit while trying to bring in his body. We had to leave him because of the intense fire which had us pinned down. That night we succeeded in bringing in Father's body.

"When we found him he had his right hand over his breast pocket. It seemed as if he were holding his Bible. He had a smile on his face, and his eyelids were closed as if asleep or in prayer.

"Every Marine in Second Platoon liked and respected Father. He refused to carry a weapon, and we were all concerned for his safety. His courage and example inspired us and helped us over many rough spots. I will never forget Father Capodanno and his love and concern for us Marines."

In a memorial service for fallen Marines, Father Capodanno once praised these young men. His eulogy said a lot about them and all of the veterans from Vietnam—the soldiers, the sailors, the airmen, the Marines—who served their country during this trying period in American history.

"We are assembled to pay homage to men we knew and admired . . . God loved them or they would not have been born. God called them when they were most prepared to go. Do not let their names become empty memories. Recall to mind all their good points, the many things we admired in them. Imitate them. In that way their lives will be perpetuated among us. Our monument to them will not be of bronze or marble, but the living monument of all the good we saw in them."

Amen, Father Capodanno, Amen.

P.S.

"IN prison," Jim Stockdale said in his office at Stanford, "when I was in isolation, as I was for about a year, if I wanted to scream at the top of my lungs, there would have been no one who spoke English to hear me, so silence was sensible. When I was in solitary confinement, as I was for three more years, silence was enforced by the Vietnamese. Any kind of noise was justification for punishment. So we lived in a silent world."

He walked around his desk—limped, really—to the bookcase next to the door to get some reading material for his visitor.

He paused and said, "When I came home, people asked, 'What do you think about America? What do you think about the mini-skirt?'

"Here I'd been in this silent room for eight years thinking about God, freedom, and immortality.

"Oh, I didn't pay much attention to that stuff. All I could think of was what a *noisy* place America was. Everybody seemed to be talking, talking, talking, about trivial matters. Then there was all of the background noise of honking horns, rock 'n' roll. I started to call it, to myself, 'the big

world of yackety-yack.' I had trouble figuring out why all
the chatter; what was worth so much talk?"

The visitor laughed, but after he left, the question
haunted him. He traveled the country from the shores of the
Chesapeake Bay to the surf at Redondo Beach looking for
an answer. He stopped at a dozen places in between until
finally the visitor stopped in Greeley, Colorado. Jim and
Maureen Bowen loaned him their basement, which was
cool and dark and safe, and there he wrote a letter.

June 17, 1988

Dear Admiral,

I've been thinking about your question, and I
thought I'd try and answer it for you. You certainly
earned it. Rip Van Winkle slept for twenty years and
woke to a new world. Although your eight years in
prison were more intense, your return to freedom must
have been as bewildering.

The Vietnam War exploded during the Sixties, by
far the most controversial decade in this country's
history. Conventional ideas, traditional institutions,
and historical perspectives were trampled by stamped-
ing events.

Few experienced so much of the war and, at the
same time, missed so much of the Sixties as you did.
When you were flying cover for the *Maddox* and the
Turner Joy in the Gulf of Tonkin in August 1964, the
Sixties were just taking off. At that time the Dow was
733, gold was selling for $34 an ounce, and the posted
price for Mideast oil was $1.80 a barrel. The federal
budget for 1964 was $97.9 billion, which was $100
million less than the 1945 federal budget. It was the
last time the budget balanced.

In 1964 and 1965, we had a lot to talk about.

Lee Iacocca was riding high at Ford with his new
Mustang and Ralph Nader was bitching about safety
violations in Detroit.

John Wayne had licked cancer and was talking to reporters. "I'm the stuff real men are made of!" And Lenny Bruce was being arrested for talking dirty.

Hollywood was talking about new television shows *The Wild, Wild West*, *The FBI*, *The Big Valley*, *I Spy*, *F Troop*, *Green Acres*, and *Hogan's Heroes*.

Yogi Berra was talking about his new job as Yankee manager. "I'd like to thank all of the people who made this necessary."

And then we crossed the Pacific on the AKA *Union* and LPD *Vancouver*, hit the beach at Da Nang and smelled Death for the first time.

We were talking about the obituaries of Herbert Hoover, Winston Churchill, Malcolm X, King Farouk, Amos Alonso Stagg, Edward R. Murrow, Stan Laurel, Adlai Stevenson, Somerset Maugham, Alvin York and Cole Porter.

Overseas they were talking about Khrushchev being booted out for Brezhnev; China exploding the bomb; charges that the Beatles were part of a "Communist Master Music Plot"; and Ferdinand Marcos being elected president of the Philippines.

Pentagon officials were talking about an old Ethiopian draft notice, circa 1935, that read:

"Everyone will now be mobilized and all boys old enough to carry a spear will be sent to Addis Ababa. Married men will take their wives to carry food and cook. Those without wives will take any woman without a husband. Women with small babies need not go. The blind, those who cannot walk or for any reason cannot carry a spear are exempted. Anyone found at home after the receipt of this order will be hung."

A Pentagon official sighed. "Now that's how to run a draft!"

Liz Taylor and Richard Burton married for the first time.

Smokers were switching to cigars—Edie Adams and the Tiparillo girl; and the Surgeon General reported on smoking.

Cassius Clay was talking and talking and talking, telling his critics after he failed his pre-induction military aptitude test, "I said I'm the greatest. I never said I was the smartest."

Martin Luther King, Jr., was presented the Nobel Peace Prize.

And from Paris Madame Nhu was hissing, "The Americans don't understand Vietnam and never will."

Outside the Mayflower Hotel in Washington, a nineteen-year-old Georgetown student celebrated the landslide victory of LBJ with too much booze, and he went outside to throw up. The doorman went over and chided him, "You can't do that here!" The kid slurred back, "Why not? I got it here!"

Bell-bottoms were in.

On Okinawa a 26-year old sergeant was trying to familiarize his young troops with night life in the Orient. He took a short sip from a bottle of rice wine and chased it with half a Coke. "That's how you drink saki." One of his eighteen-year-old Marines said, "Gimme that!" and opened a fresh bottle and drank half of it. "Aren't you going to chase it?" the sergeant asked in awe. The kid downed the rest of the bottle and said, "Now that's how you drink saki!"

The Pope came to America and someone said God was dead.

There was the New York City Blackout, the first one.

On campuses we were talking about free speech and free love, birth control and cohabitation, ". . . love leasing and super going steady."

And during Operation Harvest Moon, Barney Bar-

num stood up in the middle of the fight and pointed out
enemy targets for the gunships.

There was a Christmas truce and the war stopped for
a moment. Marine Corporal Mike Wilson, my buddy
from Greeley High School, was on patrol with Bravo,
One-Nine, just after the truce had ended, and the
Marines came across some VC. Mike's lieutenant
decided not be the one to fire first—I guess he was
hoping that the peace would last; it didn't. The
lieutenant got shot in the stomach; the point man got
shot in the leg; and Mike ran forward, picked up the
wounded point man, and on the way back, got shot in
the back.

And by the end of 1965, there were over 200,000
Americans in Vietnam and 23,000 marched in Washington against the war.

In 1966 and 1967 we were talking about: Truman
Capote's new book *In Cold Blood*; the rise of *Batman*
and the fall of *Ozzie and Harriet*; and in the theaters it
was *Dr. Zhivago*, *A Thousand Clowns*, *The Spy Who
Came In From The Cold* and *Thunderball*.

Timothy Leary was talking about drugs.

A teenage girl was saying, "The boys I know look
more like girls than the girls I know."

Marshall McLuhan was saying ". . . if it weren't
for the hot media, the war in Vietnam would be over in
an hour."

David Brinkley was saying, "The star system, as
applied to the reporting of the news, takes the form of
one man or two men, appearing every day in the role
of the all-wise, all-knowing journalistic superman, and
it is absurd."

And everybody was talking about the hippies.

Lyndon Johnson was talking about the polls; Mao
was talking about China's Cultural Revolution.

Negroes were talking about Black Power; Mexican-

Americans were talking about Brown Power; and the
older citizens were talking about Gray Power.

William O. Douglas was divorcing his third wife
and taking a twenty-three-year-old for his fourth.

And your wife, Sybil, and the other POW wives
were talking to whomever would listen about their
husbands' plight; the government wasn't saying much
about the prisoners publicly.

Jackie Kennedy was in Hawaii and saying, "I had
forgotten and my children have never known what it
was like to discover a new place unwatched and
unnoticed."

In Austin, sniper Charles Whitman killed his mom
and then went on a rampage.

In Washington, everyone was talking about the fall
of Adam Clayton Powell and Ferdinand Marcos was
addressing Congress.

And, yes, the mini-skirt vs. the maxi-skirt.

In Canada, draft dodgers from America were talking
about Vietnam; and in Vietnam, LBJ was talking to the
troops.

In Boston the hot topics were a strangler, eighteen-
year-old Bobby Orr, and Carl Yasztremski.

There was the SDS and Super Bowl I.

And deaths included Walt Disney, Goose Tatem,
Henry Luce at *Time*, Spencer Tracy, J. Robert Oppen-
heimer, Jayne Mansfield, and Vivien Leigh—and before Challenger there was the Apollo tragedy.

Everybody was buzzing over the rise in the federal
budget to $169.2 billion.

New Orleans District Attorney Jim Garrison was
talking conspiracy in the assassination of John
Kennedy; there were go-go girls; Reagan running for
President; the defection of Joe Stalin's daughter; the
new *Dean Martin Show*; and why the POWs in Hanoi
were "confessing."

In the hills around Da Nang, the call went out for

volunteers for the Marine Corps Band and a young grunt's hand went up and he was trucked to the air base to audition. The man before him played the flute symphonically and when asked what instrument he wanted to play in the band, this combat-weary Marine said confidently, "The flute!" However, when he blew into the flute, a razzberry came out and the band director snarled, "You dumb son of a bitch, you can't play the flute." The Gyrene said, "They didn't ask me that; they asked if I wanted to be in the band, and yeah, I want to be in the band!"

The exasperated director droned, "You don't know how to play."

Bob fired back, "I CAN LEARN!"

In Israel, a Palestinian refugee was telling the world, "Even if the present crisis with Israel should end in a debacle like the Suez Canal, we wouldn't give up our hopes. Neither we nor our children will ever stop dreaming about Palestine. If you doubt it just remember the example of the Jews. They waited two thousand years."

Support for the war was growing despite protests, and the troop level in Vietnam was at 470,000.

The Panama Canal was winning sovereignty, and in Newark it was Battlefield U.S.A. and revolution.

Dr. Spock was talking about the war and getting into trouble; kids were experimenting with drugs and getting stoned; and women were taking the pill, jumping into bed and not getting pregnant.

Muhammed Ali was being convicted for refusing induction while auto-insurance rates soared.

Dark Shadows, The Flying Nun, The Guns of Will Sonnett, High Chapparal, and *NYPD.*

Also in 1967, there was a Peace march being planned on Washington, the assassination of American Nazi George Rockwell, the cancelling of *What's My Line?,* Dean Rusk's daughter marrying a "Negro," the

Jimi Hendrix Experience, the new Alberta oil field that
might cause oil prices to go up to $2.55 a barrel, peace
protests across the country, a march on the Pentagon
and photographs of POWs in *Life* magazine.

John Bobo died protecting his men; Father C. died
praying for his; and Larry Smedley died charging the
enemy.

In Iran, they were talking about "Booming Teheran"
and the coronation of a king.

At the U.N., Resolution 242 was adopted calling for
the withdrawal of Israeli forces from occupied territo-
ries and for Arab recognition of Israeli sovereignty
"within secure and recognized boundaries."

At USC they were talking about O. J. Simpson. And
Latimer died in Stumpy's arms.

Cardinal Spellman and Otis Redding died; Westmoreland sees "the beginning of the end"; and a
Marine father volunteered for Vietnam to get his son
out of danger. (He said first sergeants live longer than
corporals.) When he landed at Dong Ha he asked
where his son's company was located and he was told
it had been in a fight the night before. "Do you know
Corporal Churchill?" the father asked. "Yeah, he was
killed."

And in 1968, boy! did we have a lot to talk about.

The North Koreans seized the U.S.S. *Pueblo* and
Laugh-In premiered the same day.

There was the first heart transplant patient, the
Reserves being called up, "Zap! There Goes Batman"
and after Tet a cartoon of LBJ in bed with a phone
saying, "What the hell's Ho Chi Minh doing answering
our Saigon embassy phone?" Terry Graves and Larry
Maxam chose loyalty over life; the soldiers cheered as
Pat Brady and his crew emerged from the foggy valley
floor with wounded Americans; and the Marines at
Khe Sahn watched in awed silence as Gene Ashley

tried again and again to get to the top of that damned
hill.

And Bill Barber ordered his regiment to stay out of
Washington, D.C., because of a peace march. Not
much talk about that.

Joe Jackson flew into the enemy-held airstrip to save
three buddies, and then he flew some milk to the
Special Forces. The Marines got some milk, too—real
milk. A mechanic from motor transport—his hands
covered with garage grime—shoved his canteen cup
elbow-deep into the pot. As grease and oil rose to the
surface, the bewildered grunt who was next in line
stared into the 20-gallon pot of marbled milk and then
at the mechanic. The grunt shrugged, put down his
unused canteen cup, picked up a metal meal tray and
began pounding on the mechanic's head.

As he was being pulled off the grease monkey,
he said, "It was so white, so clean. He ruined it!"
The mechanic was revived and he got back in line; the
grunt was psychoanalyzed and he got back to the
jungle.

We were also talking about Black Jack Pershing's
grandson being KIAed; Michael Rockefeller disap-
pearing in New Guinea, the furor over Pet Clark
touching Harry Belafonte on an NBC Special (the ad
man said that a black man touching a white girl would
reflect poorly on Plymouth), Cary Grant using LSD,
the abortion revolution, a beleaguered LBJ dropping
out of the race, Jim Garrison threatening to subpoena
Bobby Kennedy, Martin Luther King, Jr., being murdered and forty U.S. cities exploding in racial violence.

The Black Panthers were in a firefight with Oakland
Police; television commercials went sexy; there was
talk about peace talks in Paris; Helen Keller died; and
Bobby Kennedy was leading in the polls when Sirhan
murdered him.

Jay Vargas carried Bill Weise to safety at Dai Do; and Jim Livingston—that salty dirt farmer from Georgia—led his company in to help Jay's.

There was the riot in Chicago, *The Mod Squad*, *Hawaii Five-O*, Detroit defeating the Cards, the Russians sending the tanks into Prague, Nixon winning and Wayne Morse losing.

There was "Light at the end of the tunnel" (somebody said, "Yeah, it's a train!"); a lady jockey; the prime rate went to 6.5; Nixon's "can-do" cabinet (Schultz at Labor, Mitchell at Justice, Volpe at Transportation, Stans at Commerce, Hickel at Interior, Laird at Defense and Rogers at State).

Al Lynch found where the rubber meets the road.

Joe Namath shaved his Fu Manchu on television for $10,000. And while he tugged desperately on Ron Playford's cartridge belt, Ron Coker . . . aw, hell.

Also in 1969 Julie married David Eisenhower; the Israelis coldly executed a raid against Beirut airport in response to a terrorist attack; the Jets upset the Colts in the Super Bowl; the federal budget was up to $195 billion; the plane hijacking epidemic; the deaths of Allen Dulles, Boris Karloff, Gabby Hayes, Ike, John L. Lewis, Judy Garland, Ho and Everett Dirksen.

Wes Fox led his men through a Dewey Canyon and then he went home to Dotti Lu and his two girls.

The Code of Military Justice was on trial, the government predicted a negotiated settlement in Vietnam by December and the Smothers Brothers were cancelled. Did you know that their dad was a POW during World War II? I believe he died in a Japanese prison.

During the fierce fighting in the northern provinces of South Vietnam, someone asked a kid how long he'd been in the Marines and he drawled, "All . . . fucking . . . day!"

There was a riot at Harvard, gun-toting militants at

Cornell, and S. I. Hayakawa had chairs thrown at him at Colorado.

Northern Ireland erupted in violence; My Lai; King Idris I was overthrown in Libya; the Dow was at 876; the Tate/La Bianca murders; peace delegations to Hanoi; The Great Woodstock Rock Jam; Billy Martin was in another fist fight. And you offered your life for the guys in the next cell.

"The Amazing Mets" won the Series, Tiny Tim married Miss Vickie on *The Tonight Show* and Charley Manson's gang was arrested.

In 1970, people were talking about the split up of the Hell's Angels and the hippies; Willie Sutton; "The Marina Oswald Story" the Yablonski murders; the Steelers signing Terry Bradshaw; and the new Watergate complex in Washington, the residents included Vince Lombardi, John and Martha Mitchell, Maurice Stans, Rosemary Woods, and the Democratic National Committee headquarters was on the Sixth Floor. *Newsweek* wrote:

> "The worst shortcoming of the Watergate, in the opinion of many of its residents, is that it is burglar-prone . . . and the live-in presence of a determined crimefighter such as the attorney general doesn't seem to matter much. There were more than two dozen thefts and fifteen burglaries last year—including the heist of $7,000 in jewels from the apartment of the President's own Rosemary Woods."

New on television were, *The Mary Tyler Moore Show*, *The Flip Wilson Show*, *The Odd Couple*, *Monday Night Football*; Smokin' Joe won the heavyweight title; the Dow was at 757.46; Jane Fonda declared war on the U.S. military establishment; My Lai won a

Pulitzer; and John Baca held the hand of a blinded Vietnam veteran in a San Diego hospital. The poor fellow had been crying.

There was Kent State, Jackson State, and the deaths of Jimi Hendrix, Janis Joplin, Jim Morrison, Charles De Gaulle and Gamal Abdel Nasser.

Women's Lib invaded the church and the Son Tay rescue mission failed. You heard about that, didn't you?

In 1971, someone described the new ruler of Libya, "A handsome man with a lean, hollow-cheeked look, Gaddafi is known for his brashness and impetuosity"; Green Beret Jeffrey MacDonald went on trial for killing his wife and children; and John Lennon said, "The dream is over. I'm not just talking about the Beatles. I'm talking about the generation thing. It's over and we gotta—I have to personally—get down to the so-called reality."

George McGovern declared; Congress quietly rescinded the Gulf of Tonkin Resolution; and just as quietly, President Nixon signed it. Nobody wanted to talk about that.

Dee Brown wrote *Bury My Heart at Wounded Knee*, the Green Berets turned over their last camp to the ARVN, Idi Amin overthrew Apollo Obote, and Grace Slick named her daughter "god".

Squeaky Fromme, twenty-two, described her life in the Manson Family; later she tried to shoot President Ford. Jackie visited the Nixons at the White House; the country was cooling; the Radicals took time out to retrench; and it was all quiet on the campus front.

Ali lost his first fight with Smokin' Joe, and for the first time anyone could remember, he wasn't talking and everybody was talking about that.

There were aerobics, the geodesic dome, Evonne Goolagong, and Senator Sam Erwin said about the snooping by the Army and the FBI: "If we are going to be a free society, the Government is going to have to take some risks. It can't put everyone under surveillance. . . ."

George C. Scott said he wouldn't accept an Oscar: "The whole thing is a goddamn meat parade. I don't want any part of it."

The Senate was bombed by radicals; a Datsun (Nissan now) was selling for $2,350; Colonel Anthony Herbert charged a general with covering up atrocities; Thomas Dewey—"Give 'em Hell Harry's" 1948 opponent—died; wages and prices were stabilized; and the FBI files were stolen from Media, PA, offices.

Mary Ann Vecchio, the girl who was pictured over Jeff Miller's body at Kent State, was in a juvenile home; Bangladesh; Ping-Pong diplomacy; a black hole in space was discovered; Disneyland East; Ulster's violent children; Chicago's Richard Daley wins again; CBS broadcast "Selling of the Pentagon"; and growing criticism of the FBI.

There were questions about whether or not Lockheed would be saved; the Harrisburg Six; the Chicago Seven; antiwar protest in Washington; Papa Doc died and Baby Doc took over; and Martha Mitchell was on the phone talking to reporters.

Ronald Reagan had a no-tax plan; the world monetary crisis exploded; Al Capp was charged with a morals violation he claimed was inspired by the political left; *Sesame Street* was under fire; rookie Vida Blue was pitching for the A's; and Frank Serpico was talking to the Knapp Commission about police corruption in New York City.

Angela Davis was charged with involvement in the San Rafael shootout; mass murderer Juan Carona was going on trial; Tricia Nixon married; and Audie Murphy died.

There was group sex; the great airfare war; *The Pentagon Papers*, Daniel Ellsberg, *The Godfather*; the

President's war on drugs; and in Albuquerque a Street-nik said, "Hey, man, the radio says we got a riot here. Let's give 'em a riot."

The Yablonski murders were solved; Dick Greogry fasted; Joe Columbo was gunned down during an Italian-American rally; and eighteen-year-olds got the vote.

Viet vet unemployment was at 14.2 percent, twice the national average; Jim Garrison was arrested and charged with taking a bribe to protect illegal pin-ball gambling; Ed Muskie began his campaign; and Louis Armstrong, Van Heflin, Nikita Khrushchev, Spring Byington, and *Look* magazine died.

Everybody was striking; men were riding around the moon in a go-cart; people were opting for pay television; Congress bailed out Lockheed; the dollar was devalued, and in 1971 there were riots at San Quentin, Rahway and Attica.

Ron Ziegler said, "The President is aware of what is going on in Southeast Asia. That is not to say anything is going on in Southeast Asia."

Cocaine had become the latest "groove"; H. Rap Brown was wounded in an FBI shootout, sky marshals and D. B. Cooper were on planes; and Jesus Christ was a Super Star.

Nebraska and Oklahoma played a football classic; Jesse Jackson broke with SCLC; and Clifford Irving wrote a hoax.

Time magazine reporters interviewed Richard Nixon for the Man of the Year cover story, and said they would tape the conversation, but presidential aides said that the White House would provide its own tapes. However, the tapes provided by the White House were so poor that half of the conversation was unintelligible.

In 1972, Henry Kissinger was jetting to China.

And in Hanoi Jane Fonda was making propaganda broadcasts against America and being photographed in an enemy antiaircraft gun position, like the one that shot you down. When the government refused to do anything about her treason, many of us began hating her.

Richard Kleindienst became Attorney General when John Mitchell took over the Campaign to Re-elect the President (CREEP); and James McCord rented an office next to Ed Muskie's campaign headquarters. At the time Muskie was the number-one Democratic contender and was leading Nixon in the polls.

Bob Hope talked to North Vietnamese officials about releasing the POWs as other celebrities avoided South Vietnam visits because, according to a USO official, ". . . [it] reflects the general community feeling on the war. Everybody's sick of it, and most don't want to be identified with supporting a military effort that is bad news for everybody."

Shirley Chisolm announced her presidential bid; the last Japanese soldier from World War II surrendered on Guam; saccharin was banned; Chris Evert, 17, beat Billie Jean King; Nixon went to China; the Berrigan trial began; and nine million cars were recalled.

Miss Vickie filed against Tiny Tim.

ITT pledged $400,000 to CREEP, and the Justice Department dropped an anti-trust suit. Ditta Beard wrote in a memo, "I thought you and I had agreed very thoroughly that under no circumstances would anyone in this office discuss with anyone our participation in the Convention including me. Other than permitting John Mitchell, Ed Reinecke, Bob Haldeman and Nixon . . . no one has known from whom that four hundred thousand commitment had come. You can't imagine how many queries I've had from 'friends' about this situation." Jack Anderson wrote about that one.

M*A*S*H was on television; the Shah of Iran cracked down on political foes; the Alaska pipeline got the go-ahead, George Wallace was shot; and Groucho

Marx said, "A man is only as old as the woman he feels."

Nixon mined the harbors; the Weathermen bombed the Pentagon; and Japanese terrorists killed twenty-six in an airport massacre. Someone lamented, "Japanese terrorists killing Italian tourists because the Arabs hate the Jews."

And in the late spring of 1972, one of the burglars caught in the Watergate break-in said, "Don't shoot! You've got us."

The Supreme Court outlawed capital punishment; Westmoreland retired; Bobby Fischer played Boris Spassky; McGovern won the nomination; and Eagleton was scratched as his veep because he had had shock treatments; the Russians bought our wheat; and the U.S. ground combat role in Vietnam ended.

Oscar Levant died. "When I was young, I looked like Al Capone, but lacked his compassion." When asked by an Army psychiatrist if he could kill, Levant replied, "I don't know about strangers, but friends, yes."

Ron Ziegler denied White House involvement in Watergate; a secret GOP campaign fund was uncovered by *The Washington Post*; and there were Plumbers in the White House.

And Olga Korbut was the talk of the town in Munich until Arab terrorists killed the Israeli athletes.

The Watergate crew was mum, and Judge Sirica was saying they were going to talk or else; in the end everyone talked but G. Gordon Liddy.

And Howard Cosell, boy, could he talk!

In October, for the first time since March 1965, there were no American battlefield deaths in Vietnam, and we were grateful for that.

Woodward and Bernstein had become the Dynamic Duo; a Louis Harris Poll showed that most voters didn't seem to care much about the Watergate affair;

and Ben Bradley at the *Post* said, "As sure as God
made apples, this story will be with us after election
day." Ben knew what he was talking about.

There was the Nixon landslide as only one state
voted for McGovern: "The Democratic People's Re-
public of Massachusetts".

And an unemployed Viet vet said, "War is hell, but
peace can be a real bitch too."

And at the end of 1972, *Life* died.

In the first couple of months of 1973 just before you
guys came home from the Hanoi Hilton, we were
talking about the White House feud with *Post*; the
heaviest bombing raid in history against Hanoi; the
death of "Give 'em Hell, Harry" and LBJ; and the
Chilian rugby players who were eating their dead.

The price of gas in the U.S. was thirty-seven cents
a gallon and the following government proclamation
was issued:

> "Suitable jobs are to be reserved, I repeat, re-
> served for Vietnam veterans. Official policy has
> been established that while waiting for work, they
> will receive the same salary they got in the
> service. Professional and specialist schools must
> reserve places for wounded veterans . . . Chil-
> dren of dead or wounded veterans are to receive
> educational privileges and special attention
> throughout their schooling."

This is how the North Vietnamese treated their
returning veterans.

And then they said you were coming home. We
talked about that and winced when you limped off the
plane. One of the magazines had a cover story after it
was all over and said, "It was a war that produced no

famous victories, no national heroes . . . and when a cease-fire finally came to Vietnam last week, the American public seemed too exhausted . . . to celebrate."

It was true, the country was too tired to cheer, but that was okay, because we, those of us who were there, knew that we had done our job and had done it well. There were 238 Medals of Honor awarded for service during the Vietnam War, including four POWs held in North Vietnam—George Day, Leo Thorsness, yourself, and Lance Sijan (posthumous).

However, there were only a few national stories at the time about these brave men. Some people didn't even know any Medals of Honor had been awarded. Then someone asked if I was ashamed to be a Vietnam veteran. I said, no, and told her part of the reason in *And Brave Men, Too*, and the rest of it here. I think she understands now.

Well, Jim, that's what we were talking about while you were away. To tell you the truth, I'm surprised we had any strength left to talk at all by the time you came home. If it doesn't make much sense, that's okay, because we were talking about that too.

I've got to go now. Next time I'm in the neighborhood, I'll drop in to see you and we can raise a glass or two, but, please, no saki.

Best regards to Sybil and the family.

I remain,

Faithfully Yours,

Jim

P.S. Jane apologized today, and I can't hate her any longer. I think that means it's over.

Appendix A
Reflections

JOHN BACA —"I'd rather hear something about saving people rather than stories about people blowing away a bunch of people—bunker after bunker, shooting and killing everybody. I guess most people want to hear that, though.

"I've had guys ask, 'How many people did you kill over there, how many civilians?' I think that because I didn't kill anyone it might disappoint some people.

"However, when they dedicated the Vietnam Memorial, I think it changed a lot of peoples' attitudes about Vietnam veterans. Walking in the parade they were saying, 'Thank you and welcome home.'

"I met one guy. He looked at me and I looked at him, and we recognized each other. He said, 'You saved my life the night you were wounded.'

"We hugged and cried.

"It was nice, very moving.

"They marched me out front with the Reserves and all of the Vietnam veterans were way in back. The weekend warriors were stepping all over my feet. I wanted to be with all of the other guys stuck in the back.

"They should have been marching up front, but some organizer decided that this was the way it had to be.

"I looked up this one guy from Kansas City or St. Louis from the 1st Cav. It was a good week. I read names off the Memorial. The chaplain read some names. It was sad, hard."

BARNEY BARNUM —"I did, and my Marines did what we were sent there to do; followed orders and, considering the restraints under which we were operating, I think we did damn well.

"We carry on our shoulders a proud tradition that has been molded by hundreds of thousands who have gone before us, and I'll be damned if we are going to let them down. There have been several times when the odds were phenomenal and how did Marines come through it? Semper Fi.

"Marines don't say that they can do the job; they do it.

"That's why Americans believe in us. I swear to God.

"That is one thing I always remembered; if I got shot, a Marine would never leave me on the battlefield. And I didn't leave anybody on the battlefield. Marines got killed going to the aid of other Marines. That is something we know and we are proud of it.

"And lead. If you can't stand up and lead, then get the hell out of the way. Someone else will do it. Don't tell your people with your hands on your hips to run around the grinder. You be up front running and let them follow you.

"Since I've been in Washington, people come to visit and I take them to The Wall, and it affects me differently every time.

"The first time I went to The Wall was during the Inauguration two years ago. Wheeew! That was a tough day, really tough. That visit shot the rest of the day. I couldn't go out. The gal I was with couldn't believe the effect it had on me.

"First of all, I say this, the location of it overpowers the design—the Lincoln Memorial on one hand and the Washington Monument on the other. What a place of honor. There is not another war memorial in Washington with that prominence. I'm proud of it and what it represents.

"Back in November, I was there with my mom and dad, and I got a little misty eyed. Sometimes, emotionally, I just go to pieces, privately.

"A couple of weeks ago I was there, and I walked away with a little bounce in my step.

"I really felt good."

PAT BRADY —"I feel sorry for anyone who misses an opportunity to serve his country during time of war. They may joke and jive about it at the time, but during later years they come to regret it. I think it leaves a great loneliness and emptiness in their lives. It is an experience you cannot otherwise have.

"We see now that the leadership in this country is being assumed by the Vietnam veteran; the veteran above all other veterans who learned the true meaning of unselfishness.

"That may be why we had such great problems with the Vietnam War. Elements in our society couldn't see what was in it for us; there was no oil, no material wealth, no threat of invasion, no world-wide specter.

"That is one war which represented possibly the most unselfish thing this country has ever done. And perhaps that is why we had such great problems. It was a totally unselfish act to go and help these people help themselves to be free.

"There was nothing in it for us. I don't see how anybody can criticize something like that. People did criticize it, but now look at that part of the world. The very thing we knew would happen if the communists took over did happen. Total, brutal subjugation of the people.

"I believe that the news media of this country showed the ugliest part of their nature during Vietnam. Their job is to tell us the truth about ourselves and, quite frankly, they didn't do that.

"When the media began to flex its muscles, it indicated the real power they had, and they ran rampant in Vietnam. The media people used to come through and write stories that had no basis of fact.

"If you had been in an action or were familiar with what really had happened and read about it or saw it on television, it wasn't even close. Many stories were fabrications.

"I can remember during those years that if I went to talk to an ROTC graduation on a college campus in uniform, I had to be escorted around campus. They feared for my safety.

"In one instance, the college president would not be seen with me, nor would he attend the ROTC graduation— outright cowardice.

"I can also remember standing in parades where politicians would turn away if they saw a camera for fear that a camera would get a picture of them standing next to me, a military guy in uniform.

"I would have gotten out of the military many years ago, but at the time I felt that I would have been irresponsible for running away from a mess.

"We went through a period in the Army where the quality of personnel coming into the Army was not very good. It was during that period that we kind of emasculated our NCO corps, took the responsibilities away from the noncommissioned officers and shifted to a higher level.

"When I came into the service, the NCOs took care of me, taught me, protected me and showed me how to be an officer and to lead men. But we got away from that and it started being handled by the officers.

"Now we are getting back on track. In fact, the quality of the men coming into the military today is superb, on the Army side of the house, anyway.

"The guy coming in today is patriotic, and he is not ashamed of it. That is a beautiful thing to see.

"Now, I am just delighted with the turn around with young people. I don't know how they would fight—they haven't been tested—but the leadership in the Army says they are the finest it has ever seen. The leadership always says that and I didn't agree during some of those years, but now I completely agree.

"Keep in mind, though, that the soldier of today would have to go some to beat the guys I served with in Vietnam, but I would go to war with this guy in a heartbeat. And pity the poor sucker who gets in his way.

"I can ride out of here pretty soon, and know that I will be secure in my old age in his care."

WES FOX —" 'Nobody likes to fight, but somebody needs to know how.'

"Someone said that was a good recruiting slogan. I think that it is dangerous for Marines to harbor those thoughts, primarily, because I don't know anybody who did anything well and didn't like to do it.

"Unfortunately, we lose our best, those who are up moving and going for it. Those who come back just aren't quite as aggressive. Britain knows that, France knows that better than anybody.

"The two times we went back to Vandergrift to provide security, we spent nights on line. But during the day, you could get the best part of your company together for classes.

"I would have a squad go out and set up an L-shaped ambush the way that it ought to be set up—put the machine gun in the proper position, put the Claymore out where it ought to be, put the patrol leader where he should be and establish the kill zone.

"I would get another squad on the trail, walk them into the ambush site and talk them through it step by step.

"What that gave me as the company commander was a company of men who thought the same way, that understood the details of what is expected of each man and what you could expect of the Marine on either side.

"I get a lot of credit for kicking ass and going forward in that fight on the 22nd. But with triple canopy jungle, the banana trees, I could never see more than three or four Marines at a time. In that kind of a situation, had it been a less cohesive unit, we would never have carried the fight forward. Especially after I lost all of my platoon commanders.

"I lost them early in the fight. So it is to the credit of every Marine—the private, the machine gunner, the rifleman, the gunfighter—that we won on the 22nd."

JOE JACKSON — "During the Vietnam War, there was no public support, only apathy. People who didn't serve during that period seemed resentful of those who did.

"The family was delighted and I was delighted to be back home after my tour of duty in Vietnam, but the attitude of the public in general was, 'You were there, so what?' It wasn't like the end of World War II when the soldiers came home, and there was a big celebration welcoming them back home.

"Today, there is a lot of support for the Vietnam veterans. It has changed almost one hundred eighty degrees. And the support seems to be growing.

"In fact, many people today are having second thoughts about not serving, but it's too late now, sport.

"Admiral Stockdale probably has the best insights into the origins of the Vietnam war, and in talking with him and others, I came to the conclusion that it should never have happened.

"However, we as military people—once a war starts—really don't have a choice.

"We took an oath."

JIM LIVINGSTON —"We didn't get beat in Vietnam, we pulled out. We were our own worst critic, and that probably is a positive aspect of our society. However, being our own worst critic, we do ourselves a real disservice in the eyes of the world.

"It is a strength, but also a weakness.

"You have to be astute enough to realize which side of the fence we were on—the strength side or the weakness side—and in Vietnam after Operation Hue City I think there was a tendency to be all on the weakness side.

" 'Oh, we're beat, we're beat, we're beat!'

"Shoot, the fight started and we won it."

AL LYNCH —"I did one tour and they wouldn't let me go back to Vietnam because of the Medal of Honor. I wanted to go back and rejoin my unit. Years later I had a lot of problems because of that. The only regret that I have with the Medal was that when my unit moved north, I stayed back. I guess we got our butts kicked real bad a couple of times.

"When I asked to go north with the guys, I was told, 'No.' When I asked to extend, I was told, 'No.' I obeyed the orders. I still wish I could have gone north, there is still a twinge, especially when I see guys who did more than I did."

"When I was executive director of the Vietnam Veterans Leadership Program and I talked to guys, I would tell them, 'There are guys who are dead, there are guys who are severely wounded, there are guys who have terrible mental problems. Those of us who are able owe it to them to live the very best lives that we can, to honor them. We have to live better, richer, fuller lives and to savor it.'

"I try every way in the world to do that. I have fun. I feel that by raising a family, by raising three good kids, by keeping them off drugs, by teaching them about God, by working with veterans, and by doing some of the things I do, it is a payback, because it honors them, the ones who sacrificed so much.

"Without the Medal of Honor, I could not do the things I do now for veterans. I've made a difference, I know I've made a difference in people's lives. That is really important. It gave guys like me, like Gary Wetzel and other guys, it made us say, 'We owe something, we pay it back.' I think that is why we do it.

"When I worked with the VA as a veterans benefits counselor, I got the job because I had the Medal of Honor. I worked my tail off for guys when they came home. I talked to them, I listened to them, I felt an affinity toward them, because we were brothers.

"I did the very best job I could. Because I got the Medal I was able to go to the hospitals, and work with the guys who came back from 'Nam. The things I did with the Vietnam Veterans Leadership Program made differences. There are three thousand veterans who got jobs because of what we did with the state of Illinois. We made them toe the mark and hire veterans. What I've had the opportunity to do with the attorney general's office for veterans made a difference.

"That's important."

KENNY STUMPF —"*Platoon* was so negative. It really bothers me that it was supposed to be 'the movie' about Vietnam.

"I was so disgusted with that movie. I saw so much bravery and the love of fellow man during the thirty-three months I was in Vietnam. We never went into a village and harassed them, but to see that movie and have the media say, 'That's the way it was in Vietnam.' Well, it wasn't.

"We did so many things for the villagers. In fact, I've got pictures at home of me chopping rice with them. I pounded the rice with them, and it was hard work!

"We really respected the Vietnamese.

"I can understand the frustrations with booby traps; we lost so many people from booby traps. But we didn't go into a village and point out a Vietnamese and say, 'It must have been you,' and blow him away.

"But what that movie said about the infantry soldier is what I disliked. But that's why Jane Fonda loved the movie; that's why the North Vietnamese loved the movie; that's why all of the antiwar people loved the movie. It was fiction, but it reinforced the negative view many had toward the Vietnam veterans.

"Certainly, there was a My Lai, but there weren't a thousand My Lais. My Lai was an unfortunate situation, but it was not the normal thing.

"Over the last four or five years, the Vietnam veterans began getting some long overdue recognition. *Platoon* knocked us back a long way."

Appendix B

Notes

CHAPTER 1

Unless otherwise noted, the material in this chapter is derived from Commanding Officer, M Company, 3rd Battalion, 3rd Marines, 3rd Marine Division (Rein) FMF to Secretary of Navy, Navy Department Board of Decorations and Medals, Subj: Award Recommendation, dated April 21, 1969; Narrative description of gallant action dated April 21, 1969, eyewitness statements April 21, 1969 from Gifford T. Foley, 2447541, CPL USMC; Clifford G. Goodau, 1232247, SSGT USMC; Willie C. Terrell, 2401723, LCPL, USMC; Jimmy D. Murphy, 2449953, PFC, USMC; Tim Barrett, 2485413, PFC, USMC; Warren E. Vanaman, 2437677, USMC; Roberto Valencia, Jr., B829441, HN, USN; Ronald L. Coker award citation, dated April 21, 1969; Reference Section, Marine Corps Historical Center, Washington, D.C.

CHAPTER 2

Unless otherwise noted, the material in this chapter was derived from James Bond Stockdale interview by Timothy S. Lowry, Coronado, California, October 22, 1986; James Bond Stockdale interview by Timothy S. Lowry, Stanford University, Stanford, California, October 28, 1986; personal memorandum from Jim Stockdale to Tim Lowry, August 17, 1988 and August 18, 1988.

CHAPTER 3

Unless otherwise noted, the material in this chapter is derived from John P. Baca interview by Timothy S. Lowry, June 23, 1984, Arlington, Virginia.

CHAPTER 4

Unless otherwise noted, the material in this chapter is derived form Colonel Harvey Barnum interview by Timothy S. Lowry, September 5, 1986, Special Projects Section, Headquarters, United States Marine Corps, Navy Annex, Arlington, Virginia; personal letter, from Colonel Harvey Barnum to Tim Lowry, dated February 10, 1987; Biographical Data, Colonel Harvey C. Barnum, Jr., United States Marine Corps; Reference Section, Marine Corps Historical Center, Washington, D.C.

CHAPTER 5

Unless otherwise noted, the material in this chapter was derived from Joe Jackson interview by Timothy S. Lowry, October 29, 1986.

CHAPTER 6

Unless otherwise noted, the material in this chapter is derived from *The Battle of Khe Sanh*, by Moyers S. Shore II, USMC, May 28, 1969, History and Museum

Division, Headquarters, U.S. Marine Corps, Washington, D.C.

CHAPTER 7

[1] The Marine Corps *Gazette* September 1987, "Memories of Dai Do" by Brigadier General William Weise, USMC (Retired) p. 42
[2] Ibid., p. 43
[3] Ibid., p. 44
[4] Ibid., p. 46
[5] Ibid., p. 46
[6] Ibid., p. 47
[7] Ibid., p. 47
[8] Ibid., p. 45
Unless otherwise noted, the material in this chapter is derived from Colonel Jay R. Vargas, interview by Timothy S. Lowry, November 4, 1986, Navy Amphibious Base, Coronado, California; personal letter from Colonel Jay Vargas to Tim Lowry February 6, 1987; personal letter from BGEN Bill Weise USMC (Ret.) to Tim Lowry June 17, 1987; personal letter from BGEN Bill Weise (rtd.) to Tim Lowry August 15, 1988.

CHAPTER 8

[1] The Marine Corps *Gazette* September, 1987, "Memories of Dai Do", by Brigadier General William Weise, USMC (Retired), p. 48
[2] Ibid., p. 49
[3] Ibid., p. 49
Unless otherwise noted, the material in this chapter is derived from: Colonel James Livingston interview by Timothy S. Lowry, January 7, 1987, Headquarters, 6th Marine Regiment, 2nd Marine Division, Camp Lejeune, North Carolina; personal letter from Colonel Jim Living-

ston to Tim Lowry February 10, 1987; personal letter
from BGEN Bill Weise USMC (Rtd) to Tim Lowry June
17, 1987; personal letter from BGEN Bill Weise (rtd.) to
Tim Lowry August 15, 1988.

CHAPTER 9

Unless otherwise noted, the material in this chapter is
derived from Colonel William Barber, USMC (rtd.),
interview by Timothy S. Lowry May, 1985; Colonel
William Barber, USMC (Ret.) interview by Timothy S.
Lowry June 1, 1986; Marine Corps Historical Center,
Washington, D.C., Reference Section, Biographical
Data, Colonel William Barber, USMC, revised 1966
HQMC.

CHAPTER 10

Unless otherwise noted, the material in this chapter is
derived from "Summary of Recommendation for Award
of Medal of Honor (Posthumous)—Eugene Ashley, Jr.",
Department of the Army, U.S. Army Military Personnel
Center, Alexandria, Virginia, undated; *The Battle for Khe
Sanh*, by Captain Moyers S. Shore II, USMC, pps.
66—68, May 28, 1969, History and Museums Division,
U.S. Marine Corps, Washington, D.C.

CHAPTER 11

Unless otherwise noted, the material in this chapter is
derived from "Award Recommendation—Terrence
Graves", from Major J. E. Anderson, Commanding
Officer 3rd Force Recon Company, 3rd Force Recon
Battalion, 3rd Marine Division, to Secretary of the Navy,
Navy Department Board of Decorations and Medals,

dated May 15,1968; "Summary of Recommendation for
Award of the Medal of Honor (Posthumous)" dated May
15, 1968; eyewitness accounts by Stephen R. Thompson,
HM3 9995919, USN; Danny H. Slocum, Cpl., 2296479,
USMC; Michael P. Nation, LCpl., 2349846, USMC;
Thomas Burns, Capt., USMCR; A.J. Mortimer, Cpl.,
USMC; David F. Underwood, Capt. USMCR; C.E.
Bergman, Capt., USMCR; Edward I. Egan, Capt.,
091560, USMCR; Marine Corps Historical Center,
Washington, D.C., Reference Section.

CHAPTER 12
Unless otherwise noted, the material in this chapter is
derived from Allen Lynch interview by Timothy S.
Lowry July 8, 1988.

CHAPTER 13
Unless otherwise noted, the material in this chapter is
derived from Commanding Officer, D Company, 1st
Battalion, 4th Marines (Rein), 3rd Marine Division
(Rein) FMF to Secretary of Navy (Navy Department of
Decorations and Medals, Subject Award Recommenda-
tion, dated February 15, 1968; Summary Description for
Award of Medal of Honor Posthumous, Larry Maxam;
eyewitness statement dated February 15, 1968, from
Michael Stick, Second Lieutenant, USMCR; Corporal
Larry Maxam (Deceased) Biographical Data, Reference
Section, Marine Corps Historical Center, Washington,
D.C., Reference Section.

CHAPTER 14
Unless otherwise noted, the material in this chapter is
derived from Sergeant Major Kenneth Stumpf interview

by Timothy S. Lowry, November 13, 1987, Irvine, California; Kenneth Stumpf interview by Timothy S. Lowry, November 14, 1987, Irvine, California; personal letter from Ken Stumpf to Tim Lowry dated August 24, 1988.

CHAPTER 15

Unless otherwise noted, the material in this chapter is derived from Lieutenant Colonel Wesley Fox interview by Timothy S. Lowry, January 6, 1987, Quantico, Virginia; personal letter from Lieutenant Colonel Wes Fox to Tim Lowry dated February 6, 1987; Biographical Data, Wes Fox, United States Marine Corps, Reference Section, Marine Corps Historical Center, Washington, D.C.

CHAPTER 16

Unless otherwise noted, the material in this chapter is derived from Biographical File—Larry Smedley, Reference Section, Marine Corps Historical Center, Washington, D.C.; Summary of Recommendation for award of the Medal of Honor (Posthumous)—Larry Smedley, Narrative of Gallant Conduct, dated December 19, 1967. Eyewitnesses: Michael Neil, 2nd Lt., 0101333, USMC; Clayton C. Christiansen, 2nd Lt., 0100116, USMCR; Michael A. Storey, LCpl, 2326908, USMC; Joseph H. Blichfeldt, Capt., 091253, USMC.

CHAPTER 17

Unless otherwise noted, the material in this chapter is derived from Recommendation For Award, October 1968, Colonel W.R. Le Bourdais, MC, 67th Medical

Group, 96337, "Character and Condition of Terrain and Weather", Brigadier General Pat Brady interview by Timothy S. Lowry, September 6, 1986, Fort Meade, Maryland; personal letter from Brigadier General Pat Brady to Tim Lowry, dated February 10, 1987.

CHAPTER 18

Unless otherwise noted, the material in this chapter is derived from Michael Butt interview by Timothy S. Lowry, January 5, 1987; Biographical Data Second Lieutenant John P. Bobo, 092986, USMCR, dated July 1968, HQMC; Commanding Officer, I Company, 3rd Battalion, 9th Marines, 3rd Marine Division (Rein), FMF to Secretary of Navy, Navy Department Board of Decorations and Medals, Subj: Award Recommendation, eyewitness statements from Raymond G. Rogers, 583291, FSGT, USMC; John P. Lange, 2023608, LCPL, USMC. Reference Section, Marine Corps Historical Center, Washington, D.C.

CHAPTER 19

[1] The Marine Corps *Gazzette* October 1985, "For God, Corps and Country" by Commander Ernest F. Passero, CHC, USN, p. 18

[2] Ibid., p. 19

Unless otherwise noted, the material in this chapter is derived from: Lieutenant Vincent R. Capodanno USN (deceased), Biographical Data, Reference Section, Marine Corps Historical Center, Washington, D.C.

P.S.

Unless otherwise noted, the material in this chapter is
derived from personal letter from Tim Lowry to Jim
Stockdale, June 18, 1988; from personal memorandum
from Jim Stockdale to Tim Lowry August 17 and 18,
1988.

Acknowledgements

In 1982 I began researching the Medals of Honor awarded for service in Vietnam. With quiet pride, I read about men who served with courage and honor during a most trying time in American history. In the spring of 1983, I threw a sleeping bag and pup tent on the back of my motorcycle and headed out to find these unacknowledged heroes.

Along the way, I was helped by many old friends and I discovered many new ones. In Leadville, Colorado, I was taken in by my old friends from college days—Rick (Vietnam vet) and Nancy Christmas.

I traded off my motorcycle for "The Orange Crushed," a battered Datsun pickup, and it was on to San Pedro, California, to formulate my plan. Plan in hand, I went to San Diego to see Ollie Wiley III, a machine gunner/ technician who served with me in the First LAAM Battalion on the hills west of Da Nang.

A couple of troopers from the 1st Cav—Herb Edwards and Jon Wallenius—came to the rescue when the thief stole all of my stuff. Herb and his wife, Kathy, bought me time, and Jon bought my vote. Too bad he didn't win.

From California I made half a dozen trips criss-crossing

the country. In Greeley, Colorado, numerous Vietnam Vets and non-vets assisted me in a variety of ways: former Marine officer Meredith P. Davidson got me to the airport on time; Jimmy Martinez (my schoolmate from Heath Junior High School and a cannon cocker in Vietnam) swapped war stories with me; a former chaplain's aide in Vietnam and high school pal, Doug Dunkel, remembered things I hadn't known; and former Navy Corpsman Ron Meltz and Dave Harvey (a London policeman and military historian) played some memories.

It was then on to Crawford, Colorado, to eat fresh venison and trout with John Pladson. After having my fill, I drove to Minnesota to see Bob Pladson and the girls, Robyn and Annie. If it wasn't for this former combat Marine and his "Patented Rides," this story would not have been told. Thanks, Bob.

Then it was on to Naperville, Illinois, and another soldier from the 1st Cav, Tim Millar. He and his wife Bev provided a secured LZ. Fine men, those Sky Troopers.

In Washington, D.C., I went to The Wall and found Latimer. Then Bob and Connie Ray shared their home in Tampa, Florida, while I sweated out the final touches.

The patience and eye for detail of Bill Weise was invaluable.

Then it was back to Greeley and Robbie Johnson's where I printed up the final draft and sent it to Ed Breslin and Jim Morris at Berkley. It was then back to California where I found the Pot of Gold at the end of my rainbow—Belinda.

A special thanks to my brothers, Joe and Mike.

The respect and admiration I feel toward Bill Barber is immense. His faith and encouragement kept me moving forward. To paraphrase Wes Fox: With a leader like that, I was in a no-lose situation; he was always there with the support I needed.

To all of these men, women and children, I will forever be indebted.

To those men of Honor who trusted me . . . I am unable to find the words.

And to all of our veterans from Vietnam—America did not send her best to Vietnam; they became her best.

TRUE ACCOUNTS OF VIETNAM
from those who returned to tell it all . . .

___PHANTOM OVER VIETNAM: FIGHTER PILOT, USMC John Trotti
0-425-10248-3/$3.95

___SURVIVORS: AMERICAN POWS IN VIETNAM Zalin Grant
0-425-09689-0/$3.95

___THE KILLING ZONE: MY LIFE IN THE VIETNAM WAR Frederick Downs
0-425-10436-2/$3.95

___AFTERMATH Frederick Downs
Facing life after the war
0-425-10677-2/$3.95

___NAM Marc Baker
The Vietnam War in the words of the soliders who fought there.
0-425-10144-4/$3.95

___BROTHERS: BLACK SOLDIERS IN THE NAM Stanley Goff and
Robert Sanders with Clark Smith
0-425-10648-9/$3.50

___INSIDE THE GREEN BERETS Col. Charles M. Simpson III
0-425-09146-5/$3.95

___THE GRUNTS Charles R. Anderson
0-425-10403-6/$3.50

___THE TUNNELS OF CU CHI Tom Mangold and John Penycate
0-425-08951-7/$3.95

___AND BRAVE MEN TOO Timothy S. Lowry
The unforgettable stories of Vietnam's Medal of Honor winners.
0-425-09105-8/$3.95

THE BEST IN WAR BOOKS

__ **DEVIL BOATS: THE PT WAR AGAINST JAPAN**
__ **William Breuer** 0-515-09367-X/$3.95
A dramatic true-life account of the daring PT sailors who crewed the Devil Boats—outwitting the Japanese.

__ **PORK CHOP HILL S.L.A. Marshall**
__ 0-515-08732-7/$3.95
A hard-hitting look at the Korean War and the handful of U.S. riflemen who fought back the Red Chinese Troops.
"A distinguished contribution to the literature of war." –New York Times

__ **AMBUSH S.L.A. Marshall**
__ 0-515-09543-5/$3.95
Vietnam's battle of Dau Tieng and the horror and heroism of guerrilla warfare—captured in firsthand accounts.
"Make[s] the reader see and feel and smell the fighting." –New York Herald Tribune

__ **PATTON'S BEST Nat Frankel and**
__ **Larry Smith** 0-515-08887-0/$3.50
The 4th Armored Division—whose everyday heroism blazed a trail of glory from Normandy to the Rhine. Here is the real war—from the dog soldier's eye-view.

__ **THREE WAR MARINE**
__ **Colonel Francis Fox Parry**
0-515-09872-8/$3.95
A rare and dramatic look at three decades of war—World War II, the Korean War, and Vietnam. Francis Fox Parry shares the heroism, fears and harrowing challenges of his thirty action-packed years in an astounding military career.
